OLE DOC METHUSELAH

AMONG THE MANY CLASSIC WORKS

by

L. RON HUBBARD

Battlefield Earth
Beyond the Black Nebula
Buckskin Brigades
The Conquest of Space
The Dangerous Dimension
Death's Deputy
The Emperor of the Universe
Fear
Final Blackout
Forbidden Voyage
The Incredible Destination
The Kilkenny Cats
The Kingslayer
The Last Admiral
The Magnificent Failure
The Masters of Sleep
The Mission Earth Dekalogy*

Volume 1: The Invaders Plan
Volume 2: Black Genesis
Volume 3: The Enemy Within
Volume 4: An Alien Affair
Volume 5: Fortune of Fear
Volume 6: Death Quest
Volume 7: Voyage of Vengeance
Volume 8: Disaster
Volume 9: Villainy Victorious
Volume 10: The Doomed Planet

The Mutineers
The Rebels
Return to Tomorrow
Slaves of Sleep
To The Stars
The Traitor
Triton
Typewriter in the Sky
The Ultimate Adventure
The Unwilling Hero

*Dekalogy—a group of ten volumes

OLE DOC METHUSELAH

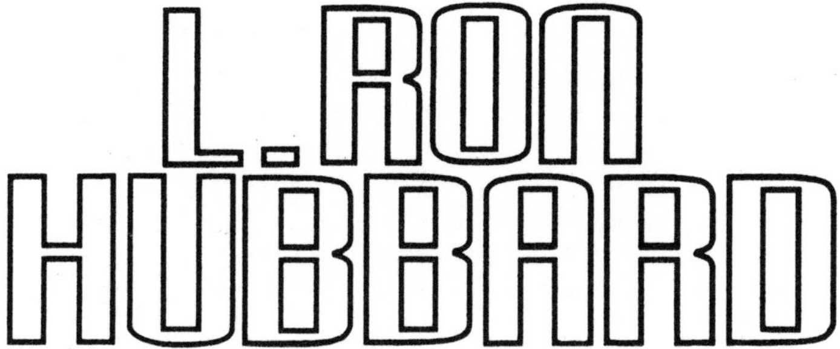

BRIDGE PUBLICATIONS, INC. LOS ANGELES

 For information, address Bridge Publications, Inc., 4751 Fountain Ave., Los Angeles, CA 90029.

10 9 8 7 6 5 4 3 2 1

Library of Congress Cataloging in Publication Data
Hubbard, L. Ron (Lafayette Ron), 1911 - 1986
Ole Doc Methuselah
1. Fiction, American. I. Title
ISBN 0-88404-653-2

CONTENTS

INTRODUCTION

It was the autumn of 1947—the tenth year of a golden age for John W. Campbell's *Astounding Science Fiction*, the magazine that had reshaped and redefined science fiction into its modern form. Campbell, coming to the editorship of *Astounding* at the age of 27 in October, 1937, had tossed out within a year or two most of the old-guard writers who had dominated the magazine, and had brought in a crowd of bright and talented newcomers: such people as Robert A. Heinlein, Isaac Asimov, L. Ron Hubbard, A.E. van Vogt, L. Sprague de Camp, Theodore Sturgeon, Fritz Leiber, Lester del Rey. They—and a few veterans like Jack Williamson and Clifford D. Simak—wrote a revolutionary new kind of science fiction for Campbell, brisk and crisp of style, fresh and lively and often irreverent in matters of theme, plot, and characterization. The readers loved it. *Astounding* was the place where all the best stories were—many of them now classics, which have stayed in print for fifty years—and both the magazine and its larger-than-life editor were regarded with awe and reverence by its readership and by most of its writers as well.

In 1947 the absolute reign of Campbell and *Astounding* was in its final few years—new magazines, new editors, new writers were coming, and by 1951 they would push the old leader aside—but no one knew that yet.the slick magazines, but the names of Asimov, van Vogt, Williamson, Sturgeon and Simak were frequently seen on the contents page in the post-war years.

And L. Ron Hubbard had returned as well.

Hubbard—whose famous writing career had begun in the early 1930's in such wild-and-wooly pulps as *Thrilling Adventures*, *Phantom Detective*, *Cowboy Stories*, and *Top Notch*, and the more prestigious magazines as *Argosy*, *Adventure*, *Western Stories*, *Popular Detective* and *Five Novels Monthly*, had been especially commissioned by publishers Street & Smith to write for *Astounding* magazine's editor John W. Campbell Jr. in 1938. At 27, just a few months younger than Campbell, he was already the author of millions of published words of fiction, and Campbell wanted him for his knack of fast-paced story-telling and his bold ideas. Soon Hubbard was a top figure in the *Astounding* of the 1940's and in its short-lived but distinguished fantasy companion, *Unknown*, with such Hubbard stories and novels as "The Tramp" (1938), "Slaves of Sleep" (1939), "Typewriter in the Sky" (1940), "Final Blackout" (1940), "Fear" (1940), "The Case of The Friendly Corpse" (1941), and "The Invaders" (1942). But then Hubbard too went off to military service, and his contributions to Campbell's magazines ceased for five years.

The extent of Hubbard's popularity among the readers of *Astounding* and *Unknown* in the first few years of Campbell's Golden Age was enormous. No better proof of that can be provided than a letter from a young reader that was published in the April, 1940 issue of *Unknown*, listing his ten favorite stories of 1939. Three of them—"The Ultimate

Adventure," "Ghoul," and "Slaves of Sleep"—were by L. Ron Hubbard. (The young reader's name was Isaac Asimov, who would soon be one of Campbell's Golden Age stalwarts himself.) So when Hubbard finally returned to the pages of *Astounding* in the August, 1947 issue with a grim three-part novel of the postwar atomic-age world, "The End Is Not Yet," reader response was enthusiastic.

But there was more to Hubbard's return than the readers of that season suspected. Even while "The End Is Not Yet" was still being serialized, Campbell began to offer them the start of another major Hubbard enterprise—the first of a series of high-spirited space adventures under the pseudonym of René Lafayette. Entitled "Ole Doc Methuselah," it appeared—without any of Campbell's customary advance build-up—as the lead story of the October, 1947 *Astounding*, which also carried the final segment of the Hubbard novel.

The "Lafayette" pseudonym was not new. Hubbard had used it at least once before, in the April, 1940 issue of *Unknown*, on a short novel called "The Indigestible Triton." The name was simply a variation on Hubbard's own—(the "L." in "L. Ron Hubbard" stands for "Lafayette")—and almost certainly was used on "The Indigestible Triton" because of the extraordinary number of Hubbard stories that had been appearing in Campbell's magazines in 1940: editors often get uneasy when one writer appears to be too prolific. Very likely the pseudonym was revived for "Ole Doc Methuselah" for much the same reason. With "The End Is Not Yet" already running in *Astounding*, Campbell would not have wanted to use the same author's byline twice in the same issue.

"Ole Doc Methuselah"—the first of the seven galactic exploits in the book you are now holding—is an entertaining adventure hearkening back to Hubbard's other genre writing—perhaps reminiscent of one of his classic westerns: The glamorous, mysterious young doctor and his comic but highly effective sidekick come riding into town to set things straight. The bad guys have set up a phony land-development scheme, saying that the railway will be coming through soon and everybody in town will get rich. But of course it's a swindle, and it will be up to the young doctor and his buddy to defeat the villains and set everything to rights.

The readers loved it. "The Analytical Laboratory," the reader-response poll that Campbell published every month, reported in the January, 1948 *Astounding* that it had been the most popular story in the October issue. (The conclusion of Hubbard's "End Is Not Yet" serial finished in second place.) Campbell himself noted, in commenting on the results, that he personally would classify the story "as fun rather than cerebral science-fiction—and its position [in the poll] testifies that any type of science-fiction, well done, will take a first place!"

Cartier's lively, boldly outlined drawings provided images of Doc and his alien slave Hippocrates as definitive as those that Tenniel did for Lewis Carroll's "Alice in Wonderland," and gave the reader a cue not to take the story *too* seriously. Everyone knew right away that Ole Doc was a high-spirited romp—Campbell and Hubbard in an unbuttoned mood, sharing some fun with their readers for some great entertainment.

Cartier, who illustrated more stories by Hubbard than anyone else, has written fondly of his association with Hubbard's work and with "Ole Doc Methuselah" in particular. "Illustrating Ron's tales was a welcome assignment," he said, "because they always contained scenes or incidents

I found easy to picture. With some writers' work I puzzled for hours on what to draw and I sometimes had to contact Campbell for an idea. That never happened with a Hubbard story. His plots allowed my imagination to run wild and the ideas for my illustrations would quickly come to mind.... It was Ole Doc's adventures that many people, including myself, recall most fondly. Readers like my depiction of Hippocrates and I always enjoyed drawing the little, antennaed, four-armed creature. Oddly enough, in 1952 my wife, Gina, found a large five-legged frog in our yard.... Needless to say, the mutant frog was instantly dubbed Hippocrates or Pocrates, for short. He resided with honor in a garden pool and was featured in many local newspaper articles. The frog's existence was as if Ron's writings and my illustrations had come to life to prove that science fiction's imaginative ideas are quite within the realm of possibility."

A month after his debut, Ole Doc Methuselah returned, with "The Expensive Slaves" in the November, 1947 issue. Again praised in the letter column of "The Analytical Laboratory," there was no question that the series had been successfully launched, and the readers of the era—I was one—looked forward eagerly to the next episode.

They didn't have long to wait. Doc was back in the March, 1948 issue with "Her Majesty's Aberration." The fourth in the series—"The Great Air Monopoly"—appeared in September, 1948. The April, 1949 issue brought "Plague," a long lead story which gave the series its first display on *Astounding's* cover. Two months later came "A Sound Investment." (Campbell, announcing that story in the previous issue, commented, "This is one series in which the continuing hero is frankly and directly labeled as being deathless, incidentally; you won't often find an author admitting that." January, 1950 saw publication of "Ole Mother Methuselah," the seventh of the Ole Doc Methuselah series.

And there the series ended. Hubbard had other projects of a whole new scope. In the May, 1950 *Astounding* Campbell published Hubbard's non-fiction essay, "Dianetics, the Evolution of a Science," and shortly afterward came Hubbard's book, *Dianetics, The Modern Science of Mental Health*. It would be many years before Hubbard would write science fiction again.

Ole Doc Methuselah—the seven stories collected here—is Hubbard's most genial book. We see amiably miraculous events described in broad, vigorous strokes. Ole Doc, in three hours of deft plastic surgery, undoes an entrenched tyranny and restores an entire world's social balance. Space pirates, land barons, vindictive Graustarkian queens, sinister magnates who make air a marketable commodity—nothing is too wild, too implausible, for the protean Hubbard. The immortal (but human and sometimes fallible) superhero and his wry, nagging alien pal are plainly destined to succeed in everything they attempt, and the key question is not *if* but *how* they will undo the villain and repair the damage that he has done.

That having been said, though, it would be a mistake to minimize these seven stories as light literature turned out by a great science-fiction writer in a casual mood. They have their roots in pulp-magazine techniques, but so did nearly everything that Campbell published in that era. In a time before network television and paperback books, the pulp magazines were the primary source of entertainment for millions of readers, and the best pulp writers were masters of the art of narrative.

The action in the Methuselah stories is fast and flamboyant and the inventiveness breathless and hectic. The mind of a shrewd and skilled storyteller can be observed at work on every page, and the stories grow richer and deeper as the series progresses—note, particularly, the touching moment in "The Great Air Monopoly" when Doc enters Hippocrates' working quarters aboard their ship. ("A bowl of gooey gypsum and mustard, the slave's favorite concoction for himself, stood half eaten on the sink, spoon drifting minutely from an upright position to the edge of the bowl as the neglected mixture hardened. A small, pink-bellied god grinned forlornly in a niche, gazing at the half-finished page of a letter to some outlandish world. . . . Ole Doc closed the galley softly as though he had been intruding on a private life and stood outside, hand still on the latch. For a long, long time he had never thought about it. But life without Hippocrates would be a desperate hard thing to bear.") And though a lot of Doc's medicinal techniques look more like magic to us, I remind you of Arthur C. Clarke's famous dictum that the farther we peer into the future, the more closely science will seem to us to resemble magic. Ole Doc is nine hundred years old—he took his medical degree from Johns Hopkins in 1946—and looks about twenty-five; but who is to say that people now living will not survive to range the starways nine hundred years from now? It may not be likely, but it's at least conceivable—and fun to think about.

The stories are good-natured entertainment; and they give us something to think about. As Alva Rogers pointed out in *A Requiem for Astounding*, his classic history of John Campbell's great magazine, "The 'Ole Doc Methuselah' stories were immensely enjoyable; there was nothing pretentious about them, they were full of rousing action, colorful characters, spiced with wit, and yet, underneath it all, had some serious speculative ideas about one possible course organized medicine might take in the future and a picture of medical advances that was very intriguing." They were well-loved stories in their day, rich with their sense of wonder; and here they are again, to delight, amuse, and amaze a new readership now.

— **Robert Silverberg**

Award-winning author, Robert Silverberg, has written over 100 books and numerous short stories—and is equally renowned as a top editor of science fiction anthologies.

— The Publisher

FOREWORD

Ole Doc Methuselah was the name by which he was known on a myriad scattered planets, for he was the most famous member of the most elite organization of the cosmos, The Soldiers of Light. But he was no soldier in the military sense, for the enemies he fought were disease, old age, and the warped psychology that spawned only in the isolation of mankind's lost planetary colonies.

This is his exciting story—and that of his strange, multi-armed companion—and of their unending journey through the trackless galaxy.

It is a series of astonishing adventures on many worlds as the greatest space medic of them all encounters double-dealing, mutation, and the unexpected that always haunts alien spheres.

In the words of Hippocrates, Ole Doc's companion: "The Soldier of Light is no ordinary physician. He is part of an organization of six hundred who have dedicated themselves to the ultimate preservation of mankind no matter the wars or explorations of space.

"There are one hundred and seventy-six trillion human beings throughout this galaxy. There is roughly one physician to every hundred and sixty of these. There are only six hundred Soldiers of Light. They give allegiance to no government, need no passport, so long as they do not engage in political activity, their persons are inviolate.

"An apprenticeship of forty years is required to become a

member of this society and membership is not confirmed even then until the applicant has made an undeniable great contribution to the health and happiness of mankind. Members of the Universal Medical Society★ do not practice as do ordinary physicians. They accept no fee. The organization is self-supporting.

"You see before you, my master, Soldier of Light seventy-seven known as Methuselah."

★U.M.S.—Universal Medical Society—the supreme council of physicians organized in the late Twenty-third Century after the famous Revolt Caduceus which claimed the lives of two billion humanoids of the Earth-Arcton Empire through the villainous use of new medical discoveries to wage war and dominate entire countries. George Moulton, M.D., Dr. Hubert Sands, the physiochemist, James J. Lufberry, M.D., and Stephen Thomas Methridge, M.D., who was later to become well known as Ole Doc Methuselah, had for nearly a hundred years kept to a laboratory studying far beyond contemporary skills and incidentally extending their work by extending their own lives, came out of retirement, issued a pronunciamento—backed with atomic and du-ray hand weapons and a thousand counter-toxins—which denied to the casual practitioner all specialized medical secrets. Thus peace came to the Empire. Other systems anxiously clamored for similar aid and other great names of medicine quietly joined them. For centuries, as the Universal Medical Society, these men, hiding great names under nicknames, who eventually became a fixed seven hundred in number, maintained a Center and by casual patrol of the Systems kept medicine as well as disease within rational bounds. Saluting no government, collecting no fees, permitting no infringement, the U.M.S. became dreaded and revered as The Soldiers of Light and under the symbol of the crossed ray rods impinged their will upon the governments of space under a code of their own more rigorous than any code of laws. For the detailed records and history of the U.M.S., for conditions governing the hundred-year apprenticeship all future members must serve and for the special codes of call and appeal to the U.M.S. in case of plague or disaster, consult L. Ron Hubbard's "Conquest of Space," 29th Volume, Chapter XCLII. René Lafayette

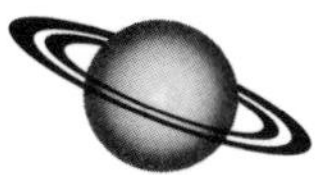

OLE DOC METHUSELAH

OLE DOC METHUSELAH

Ole Doc Methuselah wasn't thinking what he was doing or he never would have landed on Spico that tempestuous afternoon. He had been working out some new formulas for cellular radiation—in his head as usual, he never could find his log tables—and the act of also navigating his rocket ship must have been too much for him. He saw the asteroid planet, de-translated his speed and landed.

He sat there for some time at the controls, gazing out into the pleasant meadow and at the brook which wandered so invitingly upon it, and finishing up his tabulations.

When he had written down the answer on his gauntlet cuff—his filing system was full of torn scraps of cuff—he felt very pleased with himself. He had mostly forgotten where he had been going, but he was going to pour the pile to her when his eye focused upon the brook. Ole Doc took his finger off the booster switch and grinned.

"That sure is green grass," he said with a pleased sigh. And then he looked up over the control panels where he hung his fishing rod.

Lord knows what would have happened to Junction City if Ole Doc hadn't decided to go fishing that day.

Seated on the lower step of the port ladder, Hippocrates patiently watched his god toss flies into the water with a deft and expert hand. Hippocrates was a sort of cross between several things. Ole Doc had picked him up cheap at an auction on Zeno just after the Trans-System War. At the time he had meant to discover some things about his purchase such as his metabolism and why he dieted solely on gypsum, but that had been thirty years ago and Hippocrates had been an easy habit to acquire. Unpigmented, four-handed and silent as space itself, Hippocrates had set himself the scattered task of remembering all the things Ole Doc always forgot. He sat now, remembering—particularly that Ole Doc had some of his own medicine to take at thirty-six o'clock—and he might have sat there that way for hours and hours, phonograph-record-wise, if a radiating pellet hadn't come with a sharp *zip* past his left antenna to land with a clang on the *Morgue*'s thick hull.

ZIP! CLANG!

Page forty-nine of the "Tales of the Early Space Pioneers" went smoothly into operation in Hippocrates' gifted if unimaginative skull, which page translated itself into unruffled action.

He went inside and threw on "Force Field Beta" minus the Nine Hundred and Sixtieth Degree Arc, that being where Ole Doc was. Seeing that his worshipped master went on fishing, either unwitting or uncaring, Hippocrates then served out blasters and twenty rounds to himself and went back to sit on the bottom step of the port ladder.

The big spaceship—dented a bit, but lovely—shimmered quietly in Procyon's inviting light and the brook rippled and Ole Doc kept casting for whatever outrageous kind of fish he might find in that stream. This went on for an hour and then two things happened. Ole Doc, unaware of the force field, cast into it and got his fly back into his hat and a young woman came stumbling, panic-stricken, across the meadow toward the *Morgue*.

From amongst the stalks of flowers some forty feet high emerged an Earthman, thick and dark, wearing the remains of a uniform to which had been added civil space garb. He rushed forward a dozen meters before he paused in stride at the apparition of the huge golden ship with its emblazoned crossed ray rods of pharmacy. Then he saw Ole Doc fishing and the pursuer thrust a helmet up from a contemptuous grin.

It was nearer to Ole Doc than to the ship and the girl, exhausted and disarrayed, stumbled toward him. The Earthman swept wide and put Ole Doc exactly between himself and the ladder before he came in.

Hippocrates turned from page forty-nine to page one hundred and fifteen. He leaped nimbly up to the top of the ship in the hope of shooting the Earthman on an angle which would miss Ole Doc. But he had no more than arrived and sighted before it became apparent to him that he would also now shoot the girl. This puzzled him. Obviously the girl was not an enemy who would harm Ole Doc. But the Earthman was. Still it was better to blast girl *and* Earthman than to see Ole Doc harmed in any cause. The effort at recalling an exact instance made Hippocrates tremble and in that tremble Ole Doc also came into his fire field.

Having no warnings whatever, Ole Doc had just looked up from disentangling his hook from first his shirt and then his thumb and beheld two humans cannonading down upon him.

The adrenalized condition of the woman was due to the Earthman, that was clear. The Earthman was obviously a blast-for-hire from some tough astral slum and he had recently had a fight, for two knuckles bled. The girl threw herself in a collapse at Ole Doc's feet and the Earthman came within a fatal fifteen feet.

Ole Doc twitched his wrist and put his big-hooked fly into the upper lip of the Earthman. This disappointed Ole Doc a little for he had been trying for the nose. The beggar was less hypothyroid than he had first estimated.

Pulling his game-fish bellowing into the stream, Ole Doc disarmed him and let him have a ray barrel just back of the medulla oblongata—which took care of the fellow nicely.

Hippocrates lowered himself with disappointed grunts down to the ladder. At his master's hand signal he came forth with two needles, filled, sterilized and awaiting only a touch to break their seals and become useful.

Into the gluteal muscle—through clothes and all because of sterilizing radiation of the point—Ole Doc gave the Earthman the contents of needle one. At the jab the fellow had squirmed a little and the doctor lifted one eyelid.

"You are a stone!" said Ole Doc. "You can't move."

The Earthman lay motionless, wide-eyed, being a stone. Hippocrates carefully noted the time with the fact in order to remind his master to let the fellow stop being a stone sometime. But in noting the time, Hippocrates found that it was six minutes to thirty-six o'clock and therefore time for a much more important thing—Ole Doc's own medicine.

Brusquely, Hippocrates grabbed up the unconscious girl and waded back across the stream with her. The girl could wait. Thirty-six o'clock was thirty-six o'clock.

"Hold up!" said Ole Doc, needle poised.

Hippocrates grunted and kept on walking. He went directly into the main operating room of the *Morgue* and there amidst the cleverly jammed hotch-potch of trays and ray tubes, drawers, masks, retorts and reflectors, he unceremoniously dropped the girl. Monominded now, for this concerned his master—and where the rest of the world could go if it interfered with his master was a thing best expressed in silence—Hippocrates laid out the serum and the proper rays.

Humbly enough, the master bared his arm and then exposed himself—as a man does before a fireplace on a cold day—to the pouring out of life from the fixed tubes. It took only five minutes. It had to be done every five days.

Satisfied now, Hippocrates boosted the girl into a proper position for medication on the center table and adjusted a lamp or two fussily, while admiring his master's touch with the needle.

Ole Doc was smiling, smiling with a strange poignancy. She was a very pretty girl, neatly made, small waisted, high breasted. Her tumbling crown of hair was like an avalanche of fire in the operating lights. Her lips were very soft, likely to be yielding to—

"Father!" she screamed in sudden consciousness. "Father!"

Ole Doc looked perplexed, offended. But then he saw that she did not know where she was. Her wild glare speared both master and thing.

"Where is my father?"

"We don't rightly know, ma'am," said Ole Doc. "You just—"

"He's out there. They shot our ship down. He's dying or dead! Help him!"

Hippocrates looked at master and master nodded. And when the servant left the ship it was with a bound so swift that it rocked the *Morgue* a little. He was only a meter tall, was Hippocrates, but he weighed nearly five hundred kilos.

Behind him came Ole Doc, but their speeds were so much at variance that before the physician could reach the tall flowers, Hippocrates was back through them carrying a man stretched out on a compartment door wrenched from its strong hinges for the purpose. That was page eight of "First Aid in Space," not to wrestle people around but to put them on flat things. Man and door weighed nearly as much as Hippocrates but he wanted no help.

"'Lung burns,'" said Hippocrates, "'are very difficult to heal and most usually result in death. When the heart is also damaged, particular care should be taken to move the patient as little as possible since exertion—'"

Ole Doc listened to, without heeding, the high, squeaky singsong. Walking beside the girl's father, Ole Doc was not so sure.

He felt a twinge of pity for the old man. He was proud of face, her father, gray of hair and very high and noble of brow. He was a big man, the kind of man who would think big thoughts and fight and die for ideals.

The doctor beheld the seared stains, the charred fabric, the blasted flesh which now composed the all of the man's chest. The bloody and gruesome scene was not a thing for a young girl's eyes, even under disinterested circumstances—and a hypo would only do so much.

He stepped to the port and waved a hand back to the main salon. There was a professional imperiousness about it which thrust her along with invisible force. Out of her sight now, Ole Doc allowed Hippocrates to place the body on the multi-trayed operating table.

Under the gruesome flicker of ultraviolet, the wounded man looked even nearer death. The meters on the wall counted respiration and pulse and hemoglobin and all needles hovered in red while the big dial, with exaggerated and inexorable calm, swept solemnly down toward black.

"He'll be dead in ten minutes," said Ole Doc. He looked at the face, the high forehead, the brave contours. "He'll be dead and the breed is gone enough to seed."

At the panel, the doctor threw six switches and a great arc began to glow and snap like a hungry beast amid the batteries of tubes. A dynamo whined to a muted scream and then another began to growl. Ozone and brimstone bit the nostrils. The table was pooled in smoky light.

The injured man's clothing vanished and, with small tinks, bits of metal dropped against the floor—coins, buckles, shoe nails.

Ole Doc tripped another line of switches and a third motor commenced to yell. The light about the table graduated from blue up to unseen black. The great hole in the charred chest began to glow whitely. The beating heart which had been laid bare by the original weapon slowed, slowed, slowed.

With a final twitch of his wrist, Ole Doc cut out the first stages and made his gesture to Hippocrates. That one lifted off the top tray which bore the man and, holding it balanced with one hand, opened a gravelike vault. There were long, green tubes glowing in the vault and the feel of swirling gases. Hippocrates slid the tray along the grooves and clanged the door upon it.

Ole Doc stood at the board for a little while, leaning a little against the force field which protected him from stray or glancing rays, and then sighing a weary sigh, evened the glittering line. Normal light and air came back into the operating room and the salon door slid automatically open.

• • •

The girl stood there, tense question in her every line, fear digging nails into palms.

Ole Doc put on a professional smile. "There is a very fair chance that we may save him, Miss—"

"Elston."

"A very fair chance. Fifty-fifty."

"But what are you doing now?" she demanded.

Ole Doc would ordinarily have given a rough time to anyone else who had dared to ask him that. But he felt somehow summery as he gazed at her.

"All I can, Miss Elston."

"Then he'll soon be well?"

"Why . . . ah . . . that depends. You see, well—" How was he going to tell her that what he virtually needed was a whole new man? And how could he explain that professional ethics required one to forego the expedience of kidnapping, no matter how vital it might seem? For what does one do with a heart split in two and a lung torn open wide when they are filled with foreign matter and ever-burning rays unless it is to get a new chest entire?

"We'll have to try," he said. "He'll be all right for now . . . for a month, or more perhaps. He is in no pain, will have no memory of this and if he is ever cured, will be cured entirely. The devil of it is, Miss Elston, men always advance their weapons about a thousand years ahead of medical science. But then, we'll try. We'll try."

And the way she looked at him made it summer entirely. "Even . . . " she said hesitantly, "even if you are so young, I have all the confidence in the universe in you, doctor."

That startled Ole Doc. He hadn't been patronized that way for a long, long time. But more important—he glanced into the mirror, over the table. He looked more closely. Well, he *did* look young. Thirty, maybe. And a glow began to creep up over him, and as he looked back to her and saw her cascading glory of hair and the sweetness of her face—

"Master doctor!" interrupted the unwelcome Hippocrates. "The Earthman is gone."

Ole Doc stared out of the port and saw thin twirls of smoke arising from the charred and blasted grass. The Earthman was gone all right, and very much gone for good. But one boot remained.

"Looks," said Ole Doc, "like we've got some opposition."

"We were proceeding to Junction City," said the girl, "when a group of men shot down our ship and attacked us."

Ole Doc picked a thoughtful tooth, for the fish he had caught had been excellent—deep-fried, Southern style. He felt benign, chivalrous. Summer was in full bloom. He was thinking harder about her hair than about her narrative. Robbery and banditry on the spaceways were not new, particularly on such a little-inhabited planet as Spico, but the thoughts which visited him had not been found in his mind for a long, long time. She made a throne room of the tiny dining salon and Ole Doc harked back to lonely days in cold space, on hostile and uninviting planets, and the woman-hunger which comes.

"Did you see any of them?" he asked only to hear her voice again.

"I didn't need to," she said.

The tone she took startled Ole Doc. Had he been regarding this from the viewpoint of volume 16 of Klote's standard work on human psychology, he would have realized the predicament into which with those words he had launched himself. Thirteen hundred years ago a chap named Malory had written a book about knight-errantry; it had unhappily faded from Ole Doc's mind.

"Miss Elston," he said, "if you know the identity of the band then perhaps something can be done, although I do not see what you could possibly gain merely by bringing them to the Bar of the Space Council."

Hippocrates was lumbering back and forth at the buffet clearing away the remains of the meal. He was quoting singsong under his breath the code of the Soldiers of Light, "'It shall be unlawful for any medical officer to engage in political activities of any kind, to involve himself with law, or in short, aid or abet the causes, petty feuds, personal vengeances . . .'" Ole Doc did not hear him. The music of Venus was in Miss Elston's voice.

"Why, I told you about the box, doctor; it contains the deed to this planet and, more important than that, it has the letter which my father was bringing here to restrain his partner from selling off parcels of land at Junction City. Oh doctor, can't you understand how cruel it is to these people? More than ten thousand of them have come here with all the savings they have in the universe to buy land in the hope that they can profit by its resale to the Procyon-Sirius Spaceways.

"When my father, Judge Elston, first became interested in this scheme it was because it had been brought to his attention by a Captain Blanchard who came to us at our home near New York and told us that he had private information that Spico was completely necessary to the Procyon-Sirius Spaceways as a stopover point and that it would be of immense value. Nobody knew, except some officials in the company, according to Captain Blanchard, and my father was led to believe that Captain Blanchard had an excellent reputation and that the information was entirely correct.

"Blanchard came here on Spico some time ago and laid out the necessary landing fields and subdivided Junction City, using my father's name and money. He circulated illustrated folders everywhere setting forth the opportunities of business and making the statement that the Spaceways would shortly begin their own installation. Thousands and thousands of people came here in the hope either of settling and beginning a new life or of profiting in the boom which would result. Blanchard sold them land still using my father's name.

"A short while ago my father learned from officials of the company that a landing field was not necessary here due to a new type of propulsion motor which made a stopover unnecessary. He learned also that Captain Blanchard had been involved in blue-sky speculations on Alpha Centauri. He visio-graphed Blanchard and told him to cease all operations immediately and to refund all money, saying that he, Judge Elston, would absorb any loss occasioned in the matter. Blanchard told him that it was a good scheme and was making money and that he didn't intend to refund a dime of it. He also said that if my father didn't want himself exposed as a crook, he would have to stay out of it. Blanchard reminded him that only the name of Elston appeared on all literature and deeds and that the entire scheme had obviously been conceived by my father. Then he threatened to kill my father and we have been unable to get in contact with him since.

"I begged my father to expose Blanchard to the Upper Council but he said he would have to wash his own dirty linen. Immediately afterwards we came up here. He tried to leave me behind but I was terrified that something would happen to him and so I would not stay home.

"My father had the proof that the Procyon-Sirius Spaceways would not build their field here. It was in that box. Blanchard has kept good his threat. He attacked us, he stole the evidence, and now—" She began to sob suddenly at the thought of her father lying there in that harshly glittering room so close to death. Hippocrates phonograph-recordwise was beginning the code all over again.

"'It shall be unlawful for any medical officer to engage in political activities of any kind, to involve himself with law, or in short, aid or abet the causes, petty feuds, personal vengeances . . .'"

But Ole Doc's eyes were on her hair and his mind was roaming back to other days. Almost absently he dropped a minute capsule in her water glass and told her to drink it. Soon she was more composed.

"Even if you could save my father's life, doctor," she said, "it wouldn't do any good. The shock of this scandal would kill him."

Ole Doc hummed absently and put his hands behind his head. His black silk dressing gown rustled. His youthful eyes drifted inwards. He thrust his furred boots out before him. The humming stopped. He sat up. His fine surgeon's hands doubled into fists and with twin blows upon the table he propelled himself to his feet.

"Why, there is nothing more simple than this. All we have to do is find this Blanchard, take the evidence away from him, tell the people that they've been swindled, give them back their money, put your father on his feet and everything will be all right. The entire mess will be straightened out in jig time." He beamed fondly upon her. And then, with an air of aplomb began to pour fresh wine. He had half-filled the second glass when abrupt realization startled him so that he spilled a great gout of wine where it lay like a puddle of blood on the snowy cloth.

But across from him sat his ladye faire and now that he had couched his lance and found himself face to face with an enemy, even the thought of the shattered and blackened remains of the Earthman did not drive him back. He smiled reassuringly and patted her hand.

Her eyes were jewels in the amber light.

Junction City was all turmoil, dust and hope. There were men there who had made a thousand dollars yesterday, who had made two thousand dollars this morning, and who avidly dreamed of making five thousand before night. Lots were being bought and sold with such giddy rapidity that no one could keep trace of their value. Several battered tramp spaceships which had brought pioneers and their effects lay about the spaceport. Rumors, all of them confident, all of them concerning profit, banged about the streets like bullets.

Smug, hard and ruthless, Edouard Blanchard sat under the awning of the Comet Saloon. His agate eyes were fixed upon a newly arrived ship, a gold-colored ship with crossed ray rods upon her nose. He looked up and down the crowded dusty street where spaceboot trod on leather brogan and place-silk rustled on denim. Men and women from a hundred planets were there. Men of hundreds of races and creeds were there with pasts as checkerboard as history itself, yet bound together by a common anxiety to profit and build a world anew.

It mattered nothing to Edouard Blanchard that bubbles left human wreckage in their wake, that on his departure all available buying power for this planet would go as well. Ten thousand homely souls, whose only crime had been hope, would be consigned to grubbing without finance, tools, or imported food for a questionable living on a small orb bound on a forgotten track in space. Such concerns rarely trouble the consciences of the Edouard Blanchards.

The agate eyes fastened upon an ambling Martian named Dart, who with his mask to take out forty per cent of the oxygen from this atmosphere and so permit him to breathe, looked like some badly conceived and infinitely evil gnome.

"Dart," said Blanchard, "take a run over to that medical ship and find out what a Soldier of Light is doing in a place like this."

The Martian fumbled with his mask and then uneasily hefted his blaster belt. He squirmed and wriggled as though some communication of great importance had met a dam halfway up to the surface. Blanchard stared at him. "Well? Go! What are you waiting for?"

Dart squirmed until a small red haze of dust stood about his boots. "I've always been faithful to you, captain. I ain't never sold you out to nobody. I'm honest, that's what I am." His dishonest eyes wriggled upwards until they reached the level of Blanchard's collar.

Blanchard came upright. There was a sadistic stir in his hands. Under this compulsion Dart wilted and his voice from a vicious whine changed to a monotonous wail. "That was the ship Miss Elston ran to. I'm an honest man and I ain't going to tell you no different."

"But you said she escaped and I've had twelve men

searching for her for the past day. Damn you, Dart. Why couldn't you have told me this?"

"I just thought she'd fly away and that would be all there was to it. I didn't think she'd come back. But you ain't got nothing to be afeared of, Mr. Captain Blanchard. No Soldier of Light can monkey with politics. The Universal Medical Society won't interfere."

Captain Blanchard's hands, long, thin, twisted anew as though they were wrapping themselves around the sinews in Dart's body and snapping them out one by one. He restrained the motion and sank back. "You know I'm your friend, Dart. You know I wouldn't do anything to hurt you. You know it's only those who oppose my will whom I, shall I say, remove. You know that you are safe enough."

"Oh yes, Captain Blanchard, I know you are my friend. I appreciate it. You don't know how I appreciate it. I'm an honest man and I don't mind saying so."

"And you'll always be honest, won't you, Dart?" said Blanchard, white hands twitching. He smiled. From a deep pocket he extracted first a long knife with which he regularly pared his nails, then a thick sheaf of money, and finally amongst several deeds, a communication which Mr. Elston had been attempting to bring to Spico. He read it through in all its damning certainty. It said that the Procyon-Sirius Spaceways would not use this planet. Then, striking a match to light a cigar he touched it to the document and idly watched it burn. The last flaming fragment was suddenly hurled at the Martian.

"Get over there instantly," said Blanchard, "and find out what you can. If Miss Elston comes away from that ship unattended, see that she never goes back to it. And make very certain, my honest friend, that the Soldier on that ship doesn't find out anything."

But before Dart had more than beaten out the fire on the skirt of his coat, a youthful, pleasant voice addressed them. Blanchard hastily smoothed out his hands, veiled his eyes, and with a smile which he supposed to be winning faced the speaker.

Ole Doc, having given them his "good morning," continued guilelessly as though he had not heard a thing.

"My, what a beautiful prospect you have here. If I could only find the man who sells the lots—"

Blanchard stood up instantly and grasped Ole Doc Methuselah by the hand which he pumped with enormous enthusiasm. "Well you've come to the right place, stranger. I am Captain Blanchard and very pleased to make your acquaintance, Mr.—"

"Oh, Captain Blanchard, I have heard a great deal about you," said Ole Doc, his blue eyes very innocent. "It is a wonderful thing you are doing here. Making all these people rich and happy."

"Oh, not my doing, I assure you," said Captain Blanchard. "This project was started by a Mr. Elston of New York City, Earth. I am but his agent trying in my small way to carry out his orders." He freed his hand and swept it to take in the dreary, dusty and being-cluttered prospect. "Happy, happy people," he said. "Oh, you don't know what pleasure it gives me to see little homes being created and small families being placed in the way of great riches. You don't know." Very affectedly he gazed down at the dirt as though to let his tears of happiness splash into it undetected. However, no tears splashed.

After a little he recovered himself enough to say, "We have only two lots left and they are a thousand dollars apiece."

Ole Doc promptly dragged two bills from his breast pocket and handed them over. If he was surprised at this swift method of doing business, Captain Blanchard managed to again master his emotion. He quickly escorted Ole Doc to the clapboard shack which served as the city hall so that the deeds could be properly recorded.

As they entered the flimsy structure a tall, prepossessing individual stopped Blanchard and held him in momentary converse concerning a program to put schools into effect. Ole Doc, eyeing the man, estimated him as idealistic but stupid. He was not particularly surprised when Blanchard introduced him as Mr. Zoran, the mayor of Junction City.

Here, thought Ole Doc, is the fall guy when Blanchard clears out.

"I'm very glad to make your acquaintance, Mr.—" said Mayor Zoran.

"And I yours," said Ole Doc. "It must be quite an honor to have ten thousand people so completely dependent upon your judgment."

Mayor Zoran swelled slightly. "I find it a heavy but honorable trust, sir. There is nothing I would not do for our good citizens. You may talk of empire builders, sir, but in the future you cannot omit mention of these fine beings who make up our population in Junction City. We have kept the riffraff to a minimum, sir. We are families, husbands, wives, small children. We are determined, sir, to make this an Eden." He nodded at this happy thought, smiled. "To make this an Eden wherein we all may prosper, for with the revenue of the Spaceways flooding through our town, and with our own work in the fields to raise its supplies, and with the payroll of the atomic plant which Captain Blanchard assures us will begin to be built within a month, we may look forward to long, happy and prosperous lives."

Ole Doc looked across the bleak plain. A two-year winter would come to Spico soon, a winter in which no food could be raised. He looked at Mayor Zoran. "I trust, sir, that you have reserved some of your capital against possible emergencies, emergencies such as food, or the cost of relief expeditions coming here."

Captain Blanchard masked a startled gleam which had leaped into his agate eyes. "I am sure that there is no need for that," he said.

Mayor Zoran's head shook away any thought of such a need. "If land and building materials have been expensive," he said, "I am sure there will be more money in the community as soon as the Spaceways representatives arrive, and there is enough food now for three weeks. By the way," he said, turning to Blanchard, "didn't you tell me that today was the day the officials would come here?"

Blanchard caught and hid his hands. "Why, my dear mayor," he said, "there are always slight delays. These big companies, you know, officials with many things on their minds, today, tomorrow, undoubtedly sometime this week."

Mayor Zoran was reassured and, shaking hands with Ole Doc and Captain Blanchard, strode off into the street where he made a small procession of his progress. People stopped him here and there and asked him eagerly for news.

• • •

Inside at the desk a small sleepy clerk woke up long enough to get out his records book, but before the transaction could be begun Ole Doc took back the two one-thousand-dollar bills.

"There are two or three things which I would like to know," said Ole Doc innocently. "I wonder if there are going to be schools?"

"Oh yes, of course," said Blanchard. "I didn't know that you were a family man."

"And will there be medical facilities?" said Ole Doc.

"Why yes, just this morning a ship of the Universal Medical Society landed here. It won't be long before they start work on the hospitals."

"But," said Ole Doc smoothly, "the Universal Medical Society does only research and major planning. Certainly they would not take cognizance of Spico."

"Well now, I wouldn't be too sure," said Captain Blanchard. "And besides we have the usual common run of physicians here, three of them."

Ole Doc repressed his humph at this and smiled. "Well, I suppose you know more about it than I do," he said. "But what about your water supply? Is it adequate?"

Here Captain Blanchard began to assume his most expansive and guileless pose and would have carried on for some time about the excellence of the water supply if Ole Doc had not interrupted him.

"You say you have three reservoirs already. Now, are these community owned or would it be possible to buy them?"

Captain Blanchard had not expected that morning that his stars would arise so luckily. His thin white hands began to twitch as though already plucking gold from the pockets of his victim. "But this would require," said Captain Blanchard, "a great deal of money. Yes, indeed, a great deal of money."

Ole Doc smiled as though this were an easy matter. "For the water company," he said, "I would be willing to pay a very reasonable amount."

The sleepy clerk was sleepy no longer. His eyes widened. Here he was observing the captains of industry at work.

"For, let us say, twenty thousand dollars," said Ole Doc, "I would be willing—"

"My dear fellow," said Blanchard, "twenty thousand dollars would not be enough to buy the piping system which we have installed."

Ole Doc shrugged. "Then I suppose that's all there is to it," he said.

Captain Blanchard's hands did a particularly spasmodic bit of twitching. "Oh no, it isn't," he said. "Oh no, indeed. I'm sure that we might be able to come to some sort of an understanding on this. Ah . . . perhaps forty thousand dollars—"

"No, twenty thousand is all the cash I have," said Ole Doc.

"Why then this is very simple; if you give us your note of hand for, let us say, twenty thousand dollars at proper interest and cash to the sum of twenty thousand dollars, why we can arrange the matter right here. I have the power of attorney, you know, to sign for all these things for Mr. Elston."

"Done," said Ole Doc, and felt himself seized immediately by the eager Blanchard who pumped his hand so hard that he nearly broke the wrist bones. The clerk was now thoroughly pop-eyed. And he was all thumbs and blots as he attempted to make out the papers for the transaction. But finally his difficulties were dispensed with and Ole Doc, signing the name of William Jones and paying across the proper sums and notes found himself the possessor, proud owner and manager of the water works of Junction City.

Blanchard seemed to be anxious to depart immediately and left Ole Doc to his own devices. For some hours the doctor wandered through the city looking in at the temporary dwellings, watching men struggle to raise out of second-hand materials livable or usable establishments. He patted children on the head, diagnosed to himself various diseases and deformities, and was generally a Haroun al Raschid.

Hope was the prevailing emotion and there was not a man there who did not consider himself a potential millionaire to such a degree that they were giving each other notes of hand payable thirty days hence to enormous sums. But so far as actual cash was concerned, from what Ole Doc could glean, there remained but a few dollars in the whole town. The rest he correctly judged was safely drowned in the depths of Edouard Blanchard's safe. The town was restricted between a river and a ridge and every inch of ground between these natural boundaries was deeded to someone other than Edouard Blanchard as Ole Doc, later in the afternoon, ascertained after a short session with the clerk. He was forced to waken the clerk several times during his inspection of the books. That gentleman was happily asleep when some of the ledgers not generally opened were closely inspected.

Ole Doc stood in the sunlight for a while, thoughtful, barely avoiding a blaster fight which broke out in a swill parlor. Finally he understood that Edouard Blanchard probably intended to leave the area for good before another dawn came.

Ole Doc had for some time been aware of shadowing of the *Morgue*. But before he went back to his ship he decided to take an unusual step.

This did not consume many minutes for there were only five space vessels in the crude port and all of these had come from more or less regular runs amongst known systems. His business transacted, he went back to the golden vessel.

That evening, after a pleasant dinner over which Miss Elston graciously presided, Ole Doc and Hippocrates left the ship on an expedition. They had reached the bottom of the ladder when Ole Doc turned to his slave.

"Hippocrates, over there on the left you behold some trees. Under them you will find a Martian. You will make a wide circuit and come up upon him while I distract his attention from in front. Without injury to the fellow you will hold him and make him prisoner. We will then put him away safely in the *Morgue* and go about our business."

Dart, squirming and shuddering a little bit in the cold, and perhaps with a premonition that he should not expect the evening to deliver anything but evil, suddenly felt himself struck solidly and expertly from behind. As he went down he half-drew a blaster but there was no chance to use it. Dreaming peacefully of his beloved canals, he was carried back to the ship and consigned to an escapeproof compartment.

In a businesslike way Hippocrates then picked up his burden and trudged after Ole Doc around the outskirts of the town toward the higher level of ground where the river had been diverted into three reservoirs which provided the water supply.

Hippocrates was under a double burden, the sack which he carried on his back and the burden which lay in his mind. As they made their way through the night, the heavy little being shaking the solid ground of Spico with every step no matter how light he intended it and Ole Doc regarding the stars with a musing eye, Hippocrates rattled off the code from start to finish. Then he began again. Soon, newer arguments for sanity occurred to him and he started to quote at length:

On Woman

The stronger the woman
The safer the man
As he ventures afar
On the Spaces that span.

For love may be lovely
In summer's soft haze
And days may be sweeter
When fond passions blaze.

But far out on Astri
With light frying hot
Adventure can't live
When there's naught in the pot.

Her sweet curling ringlets
Can't warm you at night
And the dew in her eyes
May but lead you to fight.

No! Take woman stronger
Than Vega's bright blare
For then you live longer
Yea, live to get there!
(Tales of the Space Rangers)

Hippocrates finished this quotation with considerable satisfaction which lasted only long enough to see that Ole Doc hadn't even heard it. He glumly subsided, despairing, for there was no mistaking the elasticity of Ole Doc's step, nor the softness of his eye.

It was a beautiful night. Spico's several moons made the ground iridescent and played in triangular patterns upon the reservoirs. Ole Doc was very cheerful. "Now there," he said, "dump a third of that sack in each one of these and back we'll go."

It was not until now that Hippocrates gave way to the most gloomy forebodings. He had seen Ole Doc busy with his tubes. He had seen this white powder gushing out into the sacks but he had not associated it with the population of Junction City. Even if his reasoning powers might be feeble, it took no great effort on his part to see that Ole Doc fully intended to poison every person there. Hippocrates hesitated.

He was trembling, so great was the effort to disobey Ole Doc. He had no conversation to match his feelings about this. He could only look mutely, appealingly, and stand still.

"Go ahead," said Ole Doc. And then, focusing more closely upon his slave he suddenly realized that that being was considerably afraid.

Hippocrates tried to begin the Universal Medical Code once more but failed.

Although it greatly taxed his strength Ole Doc picked up the bag and began the task himself. The white powder went instantly into solution and one could see it spreading far out across the reservoir in the moonlight. When he had treated all three of the repositories he gave the empty sack back to Hippocrates. Such was the manner of the giving that Ole Doc's anger was clearly demonstrated in it.

All the way back to the *Morgue* Hippocrates lagged behind, head heavy against his barrel chest, gypsum tears dripping slowly onto his doublet. It was the first time Ole Doc had ever been angry with him.

The strains of various instruments and occasional shouts came on the night wind from the more lawless quarter of Junction City. Closer at hand a campfire burned and about it clustered the flame-bathed faces of pioneers. They listened to a faint and plaintive Magri song which hung over them like some sad ghost of night.

Ole Doc passed close to the group but paused to listen to the woman who sang. In his present mood he could understand the notes if not the words of the melody. They called before his eyes the cascades of bright hair which he supposed waited for him over at the *Morgue.* A wind was blowing softly from Spico's white plains but there was a chill in it and those about the fire huddled closer. They listened in deeper silence.

An eager-faced young Earthman noticed Ole Doc and made way for him in the circle. Ole Doc stumbled against the hydrant which studded this as well as every other lot in Junction City. These people had no home he observed nor lumber with which to build one. They were living instead on the bare ground using blanket screens to protect their dressing. There were several children sprawled even now outside the ring and one of them whimpered and a woman went to it.

The song was done and the young man, offering his tobacco to Ole Doc, said with a smile of camaraderie, "Where's your lot, stranger? Close by?"

"Pretty close," said Ole Doc.

"How many in your party?" said the young man.

"Just myself and a slave."

A woman nearby leaned over with a laugh, "Well, a young fellow like you," she said, "is going to need help when it comes to putting his house together. Why don't you come and help us and then when you get ready we'll help you?"

The young man laughed, several of the others joining in. "That's a fair bargain," he said. "There are fourteen of us and only two of you. That's a pretty good ratio."

The woman looked smilingly on Ole Doc. "We got to remember this is a new country," she said, "and that we're all neighbors. And that if we don't help each other out then we'll never make anything of it."

Ole Doc looked around. "I don't see any building materials here yet," he said.

The young man shook his head, "Not yet. We're looking around to find a job. It took what money we had to buy our passage and get the lot you're sitting on."

An older man across the circle joined in. "Well, according to Captain Blanchard, that atomic power plant should be going up any day now and then we'll all have work. If we don't build a palace first off, why I guess that can wait for a while. A solid roof is all I ask. This one we got now leaks." He looked up at the stars.

They all laughed and the old man who had just spoken, finding the strain too much for him, began to cough. He did so alarmingly, as though at any moment he would spray his soul out on the ground before him. Ole Doc watched, eyes narrowed, suddenly professional. He stood up.

"You want to watch these cold nights, old man," said Ole Doc. He fumbled through his pockets but it was Hippocrates behind him who found what he sought. The small black kit had been stowed in his boot pocket.

Ole Doc took it out now and selected from it a very small but extremely potent pill. He skirted the fire and gave it to the old man.

"Take this and you'll feel better."

There was some question in the eyes about him and considerable reluctance on the part of the old man. For all beware the unhappy human frailty of trying to administer to everyone else's diseases.

"Go ahead," said Ole Doc, "I'm a physician."

The old man took the pill then and swallowed it.

"That ought to cure you in an hour or so," said Ole Doc. "And if you keep yourself dry and warm, your asthma shouldn't be coming back on you very soon."

There was renewed attention about the circle. "Well, by Saturn," said the old man, "I never heard of no pill that'd cure asthma in two or three hours. What kind of a doctor do you be?"

Unbidden, phonograph-record-wise, Hippocrates was only too glad to answer this question. " 'The Soldier of Light is no ordinary physician,' " he announced in his shrill voice. " 'He is part of an organization of six hundred who have dedicated themselves to the ultimate preservation of mankind no matter the wars or explorations of space. There are one hundred and seventy-six trillion human beings throughout this galaxy. There is roughly one physician for every hundred and sixty of these. There are only six hundred Soldiers of Light. They give allegiance to no government, need no passport, so long as they do not engage in political activity, their persons are inviolate.

"'An apprenticeship of forty years is required to become a member of this society and membership is not confirmed even then until the applicant has made an undeniably great contribution to the health and happiness of mankind. Members of the Universal Medical Society do not practice as do ordinary physicians. They accept no fee. The organization is self-supporting.'

"You see before you my master, Soldier of Light seventy-seven, known as Methuselah."

Before Ole Doc could stop them, all the members of the circle about the fire had risen to their feet and the men had uncovered their heads. Not one person there had failed to hear of the organization and several had heard of Ole Doc. None of them had ever before been privileged to behold a member of this awesome and sacred society.

Embarrassed and a bit out of patience with his faithful slave, Ole Doc left hurriedly. He was angry in the realization that it was he himself who was at fault, for he had never attempted to educate Hippocrates into intrigue. He doubted that anyone could possibly impress upon the fellow that Ole Doc could or would do anything which could not be published on every visioscreen in the galaxy. True, there had been some peccadillos in the past but this was before the time of Hippocrates. However, for all his good intentions, he could not bring himself to address the slave in friendly terms and so walked on harshly ahead of him.

Hippocrates, disconsolate, outcast the second time, dropped far behind and finally sat down on a stone beside the path to try to exude his misery into the night and so be rid of it.

By himself Ole Doc reached the ship. He was all the

way into the dining salon before he fully recognized the fact that it was empty. Miss Elston was gone.

At first he thought she might have gone out to take a turn in the night but then a piece of paper, icy white on the salon table, told him this was not the case. It was in Miss Elston's handwriting.

> Please do not try to find me or come for me. I am doing this of my own accord and I have no wish to get you into trouble knowing very well that you could be cast out of your society for engaging in political affairs.
>
> Alicia Elston

Ole Doc read it through twice, trembling. Then throwing it savagely into the corner he dashed to the cabinet where he had enclosed Dart. That worthy was gone. Belatedly he bethought himself that the Martian might well have had his pocket radio phones concealed about him.

The cabinet containing Elston, being unknown, was, of course, undisturbed.

From a locker Ole Doc grabbed a blaster, fifty rounds and a medical case. Still buckling it on he ran across the field where the *Morgue* stood. He headed straight for the building where he had that day seen Blanchard.

Blanchard's white hands fluttered in the night gesticulating before the face of the tramp rocketship captain. Now they threatened, now they pleaded, now they rubbed thumb against fingers in the money sign but whatever they did the hard-bitten old master of the spaceship remained adamant.

Dart squirmed and wriggled nervously as he regarded

the odds in the form of five armed spacemen which they faced.

The captain stood sturdily on the lower step of the air lock and grimly shook his head. "No, Mr. Blanchard, I cain't do nothing like that. I gotta yella ticket, I tell ye. I cain't clear until it's turned white by him that wrote it."

"But I tell you again and again," cried Blanchard, "that I can get a physician here in Junction City who'll give you a white ticket that will get you through any planetary quarantine you face."

"Naw sir, you ain't no regular port and if there's disease to be carried I ain't carryin' it. Nawthing can make me go up against a yella ticket signed by a Soldier of Light."

Sudden intelligence shot through Blanchard's face. His hands stiffened, clenched. "How can this be? When did it happen?"

"Just afore sundown, Mr. Blanchard. He come here and he give me the ticket and he give everybody else the same yella ticket. And while he didn't say *wot* disease, and while he didn't even say there *was* disease, a yella ticket from a Soldier of Light is good enough for me. I don't go nowhere and I don't take you nowhere, and there's no use askin' it cause I'd make myself and my crew an outlaw for all the rest of my days if I was to do it. There ain't no planetary port anywhere in the galaxy that'd receive us with a yella ticket from him."

Anger displayed the extent of Blanchard's defeat. "I can show you there is no disease," he cried wildly. Then, bethinking himself that a more proper frame of mind would better suit his ends he calmed.

"How could you get rid of such a thing as a yellow

ticket? Supposing the Soldier of Light himself were to be stricken by the disease? Supposing he were to die? Then what? Supposing any number of things happened? Supposing Junction City burned down? Supposing, well, you can't stand there and tell me that you would then refuse to leave."

"Oh, that would be different, Mr. Blanchard. But them conditions ain't nowise appeared. While there's a Soldier of Light alive and well and as long as I holds his yella ticket I don't go no place. There's no use offering bribes and there's no use using threats. *I ain't going!*"

The space door shut with a clang.

If Blanchard's eyes had been acetylene torches they would have cut it neatly through but they were not. He and Dart, followed by three outlaws who carried amongst them a quantity of baggage and a peculiarly noisy chest, made their way back towards the Comet Saloon.

They had not gone nearer than the outskirts of the platted town when they encountered two pioneers at one of the innumerable water hydrants which Blanchard had used as props to give stability to his swindle.

They had just drunk when one of them said, in a sour voice, "Look at that damned sky. Goin' to rain, sure as hell."

Blanchard glanced up. The fine brilliance of the stars was not marred by a single cloud anywhere.

"Rain, hell," said the other pioneer, "it'll probably hail or sleet. I never saw a worse lookin' night!"

"My old woman," said the first, "she'll probably die if it turns cold. She's doin' awful poor."

"And you never saw ground," said the second, "harder to dig a grave in."

This gloomy dissertation caused Blanchard to walk

faster. The soft turf yielded, the night was fine. But there was chill in the wind which was not temperature. A lot depended upon the state of mind of these people.

Near the river he paused and let the three carriers come up. They jostled to a halt in the starlight.

"Men," said Blanchard, "I expect there's going to be a little trouble."

This did not amaze the three or bother them. They had been spawned in trouble. Their mental reaction was that Blanchard could be shaken down for a little more now. Not so Dart. He shifted his mask uneasily and mopped behind it with a silk cloth and squirmed. He felt rivulets of perspiration running inside his mailed jacket and yet he was chilly.

"Dart and I," said Blanchard, "have a task to perform, after which we will get a white ticket for the captain back there. The three of you leave your baggage at this point and go to the saloon. We will join you."

"What'll we do with this chest?" said one. He looked at the river.

There were muffled beatings coming from within it now. It was true that someone might come near it and investigate.

Blanchard waved a careless hand. "Make sure she's silent and then throw her in. Things are too complicated now for any part of that." He motioned to Dart and went on.

The three opened the chest and stood for a moment looking down at Alicia Elston.

Dart felt the chill deepening into his brittle bones as he slithered after his master. He looked out at the stars which winked and glared and saw, suddenly, that all this immensity was small indeed. Hardly a livable planet in this galaxy remained where a Soldier of Light had not trod. A thin, luminous wheel faintly beckoned—but it was difficult to get passage on an intergalactic ship. Passports, money, time. And a man with a slave passport such as his would not get far. The very stars seemed to be crowding down against him, pressing into his skull. He clawed suddenly at his mask for his breath was quick, and the abrupt flood of oxygen into his lungs made his pointed ears shrink and ring and the path before him blurred.

Blanchard cursed him as he stumbled and would have said more except for the hum of voices, hive-like, which came from the main section of the town. Uncertainly, Blanchard paused. He hesitated for some time at the edge of the field where stood the *Morgue,* rubbing his sweating palm against the butt of his blaster. The hum increased and there were angry shouts.

Pointing at the crude landing tower beside them, Blanchard ordered Dart up, watching his slave intently.

From the top, Dart viewed the town square and held on hard.

"Well?" yelled Blanchard.

"It's a big mob!" Dart shouted back. There was hysteria in his voice. "That Soldier is up there on a platform talking to them! He's got a portable speaker but I can't hear—"

A renewed and savage howl came from the town, blotting Dart's words. Blanchard started across the field to the *Morgue.*

He scouted the big ship for a moment and then boldly, with past familiarity, wrenched open the port and went into the main control section. His eyes scorched over the walls until they found the long-range weapon rack. He wrenched a missile thrower from its clamps and fitted its telescopic sight upon it. A moment later he was back at the landing tower and climbing.

His white fingers trembled as they gripped the hewn crossbars, for he was well aware of the crime he contemplated and all that it might involve. But his fingers did not tremble when he leveled the missile thrower and there was only bitter calculation in his eye as he gazed through the scope, into the lighted square.

Ole Doc's image wavered in the glass and then steadied. The finder against height registered six hundred and eighty meters. The sight whined for an instant and then flashed green. As the sight opened again, the entire square leaped into the widened, spotter field and the black light of the sight itself came back with all images clear and close.

There was a crash of fire against the pillar on Ole Doc's right and he reeled. Sprays, like orange plumes, radiated down into the crowd and slammed men and women to earth. The material of the platform began to burn and at its base small green puffs bloomed where the dust was burning.

With considerable pride, glowing with the pleasure of good marksmanship, Blanchard looked long at the motionless figure of the doctor about whom fire shoots began to sprout, first from the planking and then from his clothes.

Dart's hysterical tugging brought Blanchard away from the sight. The slave was gesturing at the river which lay on their right.

Bright starlight showed on two bodies which bobbed there, traveling evenly in the quiet current. A moment later a third crossed the light path of an enormous star. The grisly trio hovered together in an eddy as though holding a ghostly conference and then, having decided nothing, drifted casually apart and traveled on.

"To hell with it!" said Blanchard. "A drunken brawl." And he would have gazed again at the square except that he was almost dislodged by Dart's fleeing down the tower with such violence that even his slight weight shook it. He was screaming shrilly.

Blanchard's nerves were grating already. His anger flashed after the running slave. It was all too clear that Dart had broken before this crime's importance. And a broken slave—

Throwing the missile weapon to his hip, Blanchard shot at the running Martian. He tossed flame before the slave but Dart bolted on. Clicking the action over to automatic, Blanchard sprayed gouts of fire around and about the escaping man. But the recoil of the weapon was such that the last blast was directed more nearly at the zenith than at the runner.

Dart, however, had been hit. He was running still but his course was erratic and shortly brought him back into a pattern of fires the weapon had made. He stumbled out of this but now his clothing burned. He stopped, tore in agony at his mask. His screams were punctuated by the slaps of the tenacious mouthpiece against his lips. He turned once more and fell heavily into a fire, sending green drops hurtling up about him. The flames flared, smoke rose, and then no longer fed, the fire guttered down and went out.

Blanchard's hands were trembling as he reached for the crossbars to swing down from the landing tower. He was not without a sense of loss, and for a moment he was appalled at the manner he had handed death to one who, while he might have been cowardly, had at least been loyal. More than this he was shocked by his own lack of self-control, a shock which was doubled by a sickness he felt at being so far thrown out of orbit with his plans.

He reached the ground and, for a moment, hesitated. But the heaviness of his cash-lined pockets and the knowledge that so far he had triumphed gave him courage. He took a deep breath of the cold night and then, with renewed assurance, reloaded his missile weapon and looked about him.

It was not until then that an idea struck him. He crouched a little as though buffeted by the renewed yells coming from the center of town. His gaze swept across the field to the *Morgue.* A white ticket? What did he need of a white ticket?

He laughed in a sharp bark. There were guns on the *Morgue.* Ray disintegrators. And while the ship would have been bested in a battle with a major naval vessel, few transports would be so well armed. And even if the ship had no guns, one could stand her on her tail above this town and the other vessels in the port and leave not one scrap of anything to tell the systems other than that space pirates had evidently been at work.

The yells seemed louder. But without a glance back, Blanchard sprinted to the *Morgue.* Soldier of Light. Well, few would question the occupant of the ship and many were the dismal planets where one could jettison such as she and buy another for half the currency that would be aboard her.

It was for an instant only that Blanchard regretted the way in which he had been forced into doing things for which a man could be enslaved and sent to the hells forever. Elston had been his scapegoat. And a good one, for Elston was dead. But even then Blanchard doubted that any blame would be attached to anyone now except the inevitable space pirates to which the System Police always assigned blame for those crimes which otherwise were never solved. And in ten minutes this corner of Spico would be subject to certain chain reactions caused by either guns or tubes.

He ran past Dart—or the charred thing which had been Dart—and, so vividly was Blanchard seeing everything, he noted that the Martian's salametal tag was glittering brightly. Blanchard paused and tore off his own. There could as easily be two men in that ash pile as one. His identification tag clinked against Dart's.

Starting up again he ran on toward the door of the *Morgue,* gleaming palely golden in the starlight.

"Blanchard!"

Despite himself he whirled, missile weapon at ready. He froze. Halfway between the landing tower and himself a man came running.

"Blanchard!"

He knew that voice. He now saw the man. It was Ole Doc! His clothing was charred, his left arm was held up by a belt. But it was Ole Doc. And behind him swarmed a dark cloud of people.

With a hasty shot, Blanchard made his pursuer dodge. In an instant Blanchard had gained the port. Cursing he brought it to and then raced into the control section. Somewhere a door clanged.

Throwing the gun down Blanchard grabbed for the panel where the starting levers and throttles stood waiting. One set was marked chemical for departure and landing on a port. The other set was marked atomic. It was the second that he thrust full ahead to "start." In about ten seconds there would be the beginning of the fission.

"Blanchard!"

About the ship the mob swung, many of them passing by the tubes.

Mayor Zoran yelled to some of the men to force the ports of the ship and two Centauri men launched their heavy bulks into the task. Somebody in the crowd yelled to keep clear of the tubes and there was an immediate swing to give them berth.

Several pocket torches appeared and turned ship and field into blazing daylight. People gaped up at the golden ship or yelled encouragement to the two Centauri men who were still working at the space port. A little boy managed to climb up to the top of the vessel and with great initiative went to work with a slingshot handle prying up the emergency entrance hatch. People noticed him and howled encouragement at him. His father bellowed at him for a moment trying to get him to come down and then, realizing he had a hero on his hands, began to point and tell people it was his son. The boy vanished into the ship and there was an immediate scream from several women who had just realized that Blanchard might be in there, still alive, after killing Ole Doc.

At this the Centauri men renewed their efforts and bent several iron bars into pretzels working on the door. Suddenly it gave way, but not through their efforts. The little boy had opened it from inside, but when a horde would have bounded through it, the child barred their way with a shrill yell of protest. A moment later the effort withdrew hastily.

But it was not the boy who had turned them. Charred and battered and breathing hard after great exertion, Ole Doc filled the space port. He was holding a small blaster in his right hand and smoke idled up from its muzzle. He became conscious of it and thrust it into his holster.

The startled silence suddenly burst. From three thousand throats volleyed a spontaneous cheer, a cheer which beat in great waves against the ship, almost rocking it. The enthusiasm fled out from the field and smote against the surrounding hills to come back redoubled and meet the new, louder bursts which sprang up amid tossed hats.

Ole Doc was trying to say something, but each attempt was battered back and drowned in the tumult. Finally, when he had for the fifth time raised his hand for silence, they let him speak.

"I want to tell Mayor Zoran—"

There were new cheers for Mayor Zoran and he came forward.

"Tell your people," said Ole Doc, "that their money is safe."

There was bedlam in answer to this.

"You had better," said Ole Doc when he could again speak, "drain your water systems, all the reservoirs. I... well— Just drain them and don't drink any more water until you do."

They cheered this, for they would have cheered anything.

When he could talk, Ole Doc called for Hippocrates. But no Hippocrates answered. People went off eagerly looking for the doctor's slave but there was no instant result.

Finally Ole Doc thanked them and put the little boy outside and, despite many yells for reappearance, kept the space port firmly closed.

Still, there was much to talk about and the crowd, half hopeful that Ole Doc would come back, hung about the ship.

Some space rangers found the ashes and the two identification tags and rumors began to fly around that it hadn't been Blanchard who had gone into the ship. New waves of pessimism went through the crowd. If that was Blanchard there, in the ashes, then what had happened to the money? Maybe it had been burned with Blanchard. People began to drift back to the ship and scream for Ole Doc to come out again.

Several lost interest and recalling the doctor's admonition to drain the reservoirs, followed the lead of a local common physician who sought some reflected glory and went off to do what they were told.

But those who remained were suddenly stricken in their tracks by the sound, peculiarly fiendish and high-pitched, of a dynamo within the ship. They first mistook it for some wail of a savage beast and then identified it. Shortly afterwards lights began to arc in the midship ports and so brilliant was their flare that they sent green, yellow and red tongues licking across the field and lighted up the rows of attentive faces near at hand.

Other dynamos began to cut in and the golden ship vibrated from bow to tubes. There were some who held that she was about to take off and so went well back from her but others, more intelligent, found in these weird manifestations no such message—nor any message at all—and so hung about in fascination.

It was the little boy, hero of the earlier episode, who again adventured. He climbed up to the emergency entrance hatch which was still open and started to climb down.

Within the instant he shot forth again, his face ghastly

in the torches. He came stumbling down the hull ladder and collapsed at its foot. One hand on the last rung kept him from sinking to the ground and in this position he was ill.

Eager people crowded about him and lifted him up, volleying questions at him. But the child only screamed and beat at them to be let go. When he was finally released he sped nimbly past the crowd and sought sobbing comfort in his mother's arms.

Rumors began to double, then. There were those in the crowd who held that some devil's work was afoot inside that ship. Others hazarded the wild theory that it had not been the doctor at all who had come to the space port, but Blanchard in the doctor's clothes. Others began to retell mysterious and awful things they had heard about the Soldiers of Light, doctors whom no one knew, who were too powerful to be under any government. Somebody began to say that the System Patrol cruisers should be informed and shortly an authoritative youth, a radioman on one of the spaceships in the other port, walked away to send the message, promising a patrol ship there before morning.

With this new stimulus reaching out, people of the town began to cluster back around the ship in great numbers and there were many ugly comments in the crowd. Finally Mayor Zoran himself was called upon for action and he was pressed to the fore where he rapped imperiously upon the space port of the *Morgue.*

The weird screaming dynamos whined on. The lights flashed and arced without interruption. An hour went by.

People remembered then something they had heard about Soldiers of Light, that it was enough to be banished for them to interfere with politics anywhere. This convinced them that something violent should be done to the man in the ship and blasters began to appear here and there and a battering ram was brought up to force the door. Nobody would risk the emergency port.

The difference between the loud whinings within and the sudden silence was so sharp that the battering ram crew hesitated. In the silence ears rang. Crickets could be heard chirping near the river. No one spoke.

With a slow moan, the space port opened from within. Bathed in the glare of half a hundred torches, a gray-haired, noble visaged man stood there. He looked calmly down upon the crowd.

"My friends," he said, "I am Alyn Elston."

They gaped at him. A few came nearer and stared. The man appeared tired but the very image of the pictures on all the literature.

"I am here, my friends, to tell you that tomorrow morning you shall have all your money returned to you or shall be given work on certain projects I envision here—and will finance—as you yourselves may elect. I have the money with me. I need the records and I am sure morning will do wonderfully well. However, if any of you doubt and can show me your receipts I shall begin now—"

They knew him then. They knew him and their relief was so great after all their suspicions and worries that the cheers they sent forth reached twice as far as those they had given Ole Doc. The rolling thunderbolts of sound made the ship and town shiver. Men began to join hands and dance in crazy circles. Hats went skyward. They cheered and cheered until there was nothing to their voices but harsh croaks. And this called for wetness and so they flooded into the town. They carried Elston on their shoulders and hundreds fought with one another to clasp his hand and promise him devotion forever.

In a very short while they would let him speak again.

And he would speak and they would speak and the available supply of liquor would drop very low indeed in Junction City.

Back aboard the *Morgue,* had they not been so loud, had sounded a strange series of thumps and rattles which betokened the disposal in the garbage disintegrator of certain superfluous mass which had been, at the last, in the doctor's road.

And now quietly, palely, the real and only hero of the affair, utterly forgotten, worked feebly on himself, trying to take away the burn scars and the weariness. He gave it up. His heart was too ill with worry. He stumbled tiredly toward his cabin where he hoped to get new clothes. Near the space port he stopped, stuck numb.

Hippocrates was standing there and in the little being's four arms lay cradled a burden which was very precious to Ole Doc. Alicia Elston's bare throat stretched out whitely, her lips were partly opened, her bright hair fell in a long, dripping waterfall. About Hippocrates' feet spread drops of water.

Ole Doc's alarm received a welcome check.

"She is well," said Hippocrates. "When I walked along the river bank I found three men taking her from a chest. I killed two but the third threw her in the river. I killed the third and threw them in but walked for many minutes on the river bottom before I found her. I ran with her to the nearest spaceship and there we gave her the pulmotor and oxygen. I made her lie warmly in blankets until she slept and then I brought her here. What was this crowd, master? What was all the cheering?"

"How did you come to find her?" cried Ole Doc, hastily guiding his slave into a cabin where Alicia could be laid in a bed and covered again.

"I . . . I was sad. I walked along the river. I see better at night and so saw them." But this, obviously, was not what interested Hippocrates. He saw no reason to dwell upon the small radar tube he had put in her pocket so he would not have to go over two square miles of Junction City at some future date when Ole Doc wanted a message sent to her. There were many things he did which he saw no reason to discuss with an important mind like Ole Doc's.

Disregarding the joy and relief and thankfulness which was flooding from his master, Hippocrates stood sturdily in the cabin door until Ole Doc started to leave.

"I don't know how I can ever—"

Hippocrates interrupted his thanks.

"You have Miss Elston, master. The spaceways are wide. We can go far. By tomorrow morning it will be known that a Soldier of Light has entered social relations and politics. By tomorrow night the System Patrols will be looking for us. By the next day your Society will have banished us or called us to a hearing to banish us. It is little time. We have provisions to leave this galaxy. Somewhere, maybe Andromeda, we can find outlaws and join them—"

Ole Doc looked severely at him.

Hippocrates stepped humbly aside. He cast a glance at the woman he had saved and at his master. He saw that things would be different now.

• • •

It was a bright morning. Dawn came and bathed the *Morgue* until every golden plate of her gleamed iridescently. The grass of the field sparkled with dew and a host of birds swooped and played noisily in the rose and azure sky.

Junction City stirred groggily. It scrubbed its eyes, tried to hide from the light, scrubbed again and with aching heads and thick tongues arose.

No comments were made on the revel. The Comet Saloon was shut tightly. Blanchard's house swung its doors idly in the wind. But no one commented. Everyone stumbled about and said nothing to anyone about anything.

So passed the first few hours of morning. People began to take an interest in existence when a System Patrol cruiser swung in and with a chemical rocket blast settled in the main spaceport.

Hippocrates, sweeping the steps of the port ladder, looked worriedly at the newcomer and then threw down his broom. He rolled into the main salon where he knew Ole Doc was.

Opening his mouth to speak three successive times, Hippocrates still did not. Ole Doc was sitting in an attitude of thought from which no mere worldly noise ever roused him. Presently he rose and paced about the table. He paid no heed whatever to Hippocrates.

Finally the small being broke through all codes. "Master, they are coming! We still have time. We still have time! I do not want you to be taken!"

But he might as well have addressed the clouds which drifted smoothly overhead. With long paces the doctor was walking out a problem. His appearance was much improved over last night for all burns had vanished the night before and the arm was scatheless. However, it lacked days until treatment time and the rule never varied. Ole Doc looked a little gray, a little worn, and there were lines about his mouth and in the corners of his eyes.

Once he walked to a cabinet where he kept papers and threw back a plast-leaf and looked at a certificate there. He stood for a long time thus and finally broke off to stand in the doorway of Alicia's cabin where the girl still slept, lovely, vital and young.

Hippocrates tried to speak again. "We can take her and the ship still has time. They have not yet come into the town to get reports—"

Ole Doc stood looking sadly at the girl. His slave went back to the space port and stared at the town.

A little wind rippled the tops of the grass. The silver-plated river flowed smoothly on. But Hippocrates saw no beauty in this day. His sharp attention was only for the group of System officers who went into the town, stayed a space and then came out towards the ship, followed by several idlers and two dogs and a small boy.

Rushing back to the salon, Hippocrates started to speak. His entrance was abrupt and startled Alicia, who now, dressed and twice as lovely as before, stood beside Ole Doc at the file cabinet.

"Master!" pleaded Hippocrates.

But Ole Doc had no ears for his slave. He saw only Alicia. And Alicia had but scant attention for Hippocrates; she was entirely absorbed in what Ole Doc had been saying. It seemed to the little slave that there was a kind of horror about her expression as she looked at the doctor.

Then Ole Doc opened up the plast-leaf and showed her something there. She looked. She turned white and trembled. Her gaze on Ole Doc was that of a hypnotized but terrified bird. With an unconscious movement she drew back her skirt from him and then steadied herself against the table.

"And so, my dear," said Ole Doc. "Now you know. Pardon me for what I proposed, for misleading you."

She drew farther back and began to stammer something about undying gratitude and her father's thanks and her own hopes for his future and many other things that all tumbled together into an urgent request to get away.

Ole Doc smiled sadly. He bowed to her and his golden silk shirt rustled against his jeweled belt. "Good-bye, my dear."

Hastily, hurriedly, she said good-bye and then, hand to throat, ran past the slave and down the ladder and across the spaceport to the town.

Hippocrates watched her go, looked at her as she skirted the oncoming officers and started toward a crowd in the square which seemed to be listening to an address by her father. The cheers were faint only by distance. Hippocrates scratched his antennae thoughtfully for a moment and then turned all attention to the approaching officers. He bristled and cast a glance at the blaster rack.

"Hello up there!" said a smooth, elegant young man in the scarlet uniform of the System Patrol.

"Nobody here!" stated Hippocrates.

"Be quiet," said Ole Doc behind him. "Come aboard, gentlemen."

The idlers and the small boy and the dogs stayed out, held by Hippocrates' glare. The salon was shortly full of scarlet.

"Sir," said the officer languidly, "we have audacity

I know in coming here. But as you are senior to anyone else . . . well, could you tell us anything about a strange call from this locale? We hate to trouble you. But we heard a call and we came. We had no details. Five people, fellow named Blanchard and his friends, ran away into the country or some place. But no riot. Could you possibly inform us of anything, sir?"

Ole Doc smiled. "I hear there was a riot among the five," he said. "But I have no details. Just rumor."

"Somebody is jolly well pulling somebody's toe," said the languid young man. "Dull. Five men vanishing is nothing to contact *us* about. But a riot now." He sighed at the prospect and then slumped in boredom. "No radioman aboard any ship here sent such a message, they say, and yet we have three monitors who heard it. Hoax, what?"

"Quite," smiled Ole Doc. "A hoax!"

"Well, better be getting on." And they left, courteously and rather humbly refusing refreshment.

It was a very staggered little slave who watched them go. The small boy lingered and gazed at the ship as though trying to put a finger on something in his mind. He was a very adventurous boy, exactly the same that had scaled the ship the night before. He frowned, puzzled.

"Man child," said Hippocrates, "do you recall a riot?"

The little boy shook his head. "I . . . I kind of forget. Everybody seems to think maybe there should have been one—"

"Do you remember anybody named Blanchard getting killed?" thrust Hippocrates, producing a cake mystically from the pantry behind him.

"Oh, he didn't get killed. Everybody knows that. He ran away when Mr. Elston came."

"You remember a Soldier of Light addressing a crowd last night?"

"What? Did he?"

"No," said Hippocrates, firmly. "He was not out of this ship all day yesterday nor last night either." And he tossed down the cake which was avidly seized.

Hippocrates stomped back into the salon.

He did not know what he expected to find, but certainly not such normality. Ole Doc was playing a record about a fiddler of Saphi who fiddled for a crown and, while humming the air, was contentedly filling up a cuff with a number of calculations.

With a gruff voice, Hippocrates said, "You poured powder in the water to make everyone forget, to be angry and then forget. And it's worn off. Nobody remembers anything. Mr. Elston and Alicia have promised not to speak. I see it. But you should have told me. I worried for you. You should have told me! Nobody will ever know and I was sick with what would happen!"

Ole Doc, between hums, was saying, "Now with the twenty thousand that I got back, and with what is in the safe, I have just enough to cruise to . . . da, dum, de da . . . yes. Yes, by Georgette, I shall!" He threw down the pencil and got up, smiling.

"Hello, Hippocrates, old friend," said Ole Doc, just noticing him. "And how are you this wonderful noon? What will you fix me for lunch? Make it good, now, and no wine. We're taking off right away for Saphi. We're going to buy us a complete new set of raditronic equipment there and get rid of all this worn out junk. Why—" he stopped, staring, "Why you're crying!"

Hippocrates bellowed, "I am not!" and hurriedly began to clear the table to spread out the finest lunch ever set before the finest master of the happiest and most won-back slave in the galaxy. In a moment or two, exactly imitating the record which had stopped, he was singing the "Fiddler of Saphi," the happiest he had been in a very, very long time.

During lunch, while he shoved new dishes about on their golden plates, Hippocrates took a moment to glance, as a well-informed slave should, at the certificate which had made that horrible, detestable woman so gratifyingly scared.

The aged, carefully coated and preserved parchment—brown and spotted with mildew from some ancient time even so—surrendered very little information to Hippocrates. It merely said that the University of Johns Hopkins on some planet named Baltimore in a System called Maryland—wherever that might be—did hereby graduate with full honors one Stephen Thomas Methridge as a physician in the year of our Lord Nineteen Hundred and Forty-Six Anno Domini.

Even if this *was* seven hundred years ago that Ole Doc first learned his trade, what of that? He knew more than any doctor graduated in the best school they had today.

Well, good riddance, though just why she should so disapprove of that school was more than Hippocrates could figure out.

He sang about the Fiddler of Saphi and forgot it in the happy scramble of departure.

HER MAJESTY'S
ABERRATION

HER MAJESTY'S ABERRATION

There is a slight disadvantage in being absent-minded. It was this regrettable failing which took Ole Doc Methuselah, highly respected member of the Universal Medical Society, some forty-five light-years out of his way and caused him to land in the Algol System on the planet Dorcon.

Hippocrates had asked him, pointedly and repeatedly, if they had taken aboard a new pile at Spico and Ole Doc had answered him abstractedly in the affirmative. But it developed, some ninety light-years out, that they were traveling on the ship's reputation and that the poor old *Morgue* had but three or four grasshopper power left in her gleaming, golden tubes.

This was annoying. Hippocrates said so and, waving his four short arms, repeated, phonograph-record-wise, a two hundred thousand-word text on fuels and their necessity in space travel. He repeated it so shrilly that Ole Doc in the pilot compartment unhooked every means of communication with the operating room where Hippocrates was delivering his secondhand oration and then used inertia converters to get down, somehow, into the Algol System.

He had never been there before, which was odd because it was not too distant from Earth—on the same side of the Earth Galactic Wheel, in fact. He had heard several things about it, now and then, for a man hears quite a bit when he has lived some seven hundred and fifty years. Somewhere near the beginning of that span he had jettisoned most superstition and thus it had not been this which prevented him, though it well might have been.

Algol had a rotten reputation around the space ports. For some thousands of years men had been looking at it and shuddering only because it winked every three days. They called it the "Evil Eye" and the "Demon Star" and so deep was the feeling that for a century or more after space travel and colonization had begun, people had left Algol alone, not even informing themselves if she had planets.

The wise knew she was a dark star rotating around a bright one, which accounted for her being a variable, but when an expedition crashed on one of her planets, when the first colony vanished, when a transgalactic flier burned in the system, people began to recall her original reputation and shun her. That, of course, made her an excellent pirate base and all six of her variously inhabitable planets were soon messed about with blood and broken loot.

"As is natural in such evolutions, she ultimately gave birth—" it said in the *United Planets Vacugraphic Office Star Pilot* which Ole Doc was reading on his knees (still holding the buttons down on his creature Hippocrates)"—to a strong ruler who ate up the lesser ones and for the past three hundred and nineteen years has been getting along as a monarchy of six planetic states governed from Dorcon." It said in the book that "there were spaceship ways and limited repair facilities, fuel and supplies to be had at Ringo, Dorcon's chief city." Certainly they would have so small a thing as a pile there.

Ole Doc started to open the switch to tell Hippocrates where they were going but received a flood instead:

"'The manual circuits must be supplied by auxiliary

hanbits of torque-compensated valadium. Five erg seconds of injected . . . ' "

Plainly Hippocrates was not pleased. Ole Doc laughed uncomfortably. He had picked the weird little creature up at an auction a century back, meaning to examine his metabolism which was gypsum, but the gnome had been so willing and his brain was so accurately gauged to remembering that somehow Ole Doc had never thought again about examinations but had succumbed to these deluges of being informed.

A gong rang. A whistle blew. A big plate before him began to *flick-flick-flick* as it displayed likely landing spots, one after another. A metal finger jutted suddenly from the gravity meter and touched off the proximity coil. The ship went on to chemical brakes. The cockpit turned at right angles to ease the deceleration of the last few hundred miles and then there was a slight bump. The *Morgue* had sat down. There was a clang inside as her safety doors slid open again, a tinkle of ladders dropping and a *click-click-click* as instruments dusted themselves and put themselves out of sight in the bulkheads.

Ole Doc unbuckled his crash helmet and stood up, stretching. The port guards were sliding open of themselves, displaying a green expanse of field, a surrounding regiment of trees and the plastic towers of a city beyond.

But the instruments were not yet through. The analyzer came out, a square massed solid in red and green bulbs which recorded the presence of anything harmful, unnatural or hostile. And while it said green to atmosphere, gravity, vegetation, food, habitations, the weather, storms, the surface temperature, the subsurface temperature, radioactive presences and a thousand others, it said *red-red-red* to soldiers, weapons, dead men, women and hostility. The strip at the bottom of the board read, "Relatively unsafe. Recommend take-off."

Ole Doc owed his continued presence in the flesh to a certain superstition about instruments. If they were there they should be observed, and, if they gave advice, it should be taken. And he was about to take off on chemical and go elsewhere nearby when Hippocrates thrust his outraged antennae into the compartment.

"'. . . momentary inattention to fissure temperatures may result in ionization of farundium particles and consequent—'"

"STOP IT!" said Ole Doc.

Hippocrates stopped it. But not because he was told. He was reading "Relatively unsafe. Recommend take-off." This gave him an impasse and while his dissertation struggled fiercely with this check, Ole Doc dropped down into his dining salon and drank the milk which waited there for him.

The ports were all open there, for the salon was beautifully designed, done by Siraglio shortly after the turn of the century, paneled in gold and obsidian and exquisitely muraled with an infinity of feasting scenes which, together, blended into a large star map of the Earth Galaxy as it had been known in his time. The ports were so designed as to permit scenery to become a portion of the mural without ruining it. But in this case the scenery did not cooperate.

Six hundred and nineteen dead men swung from the limbs of the landing field trees. They were in uniforms bleached by suns and snows and their features were mostly ragged teeth and yellow bone. The blasts of the *Morgue*'s landing had made a wind in which they swung, idly, indolently as though in their timeless way they waltzed and spun to an unheard dirge.

Ole Doc set down the milk. He looked from flowering beds, well-groomed grass, splendid walks back to the hanging dead.

"Hippocrates!"

The gnome was there instantly, all five hundred kilos of him.

"Stand by the ship. If anyone approaches her but myself, turn on Force Screen Alpha. Keep in communication with me and the ship in readiness to blast. Questions?"

Hippocrates was too thwarted to reply and Ole Doc changed into a golden tunic, threw a sun-fiber cloak about his shoulders, buckled twin blasters around his waist and stepped down the ladder to the ground.

A man develops, after a few score years, certain sensitivities which are not necessarily recognized as senses. Carrying on the business of the Universal Medical Society was apt to quicken them. For though the members of the society possessed amongst them the monopoly of all medical knowledge forbidden by the various systems and states and although they had no sovereign and were inviolate, things happen. Yes, things happen. More than a hundred ebony coffins lay in the little chapel of their far off base—Soldiers of Light who had come home forever.

He directed, therefore, his entire energy to getting a pile and escaping Ringo within the hour if possible. And, guided by the sound of repair arcs and hammers, promptly brought himself to the subsurface shops beside the hangars of the field.

And at the door he halted in stupefied amazement.

There were ten or twelve mechanics there and they did mechanics' work. But they were shackled one to the next by long, tangling strands of plastiron which was electrically belled every few yards to warn of its breaking. And overseeing them was not the usual supereducated artisan-engineer but a dough-faced guard of bovine attention to the surroundings.

Ole Doc would have backed out to look for the supply office, but the guard instantly hailed him.

"Stand where you be, you!" He advanced, machine blaster at ready and finger on trigger. "Hey, Eddy! Sound it!" A gong struck hysterically somewhere in the dark metallic depths of the place.

It was a toss-up whether Ole Doc drew and fired or stood and explained. But an instant later a barrel was digging a hole in his back.

Now if the President of the Vega Confederation had been so greeted by his lackey, he could not have been more amazed than Ole Doc. For though he was occasionally offered violence, he was almost never accosted in terms of ignorance. For who did not know of the Soldiers of Light, the Ageless Ones who ordered kings?

This pair, obviously.

They were animals, nothing more. Mongrels of Earth and Scorpon stock, both bearing the brands of prisons on their faces.

"He ain't got a chain," said Eddy.

"Must've landed," hazarded the guard, straining his intellect.

"If you will please—" began Ole Doc.

"They'll be here in a minute, bud," said Eddy, planting his thick boots squarely in Ole Doc's path. He reeked of Old Space Ranger and was obviously a victim of an unmentionable illness.

They were there in less than that. An entire squad sled of them, complete with dirty uniforms, unshaven faces, yellow eyes and shiny weapons.

"Get in, pal," said Eddy, disarming Ole Doc with a yank.

"Ain't he pretty, though," said a young corporal.

"Get in!" insisted Eddy.

Ole Doc saw no sense in a chance killing. It was not that serious yet. People weren't entirely stupid on Dorcon. They couldn't be!

He mounted the sled which promptly soared off toward the city, ten feet above the ground and traveling erratically. In the glimpse he had of the blue-green pavements and yellow houses of the suburbs, Ole Doc was aware of neglect and misery. A number of these inhabitants were evidently of Mongolian origin for the architecture had that atmosphere, but now the once-gay pagodas looked more like tombs, their walled gardens gone to ruin, their stunted trees straggling out from broken bonds. The desolation was heightened by the hobbling gait of a few ancient inhabitants who dodged in fear below the sled. It shocked Ole Doc to see that each was chained to a round ball.

The sled swept on toward the blue towers, but, as it neared, the first illusion of palace gave way to a gray atmosphere of prison. For the government buildings were all enclosed within many walls, each complete in its defenses, each manned like some penitentiary on Earth. Here was prison within prison within prison. Or defense within defense within defense. And the central portion, instead of being a courtyard and keep, was a metal-roofed dome, wholly bombproof.

But the sled had no business within. It bounced to a landing outside the guard house of the first walls and there

Ole Doc was thrust into the presence of a dissolute young man.

Tunic collar unbuttoned to show a dirty neck, greasy hair awry, he sat with heels amongst the glasses and bottles on his desk. Obviously he was of that decayed school which thought that to be dashing one must be drunk.

"Where's identity card?" he hiccoughed.

Ole Doc, naturally, had no such thing. But the rayed gold medallion around his neck was a passport to the greatest kingdoms in the universe.

"What's that?" said the young officer.

"My identification," said Ole Doc. "I am a member of the Universal Medical Society."

"The what?"

"I am a physician," said Ole Doc patiently.

The young man thereupon altered. He looked bright and interested. He brought his feet down off the desk, upsetting several glasses and bottles and snatched up an antique gadget Ole Doc recognized dimly as a telephone.

"I got a doctor out here, Sir Pudno. How do you like that, huh? . . . Sure he looks like one. Why do you think I'd say so? . . . Okay, Sir Pudno. Right away."

In the wake of the reeling young officer Ole Doc was then delivered through eighteen separate ramparts, each gated, each guarded, until he came at last to a stairway which led underground. The officer having navigated this without falling, Ole Doc was ushered—or rather shoved—into a chamber done in blue silk, a particularly gloomy place which had for furniture but one bed and one chair.

Sir Pudno was getting out of bed. He was a flabby, fat

Mongolian of no definite features. He rolled himself up in a food-spattered dressing gown, sat soddenly in the chair and stared at Ole Doc.

"You really a doctor, Mac?" said Sir Pudno.

"I am. If you have some one to be treated, I shall be happy to oblige you. However there is a matter of a pile I need. I landed here—"

"Clam it, Mac," said Sir Pudno. "We'll go right up to Her Majesty."

He tucked his fat into a seam-strained uniform and then Ole Doc was thrust after him into a chamber which was more like a powder magazine than a throne room. It was huge and once it had been pretty. But all the murals and mirrors had been removed and in their places were sheets of steel. No sunlight entered here and the pale blue gleam of lamps thickened the gloom.

The dais was thickly curtained and into the curtains had been set the kind of glass which admits light and therefore sight only one way. Someone or something sat behind on a throne.

Sir Pudno saluted and bowed. "Your Majesty, by great good luck I've been able to get a doctor up here."

"At how much cut of his fee?" said the person behind the curtain. The voice was rasping. Her Majesty was in no good mood.

"There's been no conversation of fee, Your Majesty," said Ole Doc. "Nor has there been any talk of services. I am a member of the Universal Medical Society and must not be detained. If you have a patient, I will do what I can without fee other than a pile for my ship. I repeat that I must not be delayed."

"He talks like he thinks he's somebody," said the person

behind the curtains. "Well, show him the young fool. And remember this, you. Cure him but not too well. What did you say you were a member of?"

"The Universal Medical Society," said Ole Doc. "We do not like governments which detain our members."

"You know your business, huh?" said Her Majesty.

"People think so," said Ole Doc. "Now take me to the patient. I have no time to waste."

"You treat crazy people, too?" said Her Majesty.

"I have been known to do so," said Ole Doc, looking fixedly at the curtain.

"You seem to be pretty young. Curly hair and pink cheeks. Would you know how to make somebody crazy, now?"

"Perhaps."

"Build a machine or something to make people crazy?" she persisted.

"That is possible. Sometimes machines aren't necessary."

"Oh yes they are. I'd pay you well if you did it."

"What?"

"Made somebody crazy," said Her Majesty behind the curtain.

"This is out of my line," said Ole Doc.

"Well, show him to the patient anyway," said Her Majesty.

It was a tortuous way Sir Pudno led them. Urging Ole Doc on ahead of him and followed by an escort of twenty guards, Sir Pudno finally brought them to a chamber some two hundred feet into the earth. It was barred and sealed and guarded in three separate depths but opened at last into a mean, damp cubicle which stank of unwashed flesh and rotting straw.

They thrust Ole Doc into the darkness with a shove against the stone which stunned him slightly and in that instant took away his kit and belt radio. The barriers clanged grimly behind him and left him ruefully rubbing his scalp in the fetid gloom.

Ole Doc pulled the tie string of his cloak and a small spotlight, which served ordinarily as a button, lighted and, when readjusted, spread a conical shaft into the mote-filled chamber. The circle lighted upon a young woman who clung to the far wall, fending the glare from the eyes of a small child in her arms. She was dressed in ragged finery, pale and soiled with long imprisonment, but humility she had not yet been taught. Chin up and nostrils flaring, she glared back at the light.

Turning, Ole Doc let the beam play over the remainder of this tiny cubicle and brought it to rest on the man.

He lay in dirty straw, face hidden by his arm. His fine, frilled shirt was ripped, his scarlet sash was blackened with grime, his trousers and small boots were white dusted and flecked with straw. Ole Doc moved a step toward him and found the woman interposed.

"You shan't touch him!"

Gently, Ole Doc removed her hand from his cloak. "I am a physician. They have permitted me to come here, saying that he is ill."

Half-doubting, she let him come nearer. He took a second button from his cloak and set it on a stone ledge where it shed a bright light over the recumbent young man.

The bright, hectic spots in his cheeks, the rattle in his lungs, the odor of him and the wasted condition of his hands cried tuberculosis to Ole Doc—and in the last stages.

He had not seen an advanced case of the disease for more than two hundred years and it was with great shock that he plumbed the ignorance of these people.

"This is dangerous!" he said. "A child in here with this. No care, no understanding. My God, woman, how long have you been here?"

She was protecting her eyes from the light but she raised them now, proud of her endurance. "Six orbits. My child is three."

"And they permitted . . ." Ole Doc was angry. He had not seen brutality such as this for a long, long time. For these people were not criminals. The woman and the man both looked highborn.

"Who are you?" demanded Ole Doc.

"This is Rudolf, uncrowned king of Greater Algol. I am his queen, Ayilt."

"Then," said Ole Doc, a little amazed to find himself not proof against surprises, "who is that who reigns?"

"His mother, the wife of Conore, dead six orbits gone."

Ole Doc glanced back at the doors. He was wondering how dangerous it might be to know too much about this. And then he decided, after one glance at the frightened child. "Start at the beginning."

"You are a stranger to all these planets, that I see well," said Ayilt, seating herself on the straw. "We know almost as little about the rest of space, for we are not rich nor brilliant and our planets are small, arid things, mostly stone with little land to till. And so I do not wonder that we are forgotten.

"We came from pirate stock—not the best to be sure.

And the mainstay of our population had been the terrestrial oriental who can live anywhere.

"Even so we had a happy government. There was not much. The last of the great revolutions was more than two hundred years ago and after that his family"—and she indicated the feverish, tossing boy on the straw—"stabilized the government. King Conore ruled justly and wisely and was much beloved by everyone. Since the beginning, because of our pirate origin, we discouraged traffic with space and it was well, for we had white and Scorpon stock and, outcast as it was, it often went bad. We had many prison colonies, but little crime. King Conore, like his forebears, was kind to prisoners. He gave them their chance in their own society and though he would not let them return to our worlds, they prospered in their way. But the terrible error was the sentencing of women to these colonies, for women, I am ashamed to say, often descend from criminal stock as criminals. And so it was that our prison settlement population was large.

"We considered prisoners hopeless. We took away any promising young. We hoped that these eugenics would serve us, and perhaps eventually wipe away all traces of our shameful origin. But now and then we erred.

"Yes, we erred. King Conore took a royal princess of the Olin line to wed, forgetting she had been born in a prison settlement, for she had been removed at the age of four and was a brilliant woman and beautiful.

"They reigned well and wisely until there came a day when new pirates came. No one knows from whence they came nor why, but they were not of this system. They are all dead now but it was said that the leader was terrestrial.

"Unsuspected they raised revolt among our Mongolians and then struck the blow themselves. During a pageant given in honor of my husband and myself, to celebrate our marriage, the rebels threw a bomb into the royal car.

"King Conore was killed outright. His wife Pauma was seriously injured about the face and was blinded in one eye. Palace guards were prompt but not quick enough to prevent the bomb. She had them hanged, six hundred and more of them. She butchered the royal servants. She cast my husband and myself into this hole. She tried and tortured to death in all more than a million people on the six planets and then the stomachs of all decent folk turned and they tried to smash her.

"We had forgotten her origin. We had forgotten the bitterness of a beautiful woman turned ugly. We had forgotten the prison settlements.

"We were set upon by convicts—or rather the planets were, for my husband and I were imprisoned here. The army, all guards, all important dignitaries were killed or disbanded by Pauma's treachery and the convicts were set in their places.

"Unlettered, revengeful, wicked, the freed prisoners began to wreck the people and the land. And they could do this for there was one convict for every three people on our planets.

"My husband and I owe our continued lives to the fear of Pauma that some other of our planets may revolt, for there is hope everywhere that my husband still may arise from this tomb and govern as did his father."

"She keeps her own son here, then," said Ole Doc.

"Why not, doctor? He opposed her first measures, trying to point out that it was exterior influence which caused the tragedy. But she was always jealous of Rudolf, for after his birth his father made too much of him and often at Pauma's expense.

"Royal line or not, Pauma was a gutter urchin. A prison settlement child. She told Rudolf that he meant to depose her and kill her. But she has to keep him here. While he lives no one dares raise a hand against Pauma for she has often threatened to execute him if this is so and then would ensue nothing but night for all Algol.

"This is why you find us here, doctor. Can you please do something for my husband? He has some fever or other and has not talked for days, for when he talks he spits blood. See, the straw is spattered with it."

"We'll see what can be done," said Ole Doc. And he called harshly for the guards and demanded that they return his kit.

Sir Pudno, outside the three barriers, argued about it. He conceived it to be full of weapons and like no doctor's kit he had ever seen. But when Ole Doc finally threatened to do nothing, the kit was passed through.

From it, when he had increased the light on the ledge, Ole Doc took a small plate and placed it on the young man's chest. By moving it about he was able to examine the lungs in their entirety, the plate only covering some two square inches at a time. He shook his head. There was little left of the fellow. He should have been dead days back. But nothing amazed Ole Doc more than the tenacity of the human body in its cling to life.

On his ship he could have done much better but he knew he could not ask that these be removed there. For Ole Doc was working for more than the health of this young king.

He took a vial of mutated bacteria mold and thrust it between the youth's lips. There was no danger of choking him for the cheeks would absorb the entire dose.

Then Ole Doc gave his attention to the woman. He was amazed, when he passed the plate over her breast to find her in such good health. Her heart was strong, her lungs perfect. The only thing she suffered was malnutrition and this on a small scale.

The child was somewhat like the mother but there was a spot upon its lungs. It cried when Ole Doc made it take another vial and the woman looked dangerous as it protested.

"Now," said Ole Doc, "I would advise you to hold your nose. This does not smell good." And he took a bomb the size of his thumb and exploded it against the floor. A dense white cloud, luminescent with ultraviolet light, sprang up and filled the chamber.

The guard without protested, opened up, rushed in and dragged Ole Doc out, thrusting blaster muzzles into his ribs. The door clanged and then the other two barriers shut. Ole Doc was hastened up the long passageway and pushed again into the throne room.

The curtains moved slightly. Now that he had some idea of what was behind them a chill came over the Soldier of Light. For it seemed that black rods of evil were thrusting out from it.

Sir Pudno saluted and bowed. "A treatment has been given, Your Majesty."

"Will he recover?" said Pauma behind the curtains.

"No thanks to you," said Ole Doc. "The boy was nearly dead from a terrible infectious disease. I would not be surprised to find that many suffer from it right here in the palace."

There was silence and a chill amongst the guards. But a laugh came from behind the curtains.

"And if you are not interested in that," said Ole Doc, "you might be interested to learn that diseases are no respecters of rank and glory and that I scent yet another in this very room."

There was silence.

Finally the curtains moved a little. "What may it be?"

"It is known as schizophrenia," said Ole Doc. "Dementia praecox with delusions of persecution. A very deadly thing, Your Majesty. It destroys both victim and executioner."

There was silence again. The silence of ignorance.

"It is a dreadful thing, born from psychic shock. I scent here a broken schizoid of the persecution type, a paranoiac as dangerous to herself as to those about her." Ole Doc thought he spoke plainly and for the life of him, after what he had witnessed below and seen outside, he could not have refrained from this. But plain as he thought it was, only some annoyed glimmering was transmitted.

"I think you mean to be insulting." The curtains shifted.

"Far from it," said Ole Doc. "I only wish to help. I speak of a thing which I know. Here, I will show you."

He faced a guard and then as though he plucked it from the air, a small whirling disc spun brightly in Ole Doc's hand. He held it under the soldier's nose and spoke in a fierce, rapid voice.

There had been a movement to stop him but the antics of the soldier an instant later startled the guards and Sir Pudno into activity. The small disc had vanished, seen by none except the soldier.

"Bow wow! Woof!" and on all fours the soldier began to gallop around the room and sniff at boots. Ole Doc turned to the dais. "You see, Your Majesty? The illness is contagious. By merely shoving at him the soldier becomes a dog."

There was fear and something more behind the curtains. "Remove the guard immediately! Come, you doctor. Do others have this here? Tell me! Do others have this here?"

With something like disgust when he realized the mentalities with which he dealt, Ole Doc faced Sir Pudno.

"I see traces of it here."

"No!" bawled Sir Pudno, backing and stumbling.

But the disc appeared and Ole Doc's voice was harsh if almost unheard even by Sir Pudno.

"Woof! Bow wow!" said Sir Pudno and instantly began to gallop around the room.

There was fear in the place now. Ole Doc took two or three steps toward the guards who had remained and then, suddenly, they bolted.

There was a scream from behind the curtains and then terrified anger as she vainly sought to order them back.

But only the barking Sir Pudno, Ole Doc and Her Majesty remained in the room.

Ole Doc was wary. He knew she must be armed. And he carefully halted ten paces from the curtains.

"I am sorry," he said soothingly. "I am very sorry to have had to disclose this to you. I know what you go through and what you have to face. Only an intelligent man would truly understand that. It must be terrible to be surrounded by such people and to know—" And the little disc was spinning in his hand.

It does not take many years for a powerful personality to acquire the trick. Ole Doc, in a purely medical way, had been practicing it for the last seven hundred. One gets a certain facility that way. And the little disc spun.

There was a sigh behind the curtains. Ole Doc flung them back.

Had he not known the things she had done, pity would have moved him now. For the sight he saw was horrible. The bomb, six orbits ago, had left but little flesh and had blackened that.

He took a glass bomb from his kit and exploded it, carefully backing from the smoke. The narcotic would do what the disc had begun.

She must have spent all her hours behind that curtain for there was her bed, her few clothes, a small dresser. And on the dresser, where the mirror should have been, was a life-size painting of her as she had been in her youth.

Indeed she had been a lovely woman.

Ole Doc rummaged in his kit, sneezing a little as the narcotic fumes drifted his way, and finally located the essentials he needed.

The work did not take long for he had a catalyst. Sir Pudno was guarding the door and growling from time to time, but admitting no one.

Ole Doc ripped the finery from her and bared her back. His all-purpose knife, in his hands, was more than a sculptor's entire rack of tools. He looked from time to time at the life-size painting and then back to his task.

The catalyst went in with every thrust of the knife and before he was finished with the back, it had already begun to heal and would only slightly scar. The shiny grease was the very life of cells and hurled them into an orgy of production.

His surgery was not aseptic, for it did not have to be. Before he was through he would guard against all that. Just now the tumbled bed, spattered with blood, and a few rags of silk made up his temporary operating table and all he required.

The work was long, for the likeness must be good, and the scar tissue was stubborn. And then there was the matter of cartilage which must be cut just so. And it took a while for the follicles of the eyelashes to set. And it required much care to restore activity to the eye nerves. But it was a masterful job. Ole Doc, three hours later, stood back and told himself so.

He gathered up the bloody sheets and thrust his patient into a sitting position on the chair. And all the while he was talking. Her eyes fixed on him now, absorbing every syllable he uttered, began slowly to clear.

Ole Doc had his eyes on the scars which soon ceased to be pink and then turned bone white. Finally they sank out of sight and something like circulation began to redden the cheeks.

It was a good thing Hippocrates was not there. Hippocrates would have said a thing or two about the unmedical quality of some of Ole Doc's statements and Soldiers of Light are not supposed to stray from medicine.

It was time now to do other things.

Sir Pudno barked his compliance and went out to order workmen up and soon a stream of these, hampered by their chains until Ole Doc had them struck off, began to restore the mirrors and paintings to the walls. Other furniture soon appeared, a little frayed from years in storage but nevertheless very brightening. The lighting was altered. New clothes were issued.

Every time anyone came in and demanded authority for

orders such as the removal of the hanging dead at the landing field, Ole Doc had only to shove a hand inside the curtains and a signature came out. It was an opportunity which he did not abuse—but he had ideas which would not remain unordered.

He was enjoying himself. But even so, all this had to be very hurriedly done.

Soon he was able to bring up the rightful king, his queen and prince and they came, blinking and dirty, to be seized without explanation and rushed away. But as they were certain of death they were too stunned to protest. They were washed and robed.

News was spreading. More and more people came until Ole Doc saw the entrance doors bulging. The corridors and courtyards were full. Rumors were flying from city to town, from planet to planet through the system.

Then Ole Doc stood the youth before him. Dressed, shaven, healthy, Rudolf bore little resemblance to the dying man in the hole a few hours before.

Rudolf would have had vast explanations.

But Ole Doc was terse. "You are going to take that throne in about five minutes and you are never going to mention a word of the last six orbits to your mother. I must have your word on that."

Dazed, the boy could only stare at him.

"You are going to retire her to a villa and keep her in luxury. Do I have your word?"

"Yes. Of course. But I—"

"You see that he does keep it," said Ole Doc to Ayilt.

"Never fear. We'll do whatever you say. My God, to think that only a few short hours ago Rudolf was dying— Truly, you must be an angel."

"Others think very differently, I fear," said Ole Doc with a grin. "Charge it up to the Soldiers of Light, the Universal Medical Society. And never breathe a word of how I've taken a hand in politics here. Now, any questions?"

They looked at him numbly but there was life and hope in them once more. "We have inherited a terrible job, but we'll do it," said Rudolf, pumping Ole Doc's hand.

Ole Doc had to restrain Ayilt from kneeling to him. Brusquely he placed the two of them on the old, restored thrones and led Pauma out from the curtains which were now destroyed.

Pauma stood looking obediently at Ole Doc until, after a few swift words, he broke the spell.

It was their show then. King and Queen on their thrones nodded graciously to the queen mother at her greeting, but before they could speak more than a few words the great doors burst inwards and the place was flooded with people, commoners, burghers, soldiers come to know where they stood, and their mouths were full of fled garrisons and a populace burst from the bonds of slavery.

They didn't notice Ole Doc. He glanced at the old queen. She, too, had been thrust back but she was preening herself before a mirror, coquettishly turning her head this way and that to admire herself.

Ole Doc grinned. Sometimes he couldn't help but be proud of his handiwork.

Shortly afterwards, in a commandeered sled, Ole Doc arrived at the supply sheds of the hangars. The place was deserted. Two guards were dead and shackles were scattered about, broken. But the supplies were all in order and Ole Doc carefully selected a small two-billion-foot-thrust pile, pocketing it.

The light seemed brighter as he walked back to the field. Then it was clear why, for the dark star had been quarter-covering the bright one on his arrival and had now spun clear.

The trees around the field were free of any burden but green leaves, and the old *Morgue* gleamed golden in the pleasant expanse. A moment after, Ole Doc stepped aboard.

Hippocrates was waiting peevishly. The little creature threw down the tome on stellar radiations he had been reading and began to shrilly berate his master for having taken so long.

"One would think piles were hard to get!" he complained.

"This one," said Ole Doc, "was."

"Let's see it," said Hippocrates, not believing.

Ole Doc showed him and the little fellow was all smiles. He bounced below to install it, singing the ribald "Fiddler of Saphi" as he went.

Shortly after, the *Morgue* was leaping out toward the Hub and all was peace aboard her.

The pile was working perfectly.

THE EXPENSIVE SLAVES

THE EXPENSIVE SLAVES

George Jasper Arlington fancied himself as an empire builder. He had gone up to Mizar in Ursa Major when he was ten and simply by dint of sheer survival had risen to grandeur on Dorab of that system. His huge bulk defied Dorab's iciness and his inexhaustible energy overrode the cold paralyzed government. It might have been said that George Jasper Arlington *was* Dorab, for nothing moved there unless his shaggy head gave the jerk.

He had overcome the chief obstacle of the place, which made for riches. In the early days of the second millennium of space travel, when mankind was but sparsely settling the habitable worlds, land was worth nothing—there was too much of it. But it is an economic principle that when land is to be had for little then there are but few men to work it and wealth begins to consist not of vast titlings of soil but numbers of men to work it. Inevitably, when man not earth is the scarcity, capital invests itself in human beings; and slavery, regardless of the number of laws which may be passed against it, is practiced everywhere.

But George Jasper Arlington, thunderous lord of Dorab, had evolved two answers and so he had become rich.

The first of these was the simple transportation plan whereby people in "less advantageous" areas were given transport to and land on Dorab in return for seven years labor for George Jasper Arlington. He had created a space fleet of some size and he could afford this. But sooner or later it was certain to be discovered that the man who could live on Dorab seven years as a laborer had not been born and so there came a time when recruits for his project answered not the lurid advertisements of George Jasper Arlington. Indeed in some systems, they threw filth at the posters.

But none of this was the business of the Universal Medical Society, for man, it seemed, would be man, and big fleas ate smaller ones inevitably. It was the second method which brought the Soldiers of Light down upon the magnificent G. J. Arlington, in the form of one of their renowned members, Ole Doc Methuselah.

Located here and there throughout space were worlds which held no converse with man. Because of metabolism, atmosphere, gravity and such, many thousands of "peoples" were utterly isolated and unapproachable. Further, they did not want to be approached for what possible society could they have formed with a carbon, one *g* being? Man now and then explored such worlds in highly insulated ships and suits, beheld the weird beings, gaped at the hitherto unknown physiological facts and then got out rapidly. For a two-foot "man," for instance, who ate pumice and weighed two tons—Earth—had about as much in common with a human being as a robot with a cat. And so such worlds were always left alone. And therein lay the genius of George Jasper Arlington, lordly in his empire on Dorab.

He had sent out expeditions to surrounding systems, had searched and sifted evidence and had at last discovered the people of Sirius Sixty-eight. These he had investigated, sampled, analyzed and finally fought and captured. He had brought nine hundred of them to Dorab to labor in the wastes—and then the employees, the overseers, of George

Jasper Arlington had begun to sicken and die. He reacted violently.

Ole Doc Methuselah, outward bound in the *Morgue* on important affairs, received the Medical Center flash.

> IF CONVENIENT YOU MIGHT LOOK IN ON DORAB-MIZAR WHERE UNKNOWN DISEASE DECIMATES PLANET. DR. HOLDEN WON INTERGALACTIC TAMERLANE CHESS CHAMPIONSHIP. MISS ROGERS WOULD LIKE A FLASK OF MIZAR MUSK IF YOU STOP. BEST. FOLLINGSBY.

Ole Doc altered course and went back to the dining salon to eat dinner. The only controls he had there were the emergency turn, speed and stop buttons, but recently the *Morgue* had been equipped with the Speary Automatic Navigator—Ole Doc had not trusted the thing for the first hundred and twenty years it had been out but had finally let them put one in—and she now responded to the command "Dorab-Mizar, capital" and went on her own way.

Hippocrates, his ageless slave, bounced happily about the salon, ducking into the galley for new dishes quoting Boccaccio, a very ancient author, phonograph-record-wise. When he had served the main course on a diamond-set platter of pure gold and when he saw that his beloved Ole Doc was giving the wild goose all the attention it deserved, the weird little creature began to chant yet another tale, "Rappachini's Daughter," wherein an aged medic, to revenge himself upon a rival, fills up his own daughter on poison to which he immunizes her and then sets her in the road of his rival's son, who, of course, is far from proof against the virulence of the lovely lady.

Although the yarn had lain quietly amongst his books—which library Hippocrates steadily devoured—Ole Doc had not heard of it for two or three hundred years. He thought now of all the advantages he had over that ancient Italian writer. Why he knew of a thousand ways, at least, to make a being sudden death to any other being.

Maybe, he mused over dessert, it was just as well that people didn't dig into literature any more but contented themselves on sparadio thrillers and washboard weepers. From all the vengeance, provincialism, wars and governments he had seen of late, such devices could well depopulate the galaxies.

But his thoughts paused at the speaker announcement:

"We are safely landed at Dorab-Mizar, capital Nanty, main space field, conditions good but subarctic cold." That was the *Morgue* talking. Ole Doc could not quite get used to his trusty old space can having a dulcet voice.

Hippocrates got him into a lead fiber suit and put a helmet on his head and armed him with kit and blasters and then stood back to admire him and, at the same time, check him out. Hippocrates was small, four-armed and awful to behold, but where Ole Doc was concerned, the little creature was life itself.

Ole Doc stepped through the space port and stopped.

In six hundred years of batting about space, Ole Doc had seldom seen a gloomier vista.

The world of Dorab had an irregular orbit caused by the proximity of two stars. It went between them and as they moved in relation to each other, so it moved, now one, now the other taking it. A dangerous situation at best, it did things to the climate. The temperatures varied between two hundred above and ninety-one below zero and its seasons were impossible to predict with accuracy. The vegetation had adapted itself through the eons and had a ropy, heavily insulated quality which gave it a forbidding air. And every plant had developed protection in the form of thorns or poisons. Inhibited by cold, every period of warmth was attended by furious growing. The ice would turn into vast swamps, the huge, almost sentient trees would grow new limbs and send them intertwining until all the so-called temperate zone was a canopied mass.

But now, with a winter almost done, the trees were thick, black stumps standing on an unlimited vista of blue ice. It was much too cold to snow. The sky was blackish about Mizar's distant glare. No tomb was ever more bleak nor more promising of death. For the trees seemed dead, the rivers were dead, the sky was dead and all was killed with cold.

Ole Doc boosted his heater up, wrapped his golden cloak about him and bowing his head to a roaring blast forged toward a small black hut which alone marked this as a field.

He assumed instantly that life lived below surface and he was not wrong. He passed from the field into a tunnel and it was very deep into this that he encountered his first man.

The wild-eyed youngster leaped up and said, all in a breath, "You are a Soldier of Light. I have been posted here for five days awaiting your arrival. We are dying. Dying, all of us! Come quickly!" And he sped away, impatiently pausing at each bend to see that Ole Doc was certainly following.

They came into the deserted thoroughfares where shop faces were closed with heavy timbers and where only a few lights gleamed feebly. They passed body after body lying in the gutters, unburied, rotting and spoiling the already foul air of the town. They skirted empty warehouses and broken villas and came at last to a high, wide castle chiseled from the native basalt.

Ole Doc followed the youth up the ebon steps and into a scattered guard room. Beyond, offices were abandoned and papers lay like snow. Outside a door marked "George Jasper Arlington" the youth stopped, afraid to go any farther. Ole Doc went by him and found his man.

He had eyes like a caged lion and his hair massed over his eyes. He was a huge brute of a man, with strength and decision in every inch of him. It had taken such a man to create all that Dorab had become.

"I am Arlington," he said, leaping up from his bed where, a moment before, he had been asleep. "I see you are a Soldier of Light. I will pay any fee. This is disaster! And after all I have done! Thank God you people got my wire. Now, get to work."

"Just a moment," smiled Ole Doc. "I am a Soldier of Light, yes. But we take no fees. I make no promises about ridding you of any plague which might be on you. I am here to investigate, as a matter of medical interest, any condition you might have."

"Nonsense! Every man owes a debt to humanity. You see here the entire human population of Dorab dying. You have to do something. I will make it well worth your while. And I am not to be deluded that there lives a man without a price.

"Dorab, doctor, is worth some fifteen trillion dollars. Of that I own the better part. We raise all the insulating fiber used anywhere for spaceships. That very suit you wear is made of it. Don't you think that is worth saving?"

"I didn't say I wouldn't try," said Ole Doc. "I only said I couldn't promise. Now where did this epidemic start and when?"

"About three months ago. I am certain it was brought here from the Sirius planet where we procured our slaves. It broke out on a spaceship and killed half the crew and then it started to work its way through the entire planet here. By—"

"Is there another doctor here?"

"No, there were only two. Not Soldiers of Light, naturally. Just doctors. They died in the first part of the epidemic. You have to do something!"

"Will you show me around?"

A look of pallor came over Arlington's big face. For all his courage in other fields, it was gone in this. "I must stay here to be near Central. The slave guards have withdrawn and there may be an uprising."

"Ah. Of slaves? What slaves?"

"The people we brought from Sirius Sixty-eight. And good slaves they've been. I wouldn't trade one for thirty immigrants. They're cheap. They cost us nothing except their transportation."

"And their food."

"No," said Arlington, looking sly. "That's the best part of it. They eat nothing that we can discover. No food expense at all. We can't have them running away—not that they'd get far in this weather. They make excellent loggers. They never tire. And whatever the disease our people got on Sirius Sixty-eight—"

"Have any slaves died?"

"None."

"Ah," said Ole Doc. "Do these slaves have their own leader?"

"No. That is, not a leader. They have something they call a *cithw,* a sort of medicine man who says their prayers for them."

"You've talked this over with him, of course."

"Me? Why should I talk to a filthy native?"

"Sometimes they can help quite a bit," said Ole Doc.

"Rot!" said Arlington. "We are superior to them in culture and weapons and that makes them inferior to us. Fair game! And we need them here. What good were they doing anyone on Sirius Sixty-eight?"

"One never knows, does one," said Ole Doc. He was beginning to dislike George Jasper Arlington, for all the fact that one, when he has lived several hundred years, is likely to develop an enormous amount of tolerance.

"I think I had better look around," said Ole Doc "I'll let you know."

But as he touched the handle of the door a red light flashed on Arlington's Central and a hysterical voice said: "Chief! They've beat it!"

"Stop them!"

"I can't. I haven't got a guard that will stand up to them. They're scared. They say these goo-goos are carrying the plague. Everybody has skipped. In another twenty minutes the whole gang of them will be in the capital!"

"I withdraw my non-slaying order. You can shoot them if you wish. But, stop them!"

Ole Doc eased himself out of the door. He stood for a little while, the cold blasts seeping down through the air shafts and stirring the abandoned papers. The gold glass of his helmet frosted a trifle and he absently adjusted his heat.

Behind him, through the partly closed door, Arlington's voice went on, issuing orders, trying to head off the escaped slaves, trying to stir the fear-paralyzed city into action.

"They sent a doc," Arlington was telling someone, a government officer, "but he's just a kid. Doesn't look more than twenty and he's just as baffled as we are. So don't count on it. . . . Well, all we know about them soldiers after all is their reputation. I never seen one before, did you? . . . That's what you keep saying, but without slaves, you might as well quit the planet. Who'd work timber? . . ."

Ole Doc looked down the empty corridors. He didn't know why he should save the planet. He had prejudices against slavery and the people who employed it. Somehow, away back in Nineteen Forty-six when he graduated from Johns Hopkins in Baltimore, Maryland, people had got the idea that human beings should be free and that Man, after all, was a pretty noble creature intended for very high destinies. Some of that had been forgotten as the ages marched on but Ole Doc had never failed to remember.

He hitched up his blasters and went out to meet the slaves.

They were at the eighteenth barrier of the city, in a tunnel of shallow roof and frozen floor and they were confronting a captain of guards almost hysterical with the necessity of keeping them back.

"Son," said Ole Doc, peering down the long corridor at the first ranks of the slaves, "you better put that machine blaster away before somebody gets hurt. I think those people have stopped being afraid."

The captain had not been aware of company. His two

men were just as frightened as himself and the three jumped about to face Ole Doc. In the darkness the buttons of the cloak were as luminescent as panther eyes.

"What language do they speak?" said Ole Doc.

"God knows!" said the captain, "but they understand lingua spacia. Who are you?"

"Just a medic that drifted in," said Ole Doc. "I hear they have a leader they call a *cithw.* Do you suppose you could get him to meet me halfway up that passageway?"

"Are you crazy?"

"I have occasionally suspected it," said Ole Doc. "Sing out."

A short parley at respectful distance ensued and the uneasy mass at the other end of the corridor stepped back, leaving a tall, ancient being to the fore.

Ole Doc gave a nod to the captain and dropped over the barrier. The cold wind stirred his cloak and the way was dark under the failing power supply of the city. He stopped halfway.

The ancient one came tremblingly forward, not afraid, only aged. Ole Doc had not known what strange form of being to expect and he was somewhat startled by the ordinariness of the creature. Two eyes, two arms, two legs. Why, except for his deep gray color and the obvious fact that he was not of flesh, he might well have been any human patriarch.

He wore white bands about his wrists and forehead and a heavy apron on which was painted a scarlet compass and a star. Wisdom and dignity shone in his eyes. Was this a slave?

In lingua spacia Ole Doc saluted him.

"There is trouble," said Ole Doc. "I am your friend."

There are but four hundred and eighty-nine words in lingua spacia but they would serve here.

The old creature paused and saluted Ole Doc. "There are no friends to the Kufra on Mizar's Dorab."

"I am not of Dorab-Mizar. I belong to no world. I salute you as a *cithw* for this I also may be called. You are in trouble."

"In grievous trouble, wise one. My people are hungry. They are a free people, wise one. They have homes and sons and lands where light shines."

"What do your people eat, *cithw?*"

"Kufra, wise one. That is why we are called the Kufra people."

"And what is this kufra, *cithw?*"

The ancient one paused and thought and shook his head at last. "It is kufra, wise one. There is none here."

"How often do you eat this, *cithw?*"

"Our festivals come each second year and it is then we feast upon the sacred food."

"What is meant by year, wise one?"

"A year, wise one. I cannot tell more. We are not of the galactic empire. We know little of the human save what we have learned here. They call our home Sirius Sixty-eight but we call it Paradise, wise one. We long to return. These frozen snows and dead faces are not for us."

"I must know more, *cithw.* Is there sickness amongst your people?"

"There is not, wise one. There has never been what you call sickness and we saw it only here for the first time. Wise one, if you are a man of magic among these peoples, free us from this living death. Free us and we shall worship you as a god, building bright temples to your name as a deliverer of our people. Free us, wise one, if you have the power."

Ole Doc felt a choke of emotion, so earnest were these words, so real the agony in this being's soul.

"Return to your places here and I shall do everything I can to free you," said Ole Doc.

The old one nodded and turned back. Shortly, after a conversation with other leaders, the slaves left the corridor. Ole Doc met the captain.

"They are going back to quarters," said Ole Doc. "I must do what I can for them and for you."

"Who are you anyway?" asked the captain.

"A Soldier of Light," said Ole Doc.

The captain and the men stood speechless and watched the golden cloak flow out of sight beyond a turn.

Hippocrates met Ole Doc, as ordered by communicator, outside the government house, carrying some fifteen hundred pounds of equipment under one arm. Hippocrates was lawful in everything but obeying Newton's law of gravity.

" 'When plague strikes an area it is usual to issue yellow tickets to all transport and then proceed on certain well defined lines—' " automatically he was quoting a manual, meanwhile looking about him at the chill, deserted squares of the subsurface city.

Ole Doc saw with satisfaction that the little fellow was dressed in a cast-off insulator, which though much too large was fine protection against anything except blasters.

Shortly, on the broad steps of the castle, the instruments were laid out in orderly shining rows, a small table was set up, a number of meters were lined to one side and a recorder was in place by the table.

Hippocrates went off in a rush and came back carrying a stack of bodies which he dumped with a thud on the steps. He kicked the wandering arms and legs into line and sniffed distastefully at the mound, some of which had been there too long.

Ole Doc went methodically to work. He took up a lancet and jutted it at the corpse of a young girl which was promptly banged down on the table. Ole Doc, hampered by his gloves, went quickly to work while Hippocrates handed him glittering blades and probes.

In an upper window of the government house the big face of one George Jasper Arlington came into view. His eyes popped as he stared at the scene on the steps and then, ill, he slammed down the blind.

At first, a small, timid knot of people had come forward but it had not taken the officious wave of Hippocrates to send them scurrying.

The abattoir then fascinated nothing but the professional curiosity of Ole Doc.

"Would have died from Grave's disease anyway," said Ole Doc looking at the table and then at the full buckets. "But that couldn't be the plague. Next!"

The lancet glittered under the flashing arc and with a neat perfection which could separate cell from cell, nerve from tissue, nay the very elements from one another, Ole Doc continued on his intent way.

"Next!"

"Next!"

"Next!"

And then, "Hippocrates, look at these slides for me."

There was one from each and the little creature bent a microscope over them and counted in a shrill singsong.

"Right," said Ole Doc. "Anemia. Anemia bad enough to kill. Now what disease would cause that?"

Phonograph-record-wise, Hippocrates began to intone the sixty-nine thousand seven hundred and four known diseases but Ole Doc was not listening. He was looking at the remains of the girl who would have died from Grave's disease anyway and then at the window of George Jasper Arlington's office.

"Next," said Ole Doc hopelessly.

It was a scrawny woman who had obviously suffered for some time from malnutrition. And Ole Doc, with something like pity, began his work once more.

The snick of blade and the drip from the table were all the sounds in the chilly street. And then a sharp exclamation from Ole Doc.

He seized the liver and held it closer to the light and then, with a barked command at Hippocrates, raced up the steps and kicked open the door of George Jasper Arlington's office.

The big man stared in alarm and then stumbled away from the grisly thing in Ole Doc's hand.

"You've got to return the slaves to Sirius Sixty-eight!" said Ole Doc.

"Return them? Get out of here with that thing. Why should I spend a fortune doing that? Get out!"

"You'll spend it because I tell you to," said Ole Doc.

"If you mean they've caused the plague and will continue it, I'll have them shot but that's all."

"Oh no you won't," said Ole Doc. "And if you see fit

to disobey me and shoot them, at least wait until I have departed. If you kill them, you'll leave the poison here forever."

"Poison!"

"There is an old tale of a man who poisoned his daughter gradually until she was immune and then sent her to kill his rival's son. I am afraid you are up against that. You'll die—everyone on this planet and you included will die if you shoot those slaves. And you will die if you keep them."

"Get out!" said George Arlington.

Ole Doc looked at the thing he carried and smiled wryly through his helmet face. "Then you don't leave me much chance."

"Chance for what?"

"To save you. For unless you do this thing, I have no recourse."

From a pocket in the hem of his golden cloak he drew a sheaf of yellow papers. Dropping his burden on the desk he seized a pen and wrote:

George Jasper Arlington
Never

"What is that?"

"A personal yellow ticket. I go now to give them to all your spaceships, all your captains, all your towns and villages. No one will come to you, ever. No one can go from here, ever. There will be no export, no import. I abandon you and all space abandons you. I condemn you to the death you sought to give your slaves. I have spoken."

And he threw the yellow paper on the desk before Arlington and turned to leave.

"Wait. Have you got that power? Look! Listen to reason. Listen, doctor. You can't do this. I haven't tried to buck you. I am trying to cooperate. I'll— Wait! What is wrong? What *is* the disease, the poison?"

"This," said Ole Doc, "is the remains of a malignant and commonly fatal tumor of this particular species of colloid. It is a cancer, Arlington. And now I am going about my business since you will not attend to yours."

"Cancer! But that's not catching! I know that's not catching."

"Look at it," said Ole Doc.

Arlington looked away. "What did you say I was to do?"

"Take all available transport and return the Kufra people to Sirius Sixty-eight. Every one of them. Only then can you live. I will have to treat your crews and make other arrangements before departure. But I will only do this if you promise that no single slave will be shot or mauled. That is vital, understand?"

"What have I done to deserve this? It will cost me half my fortune. I will have no laborers. Isn't there—"

"There is not," said Ole Doc. "I suggest you employ the best engineers in the Galaxy to provide machinery for your timber work. When you have done that I will send you a formula so that human beings can stand the cold for a short time without injury. I will do this. But there is your communicator."

George Jasper Arlington began to look hopeful. But it was fear which made him give the orders, fear and the thing in Ole Doc's hand.

• • •

Four hours later, at the main spaceport, Ole Doc finished giving his orders to the departing crews. They were men of space and they knew their galaxies. They listened reverently to the commands of a Soldier of Light, painted their clothing and helmets as he told them, fixed their compartments at his orders and then began the loading of the suddenly docile slaves.

In the semidarkness of the subsurface hangars, a few moments before the first ship would burst out into the freedom of space, on course for Sirius Sixty-eight, Ole Doc nodded to the *cithw.*

The ancient one would have shaken Ole Doc's hand but Ole Doc adroitly avoided it, smiling through his visor.

"We are grateful," said the ancient one. "You have delivered us, Soldier of Light, and to you we shall build a shrine so that all our people may know. To you we shall send prayers as to any other god. You have delivered us."

Ole Doc smiled. And from his kit he took a certificate, brilliant yellow, of eternium satin. It stated:

Quarantine!

Know all wanderers of space, all captains of ships, generals of armies, ministers of governments, princes, kings and rulers whatsoever that this

Planet Sirius Sixty-eight

Has been declared in perpetual quarantine forever and that no inhabitant of this planet is to depart from it for any cause or reason whatsoever until the end of time.

By my hand and seal, under the watchfulness of God, by the power invested in me, so witness my command:

ODM
Soldier of Light

"Enshrine this," said Ole Doc when he had explained it. "Enshrine this and forget the rest. And show it to all who would come for you and be deluded by your manlike appearance into thinking you could be slaves. None will violate it for the men who conquer space are not the men who rule its petty planets and they know. Good-bye, then. God bless you."

The ancient one clutched at the hem of his cloak and kissed it and then, certificate securely clutched, boarded the first ship.

Six minutes later the port was empty and the slaves were gone.

But the work of Ole Doc was not yet done and through sixteen wearisome hours he labored over the inhabitants of the city who had contacted the slaves even indirectly. Fortunately it took but a short time to correct, with proper rays, all the effects that might have been made.

George Jasper Arlington, there on the steps where the station had been set up, looked with awe at Ole Doc.

"I never met one of you guys before," said Arlington. "I guess I must have been mistaken. I thought you were just some kid even if I'd always heard about the Soldiers of Light. They sure take you in young."

"They do at that," said Ole Doc, seven hundred and ninety-two Earth years young.

"Can't you tell me more about what was wrong?"

"I don't mind telling you," said Ole Doc, "now that they've gone. Slavery is a nasty thing. It is an expensive thing. The cheapest slave costs far too much in dignity and decency.

For men are created to do better things than enslave others. You'll work out your industries some better way, I know."

"Oh, sure. You got a swell idea. But can't you tell me what was wrong?"

"Why, I don't mind," said Ole Doc. "it was a matter of metabolism. All creatures you know, haven't the same metabolism. They run on various fuels. In the galaxies we've found half a hundred different ones in use by plants, animals and sentient beings. My man there runs, weirdly enough, on gypsum. Others run on silicon. You and I happen to run on carbon, which is after all a rather specialized element. Earth just got started that way. Your slaves had a new one. I knew it as soon as I saw that healed cancer."

"Healed?"

"Yes. Only the woman was healed too well."

"I don't get it."

"Well," said Ole Doc, "you will. There was a fine reason not to shoot the Kufra people or to keep them."

"Well?"

"Why, they had a very efficient metabolism which accounted for their great weight and physical composition, also for their endurance and their apparent small need of food. They," said Ole Doc quietly, "had a plutonium metabolism."

"A plu . . . oh my God!"

"On their planet, so close to the Sirius twin, everything is upper scale and plutonium is the carbon of higher range. So you couldn't have shot them or buried them in mass graves, you see. They were, I think, rather expensive slaves."

In a voice of hushed respect Arlington said, "Is there anything I can give you?"

"Nothing," said Ole Doc. And then, "Oh yes! You have

Mizar musk here. I'll take a bottle of it for a friend."

Which was how Miss Rogers received a full hogshead of Mizar musk and why the Soldiers of Light, wandering through a thousand galaxies, bear to this day the right to forbid the transportation of slaves from anywhere to anywhere on the pain of any one of those peculiar little ways they have of enforcing even their most capricious laws.

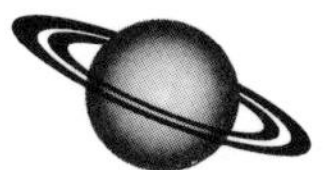

THE GREAT AIR MONOPOLY

THE GREAT AIR MONOPOLY

Ole Doc sat in the cool sunlight of Arphon and pulled at a fragrant pipe. The *Morgue,* his ship-laboratory, sat in lush grass up to its belly beside the sparkling lake and from its side came out an awning to make a stately pavilion for the master.

Sun[12] was thirty degrees high and Arphon's autumn sucked hungrily at the warmth, even as Ole Doc sucked at the pipe. He was getting away with something with that pipe. His little super-gravitic slave Hippocrates was bustling around, all four hands busy, now and then coming to a full stop to lower his antennae at Ole Doc in disapproval. It was not of his master that he disapproved, it was the pipe.

"What if it is his birthday?" growled Hippocrates. "He shouldn't. He said he wouldn't. He promised me. Nicotine, *ugh!* and three whole days until he takes his treatment. Nicotine on his fingers, poisoning him; nicotine in his lungs. Poison, that's what it is. In the pharmacopoeia . . . !!" And he rattled off a long, gruesome list of poisons for, once going, his phonograph-record-wise mind went on into Nilophine, Novocaine and Nymphodryl. Suddenly he realized where all this was heading and in anger with himself now as well as Ole Doc, got back to work with his birthday party preparations. They were very intricate preparations. After all, there had to be nine hundred and five candles on that cake.

Ole Doc paid his little slave no heed. He sat in the sunlight and puffed his pipe and occasionally made intricate calculations on his gold cuff—his filing case was full of torn cuffs containing solutions which would have rocked even his brothers of the Universal Medical Society, much less the thousand and five humanoid systems in this one galaxy.

He didn't hear the clanking chains or the bark of the guards on the march, even though they came closer with every second and would pass hard by the ship. It was nothing to Ole Doc that Arphon was a boiling turmoil of revolt and murder. In the eight hundred and eighty years since he had graduated from Johns Hopkins medical school in Baltimore, Maryland, First Continental District, Earth, Orbit Three, Sun^{1}, Rim Zone, Galaxy^{1}, Universe—or 1, 316^{0}, 1 m. ly hub^{1}, 264–89, sub-3^{28}, which will find it for you on the space charts if you are going there—he had seen everything, done everything, felt everything, tasted everything, been everything including a Messiah, a dictator, a humanoid animal in a glass dome and a god, and there were few things left to amaze or interest him.

He supposed some day he would crack up or get shot or forget his regular youth treatments for a month and wind up in the quiet crypt where sat the nine hundred coffins of black ebony and gold containing all the mortal remains of Soldiers of Light who had departed the service in the only way possible and whose brothers had carefully brought them home.

He calculated from time to time and filled his pipe. After a while, when dinner was over, he'd go to the lake, make an artificial dusk and try out his battery of flies on the trout. Just now he was calculating.

It had come to him that morning that negative could be weighed and if this were so, then it could be canned and if that were true, he could undoubtedly surprise his colleagues at the Center some two hundred million light-years away by making painless amputations so that new limbs could be grown.

He had just come up to his ninety-sixth variable when Hippocrates heard the chain gang. The little slave was ashamed of himself for being too busy or too provoked to heed sounds audible to him these past sixteen and two-tenths minutes.

Hippocrates jumped to the panel, making the *Morgue* rock with his great weight and four-handedly threw on a combination of switches which utterly camouflaged the *Morgue,* screened Ole Doc without making him invisible, trained outward a brace of 600 mm. blasters rated at a thousand rounds a second and turned down the oven so that his cake wouldn't burn. These four importances attended to, Hippocrates hung invisible in the door and eyed the column with disfavor as it came in sight.

Ole Doc saw it at last. It would have been very difficult to have avoided it, seeing that the vanguard—a huge Persephon renegade—would momentarily stumble against the screen, the limit of which he was paralleling.

It was a weird sight, that column. The lush grass bent under white human feet and became stained with red. Clothing ripped to nothing, eyes sunken and haunted, bent with iron fetters and despair, the hundred and sixteen people captive there appeared like shades just issued forth from hell for a bout with Judgment Day.

The guards were brutish humanoids, eugenicized for slave tending. And this was odd because Ole Doc himself a hundred or was it fifty years before had thought the practice stopped by his own policing. These ape-armed, jaguar-toothed devils were like humans mad with a poisonous stimulant or like Persephons dragged from their pits and injected with satanic human intelligence. Their pointed heads were as thick as helmets, their necks were collared with an owner's mark, their shoulders and shaggy loins girded about with blasters and brass cases and their elephant-pad feet were shoed in something resembling spittoons. Whoever owned and controlled that crew who in turn controlled these human slaves must be a very rough lad himself.

Ole Doc raised a microglass to his eye and read the collar brand. It wasn't a man's name, it was a commercial company stamp. "Air, Limited."

Maybe they would have gone on by and nothing whatever would have been written in the *Morgue*'s log. But then Ole Doc saw her.

She was slight, but strong enough to bear this iron. She was curved just so and thus. And her eyes and nose and mouth made a triangle, just . . . well, and her hair flowed away from her face and down her back.

Ole Doc sat up and the pipe dropped unheeded to the ground. He looked harder. The lines before and behind her vanished. The guards vanished. The grass, the sunlight, all Arphon vanished. And there was this girl. Ole Doc stood up and his knees wobbled a little which was odd because Ole Doc was in a physical recondition far superior to most men of twenty-five.

She saw him and for an instant, as she looked and he looked, broke her stride. The slave behind her was old and stumbled. The slave ahead was jerked back by his collar. The Persephon humanoid whirled off the screen he had just bumped and came around to see the tangle. And down came his brass rod.

It never touched the young lady. Ole Doc had not practiced drawing and hip shooting for about four hundred years but his hand had not forgotten. That Persephon humanoid sort of exploded into a mist. His arm flew up sixty yards, turned at the top and came down with a thump on the *Morgue*'s screen where it lay, dripping, suspended in air. The guard's blaster belt went off after an instant like a chain of small cannons and blew tufts of grass in the air. The hole smoked and the other guards came up sharply, gaped and as one faced about with guns drawn looking for their quarry.

It was not quite fair. Ole Doc was out of the screen where he could shoot without deflection and he was shooting. And even if he was a fine target it was still not sporting. He had five Persephons only to shoot at him and then there were four, three, two, none. And patches of grass smoked and there was silence. A final belt cartridge exploded in a hole and there was silence again.

The Persephons never knew they had had the honor of being shot by a Galactic Medalist in short arms.

The slaves stood still and shivered. A wild one had pinked an old woman at the end of the column and she was sitting down staring at her own blood. The rest were gazing miserably at this new menace who had risen up from the tall grass. Ole Doc found he was shaking with the excitement and he disliked finding it so for he had often told himself that one should never get a thrill out of killing, that being a barbarous sort of joy and besides at the end there it had been but five to one. He picked up his fallen pipe, jammed it into his mouth and took a drag. The slaves screamed and fell back from this smoking monster, the tobacco habit having been extinct most everywhere for hundreds of years.

Hippocrates grunted with disgust. He had not been able

to more than slew the 600 mm. into position and had not had the satisfaction of shooting even one round.

He came out. Shrilly shrewish, he said: "You ought to know better. I have told you and told you and told you and you ought to know better. You'll get hurt. I've said you'll get hurt and you will. You leave that to the bravos and buckos. It says right in your code that 'Whosoever shall kill large numbers of people solely for satisfaction shall be given a hearing and shall be fined a week's pay, it being the mission of this Society to preserve mankind in the galaxy—' " He brought up short. His terror for Ole Doc had brought him into an error of quoting the Parody Code. It actually said " . . . kill large numbers for experimentation shall . . . " This fussed him so that he shut off the force screens and came down and would have carried Ole Doc straight back into the ship for a take-off had not his revered master been staring so hard, pipe again forgotten.

Hippocrates took the pipe. He looked for the objection. He knocked out the bowl. He looked again, more wonder in his antennae waves, and slyly broke the pipe to bits. Still no objection. Hippocrates poured out the contents of the pouch and heaved bits and leather as far as his very powerful arms could throw. Still no objection. Hippocrates walked all the way around Ole Doc and stared at him. His master was staring at the line of slaves.

No, at the center of the line. And someone there was staring as though hypnotized.

"Oh," moaned Hippocrates, seeing plenty of trouble. "A girl!"

Now it was no plan of Ole Doc's to inspect Arphon of Sun^{12}. He was on his leisurely way to hand a deposition warrant to a System Chief over in Sub-Rim 18, 526^{0}, that worthy having failed to respect Section 8, Paragraph 918 of Code 94 of the Universal Medical Society. And if Arphon has slaves like this, it was theoretically none of his medical business.

But she was staring at him.

He flushed a little and looked down. But he was caped in gold and belted in scarlet with metal wings on his yellow boots and was decent.

Hippocrates sighed with the depth of resignation. He went over and chopped the girl out of the line with a simple twist of the iron links, bare-handed. Then he set her bodily to one side and to the rest made pushing motions with his hands.

"Shoo! Shoo!" said Hippocrates. "You are free. Go!"

"Nonsense," said the girl in a voice which made tingles go up and down Ole Doc's spine. "How can they go anywhere? They have no money to pay the air tax."

"The air—" Hippocrates gaped at her. She was just a human being to him. Personally he liked machines. "Nonsense yourself. The air's here and the air's free. Shoo! SHOO! You stay," he added over one of his shoulders to the girl. "Shoo!"

And the slaves sank down and began to inch forward on their knees to the little slave. "No, no," they cried. "We cannot pay the tax. We have sickened already in our homes when the air was shut off. We cannot pay. We are repossessed and on our way to remarketing. Don't send us away! Help us! Money, money! You pay our tax and we will work—!"

"Master!" cried Hippocrates, scuttling back. For there were definite limits on his skills and when these were reached he had but one god. "Master!"

But the slaves just came on, inching forward on their knees, hands pitifully upraised, begging and whining and Hippocrates fell hastily back again.

"Air, air. Buy us air! You pay our tax. Don't send us away!"

"MASTER!"

Ole Doc paid no heed to his slave now behind him, to the pathetic cries, to the creeping throng or to anything else on Arphon for that matter. He was still staring at the girl and now she blushed and pulled the rags of a robe around her.

That did it. "Put her in the ship!" said Ole Doc. "The rest of you get out of here. Go back to your homes! Beat it!" But this relapse into the vernacular of his youth had no effect on the crowd. They had crept forward, leaving flattened grass behind them.

Suddenly an old man with a ragged gray stubble and thin chest caught at his throat, rose up and with a wild scream cried, "Air! Air! Oh—" And down he went, full length into the grass. Two others shortly did the same thing.

Ole Doc sniffed alertly. He looked at his third cloak button but it was still gold and so the atmosphere was all right. He sniffed again. "Test for air," he said to Hippocrates.

The little fellow leaped gladly into the *Morgue* and in his testing brought visibility back to the ship. He saw, through the port, that this startled half a dozen of the slaves out there into fits and the fact made him feel very superior. He, master of machinery, tested for the air. And it was good.

Ole Doc pulled down his helmet to cover his face and walked forward. He rolled over the senseless antique of sixty-five winters and examined him for anything discoverable.

He examined several more and from the eighth, who just that instant was half-blind with airlessness and the flash of Ole Doc's U.M.S. gorget, flicked out a specimen of spittle and passed it to Hippocrates.

"Culture it," said Ole Doc.

"Negative," said Hippocrates six minutes later, still carrying 'scope and speed culture flask. "Bacteriologically negative."

"Air!" screamed the old man, reviving. And an instant later She went down on her face and didn't move.

Ole Doc had her in the ship in about ten seconds. Hippocrates threw a force cordon around the rest and four-handedly went through them spraying a sterilizer all over them with two hands and breaking their chains apart with the remaining sets of fingers.

"Air!" they whined and gasped. "Air, air, air!"

Ole Doc looked sadly down at the girl on the table. She was fragile and lovely, stretched there on the whiteness of the *Morgue*'s operating room. She was in odd contrast to all these brilliant tubes and trays, these glittering rods and merciless meters. Ole Doc sighed and then shook off the trance and became a professional.

"There's such a thing as malnutrition," he said to Hippocrates. "But I never heard of mal-oxygenation. Her chest— Here, what's this?"

The tag had been clipped solidly through her ear and it read, "Property of Air, Limited. Repossessed Juduary 43rd, '53. By order of Lem Tolliver, President, Air, Limited."

That offended Ole Doc for some reason. He tore it off and put a heal compress on the small, handsome ear. When he removed it five seconds later there were no scars.

Ole Doc read the tag again and then angrily stamped

it under foot. He turned to his job and shortly had a mask on the girl which fed her oxygen in proper pulsations and gave her a little ammonia and psi-ionized air in the bargain.

He was just beginning to take satisfaction in the way her lovely eyes were flickering as she came around when Hippocrates leaped in, excited.

"Ship landing!" blurted the little fellow. "Guns ready. Tell me when to shoot."

"Whoa," said Ole Doc. "Force screen them off until you see what they are at least. Now, there you are, my dear."

She struggled up and pulled off the mask. She looked mystified at her surroundings until she heard others calling for air outside. Then she flicked her eyes at Ole Doc and it was his turn to sigh.

"Ugh!" said Hippocrates. "Nicotine, women! You never live to be ten thousand, *I* bet. Next, rum!"

"Fine idea," said Ole Doc. "My dear, if you'd like to step this way—"

Hippocrates watched him open doors for her. He knew Ole Doc would take her to a stateroom where she could shower and shift into Ole Doc's robe. And then in the salon that Michalo had newly designed, they'd sit in soft lights and talk above the whine of violins. *Ugh!* It had been exactly nineteen years and six days since Ole Doc had shown any interest in a woman— The little slave paused. He grinned. After all, this was Ole Doc's birthday. It was hard enough to live hundreds of years with nothing ever exciting any more. Hippocrates knew, for his people, gypsum metabolism though they were, normally went utterly stale at twelve thousand and faded into complete boredom. Humans lived faster in the head—

He grinned and swung up into a gun turret. Let him have his birthday and three cheers for it.

But the ship called Hippocrates back sharply. And he was again intensely annoyed with Ole Doc. Women. Now look at the trouble that was coming. The ship was a Scoutcraft Raider for atmosphere travel and it had enough armament to slaughter a city and it was manned with humans who, even at this distance, looked extremely unreliable.

It landed on the edge of the screen and five guards leaped down, blasters ready to cover the debark of a huge-shouldered, black-garbed man. Hippocrates was reminded of a vulture and almost whiffed the odor that always clings to those birds. He turned on the near screen and disregarded the fact that its force kicked about twenty slaves a dozen feet or more outward from the *Morgue.*

The five scouted the grass, found the holes where the guards had been and fished up bits of melted brass. They stood and glared at the slaves who, seeing the ship, had begun to howl and plead and creep toward that as they had toward Hippocrates.

The big human stopped and looked at the *Morgue.* Its stern was toward him and he didn't see the crossed ray rods on the nose or the meaningful letters *U.M.S.S. Morgue, Ole Doc Methuselah.*

"You better stop," said Hippocrates in the high turret.

The men stopped.

The big human looked up at the turret. He signaled his men to fan out and for his ship to depress its heaviest cannon. Hippocrates shivered a little for he was not sure his screen would hold against the size of those muzzles.

"I'm Big Lem Tolliver!" shouted the human. "This is Air, Limited talking and if you got a good reason why my Persephons ain't alive, spill it, for I ain't withholding my fire long."

"You better go away!" yelled Hippocrates in derision. "If my master sees you, he'll cut you open to see the size of your liver or drill holes in your skull to equalize the vacuum. You better go!"

"Only a hundred and fifteen in this gang," said a shrunken human being who reached only to Tolliver's elbow but who served him as a lieutenant of sorts. "According to the radio report, that's one missing."

"Search the ship!" said Big Lem Tolliver.

Hippocrates swooped down with his 600 mm. "Stop and go away. This is the U.M.S.S. *Morgue* and we specialize in dead men named Lem Tolliver."

He thought this was pretty apt. After all, he'd never imagined being able to convert lines from "Tales of the Early Space Pioneers." He was a success. It stopped them.

"Spacecrap!" said Lem Tolliver in a moment. "That's no U.M.S. ship! You'd never steal a slave if you were."

"Slaves are U.M.S. business, pardner," said Hippocrates. "And even if they weren't, we'd make it our business, son. You going to go along and tell your mama to wipe your nose or am I going to have to wipe it myself—with 'sploders? Now git!" He was certainly converting well today.

"Up there, Tinoi. Search it and if they've got the missing one, haul her out. And then we'll see about the murder that's been done here amongst our people."

Tinoi, the shrunken one, hung back. He'd never had a taste for 600 mm. stuff himself. Let them as would be heroes, he valued his daily issue of *doi*.

Hippocrates saw the hesitation and grew very brave. He spanged a dozen 'sploders into the earth before the group and would have shot a thousand more as warning if the Scoutcraft Raider, ordered so, had not replied with a resounding vomit of fire.

The *Morgue* reeled as the screen folded. The top turret caved into tangled smoke. The side port fused and dripped alloy gone molten. And Big Lem Tolliver looked on in some annoyance for there went his chance of recovering the missing repossessed slave.

The men went about collecting the hundred and fifteen and forming them into lines. They were bitter because they could not imagine what had burst these perfectly good chains and they had to tie lines through the broken links.

"Air!" moaned the prisoners.

"Stow it," said Big Lem. "We'll teach you to breathe air you didn't pay for. Form 'em up, boys, and get them on their way. That spaceship, or what's left of it, is a shade too hot for me."

"You ain't goin' to make me escort them," said Tinoi. "It's a heck of a walk to Minga. I bought them Persephoncastes to do the walking."

"If I say walk, you'll walk," said Big Lem. "And if I say walk straight out into space, you'll walk. And if I say hoof it from here to Galactropolis, you'll walk every condemned light-year of it barefoot. If I can't have my orders obeyed, who can? And if you can't obey Big Lem Tolliver, you can't obey nobody. Who thought up this company? Who makes it work? Who handles all the paper work and hires politicians and abdicates kings when he chooses? Who keeps the whole confounded planet running and your belly full. Lem Tolliver, that's who. And what's Air, Limited but Lem Tolliver? And what's Arphon but Lem Tolliver? And that makes me a planet."

This syllogism caused a return of good humor. He expanded, rocked on his heels and looked down at Tinoi. "Yessir. That makes me Arphon, or mighty doggone near. Well, Tinoi, do you walk?"

"Guess so, Arphon," grumped Tinoi and appeared very beaten about it. He knew better than to appear elated. Somebody else would have got the detail if he hadn't objected and it would be fine to breathe something else besides the ozone stink of the Scoutcraft Raider. Too, he could always sell a slave or two to some farm and turn in a death report. "Guess I'll have to," mumbled Tinoi, "but I'll need two gunners and a marine off the ship, and don't go making me take Connoly along."

"That's Connoly and two marines you'll get," said Tolliver. "Now line 'em up and get—"

"Wait," said Tinoi, forgetting his elation about Connoly who could surely build them litters for the slaves to pack. He stared at the smoking side of the spaceship. "There's somebody alive."

And indeed it appeared to be the truth. Crawling backwards out of the smoke came a seared being, tugging at the boot of a second. Tinoi was all action. He swooped in, holding his breath against the fumes and snatched up the obviously live one.

Coughing and beating out a burning spot on his coat, he let her slide into the grass. "There's the missing one," he said. "Now we can get on our way."

Big Lem looked down at her and made a disdaining face.

She was very badly singed property, an enormous burn blotting out almost all of her face and destroying one eye. Wounded and bedraggled, it was plain that she would no longer gladden the eyes of man.

Tinoi looked at her tag, the one around her ankle, then stared at the ear where the repossession tag should have been and was not. He looked at his boss. "This is Dotty Grennan, the one they picked up 'specially for you. She sure is spoiled for looks."

"Throw her into the line. Some men will buy anything," said Big Lem.

"Don't guess she'll be able to walk much," said Tinoi.

"What's that to me? Throw her in. Captain! Captain! Here, you Foster. Get up there and tell my captain to send Connoly and two marines out here and stand by to take off."

The man named Foster leaped up into the Scoutcraft Raider with the message and came back shortly eating a chocolate bar to walk the line up.

"Air," moaned the slaves. "Air!"

"Shut up, you repossessed mothers' sons," said Tinoi, beating them into line with the butt of his blastick. "Form up, form up or I'll give you a lot more air than you'll ever be able to use." He tried four times to make an old man stand on his feet and then left off profanity, and held an open hand toward Tolliver.

"I'll have to have a few charges," said Tinoi. "After all, it's bad enough to walk to Minga without having to drag a hundred and sixteen passed out repossessions."

"It's a waste of company money," said Big Lem. But he signaled Connoly as the big gunner came out of the Raider and Connnoly went back for charges.

These were small cyclinders with "A.L." painted in red

on them, and when they were exploded around the slaves, sent off a greenish spray which hung foggily about them. Tinoi stepped clear and waited for the murk to dissipate and then, when the slaves had revived, turned to and lined them up without further delay.

Big Lem watched the crowd move off. He knew Tinoi would probably be carried most of the way in litters made by Connoly and he understood what would happen to a couple of those younger girls. And he knew a dozen would be sold and reported dead. But Lem Tolliver could appreciate that kind of loyalty and wouldn't ever have understood another kind of man. He grinned as the last of them disappeared in the trees and without another look at the smoking spaceship, boarded the Southcraft Raider and took off.

An hour later Ole Doc came to himself lying in the grass where the girl had pulled him. For a little while he lay there and enjoyed the cool fragrance of the soft blades around him. It was quite novel to be alive and to be so glad to be alive.

After a little he rose up on his elbows and looked at the *Morgue.* The alloy had stopped dripping and the smoke had cleared away but the poor old ship looked ready for a spare parts house. The upper turret had been straight-armed back, a ten-foot hole lay under her keel and the keel was bent, and the near port had been melted entirely out of line. And then he took heart. For she wasn't hulled that he could see and her tubes at one end and her texas on the other were untouched. He started to spring up but the second he put weight on his right hand it collapsed and he felt sick.

He looked down and saw that his palm was seared away and his wrist sprained or broken. He felt rapidly of his shoulders and chest but his cloak had protected him there. One boot was almost seared off but his ankle and foot were uninjured. Aside from singes, his wrist and hand, he had survived what must have been a considerable conflagration. He came up swiftly then and went through the hot door. Small spirals of smoke were rising from the salon upholstery. One huge gold panel had curled off its mountings from heat and a silver decanter was lying in a puddle on the charred rug, struck squarely by a ray translating itself through the hull.

But the young woman was gone and Ole Doc, looking back at the trampled meadow through the misshapen door understood suddenly how he must have got out here. No calloused space ranger would have tried to rescue him. Either the girl had tried or Hippocrates—

"Hippocrates!" "Hippocrates," "Hippocrates," echoed the empty cabins.

Ole Doc raced into the texas and looked around. He went aft to the tube rooms and found them empty. And he had nearly concluded that they must have taken his little slave when he thought of the jammed turret.

The ladder was curled into glowing wreckage and the trap at the top had fused solidly shut from the impact of a direct hit. Ole Doc stood looking upward, a lump rising in his throat. He was afraid of what he would find behind that door.

He went casting about him for a burning torch and was startled by a whir and clang in the galley as he passed it. In a surge of hope he thrust open the door. But little Hippocrates was not there. Pans, spoons and spits were just as he had left them. A bowl of gooey gypsum and mustard, the slave's favorite concoction for himself, stood half eaten on the sink, spoon drifting minutely from an upright position to the edge of the bowl as the neglected mixture hardened. A small, pink-bellied god grinned forlornly in a niche, gazing at the half-finished page of a letter to some outlandish world. The whir and clang had come from the opening oven door on the lip of which now stood the ejected cake, patiently waiting for icing, decorations and nine hundred and five candles.

Ole Doc closed the galley softly as though he had been intruding on a private life and stood outside, hand still on the latch. For a long, long time he had never thought about it. But life without Hippocrates would be a desperate hard thing to bear.

He swore a futile, ordinary oath and went to his operating room. His hand was burning but he did not heed it. There was an amputator in here some place which would saw through diamonds with cold fire. He spilled three drawers on the floor and in the blinding glitter of instruments finally located the tool.

It wasn't possible to reach the trap without taking away the twisted ladder and for some minutes he scorched himself on the heated metal until he could cut it all away. Then it occurred to him that he would have no chance of getting Hippocrates down if there was anything left of him for that little fellow weighed five hundred kilos even if he was less than a meter tall.

Ole Doc found rope and mattresses and then, standing on a chair, turned the cold fire on a corner of the trap. He stopped abruptly for fear the excess jet would touch Hippocrates' body on the other side and for a while stood frowning upward. Then he seized a thermometer from his pocket and began to apply it all over the steel above him. In a minute or two he had found a slightly higher temperature over an area which should compare with the little slave's body and he chalked it off. Then, disregarding the former lines of the trap, jetted out five square feet of resistant metal as though it had been butter. The torch was entirely spent when he had but an inch to go but the lip had sagged from weight enough for him to pry down. A moment later he was crawling into the turret.

Hippocrates lay curled into himself as though asleep. He was seared and blackened by the heat of the melting girder which had buckled and pinned him down.

Ole Doc hurriedly put a heart counter against the slave's side and then sagged with relief when he saw the needle *beat-beat-beat* in faint but regularly spaced rhythm. He stood up, feeling his own life surging back through him, and wrenched away the confining girder.

Carefully, because he had never made any study of the slave's anatomy—which anatomy had been the reason Ole Doc had bought him at that auction God knew how many, many scores of years ago, two centuries? three?— Ole Doc trussed the little fellow in a rope cradle and by steadying the standing part over a split jet barrel, began the weary task of lowering the enormous weight down to the mattresses below.

It took a full twenty minutes to get Hippocrates on an operating table, but when that was done, Ole Doc could examine him in perplexity. Other than diet, which was gypsum, Ole Doc knew nothing about the slave.

The antennae were not injured. The arms were bruised but whole. The legs appeared sound. But there was a chipped look about the chest which argued grave injury. Hippocrates was physician to himself and knowing this Ole Doc went back to the tiny cabin off the galley.

He found some amulets which looked like witchcraft and a bottle which his keen nose identified as diluted ink with a medical dosage on the label. He found some chalky-looking compresses and some white paint.

Completely beaten he went back and sat down beside the table. Hippocrates' heart was beating more faintly.

His anxiety becoming real now, like a hand around his throat, Ole Doc hurried to the galley. He had seen Hippocrates tipsy a few times and that meant a stimulant. But it wasn't a stimulant which Ole Doc found.

The letter was addressed in plain lingua spacia.

Bestin Karjoy,
Malbright, Diggs Import Co.
Minga, Arphon.
By Transcript Corporation of the Universe charge U.M.S. O.D.M.

Dear Human Beings:

Forty-six years ago you had one Bestin Karjoy of my people doing your accounts. Please to give same Bestin this message. Hello Bestin. How are you? I am fine. I have not been feeling too good lately because of the old complaint and if your father still employ with you, you tell him Hippocrates needs to come see him and get some advice. My master got birthday today so I give him happy birthday with nine hundred and five candles which surprise you for human but you know how big and famous he is and anyway I can come in gig tonight

> and see you about dawn-dark halfway on park front because I don't know where you really live and your father . . .

The cake must had demanded something there for it stopped in a blot.

"At five dollars a word outer space rates!" exclaimed Ole Doc. But when he had read it through he was willing to have it at five hundred a word.

He hastened back to the operating table and put the gypsum and mustard close to hand, stacking with it water, the diluted ink and a call phone turned on to the band of his own, propping up a note:

"Hold on, old fellow. I'm returning with your friend Bestin or his father. I'll stay tuned on this phone."

His hand annoyed him as he tried to write with it and when the note had been placed he plunged his arm to the elbow into a catalyst vat and felt the painful prickling which meant a too-fast heal. It would scar at this speed but what was a scar?

He saw the gig, which had been on the side away from the blast, was uninjured, and he had almost launched it when he saw it would never do to go demanding things in his present charred state.

Impatiently he threw on a new shirt, boots and cloak and thrusting a kit and a blaster into his belt, lost no further time.

The gig was a small vacuum-atmosphere boat, jet powered and armed. It was capable of several light-years speed and was naturally very difficult to handle at finites like ten thousand miles an hour. Ole Doc went straight past

Minga twice before he properly found it, glimpsed it just long enough to see the landing strip in the middle of town and put the gig down to paving at three hundred and eighty.

Ordinarily Ole Doc disliked middle-sized towns. They didn't have the chummy, "hello-stranger" attitude of the pioneer villages of space and yet lacked any of the true comforts of the city. Built by money-hungry citizenry around a space repair yard, such towns were intent upon draining off the profit of the mines and farms incoming and outgoing. They were, in short, provincial. A rover port had some color and danger, a metropolis had comfort and art. Such as Minga had law and order and a Rotarian club and were usually most confoundedly proud of being dull.

And so Ole Doc didn't give Minga much of a glance, either passing over or walking in. Brick fronts and badly painted signs—houses all alike—people all— But even Ole Doc in his rush had to slow and stare.

Minga was a city, according to the Space Pilot, of ninety thousand people where "a limited number of fuel piles, ice, fresh water, provisions and some ship chandlery can be obtained" and "repairs can be made to small craft in cradles with capacity under one hundred tons" and "the space hospital is government staffed by the Sun^{12} Navy with limited medical stores available" and "two small hotels and three restaurants provide indifferent accommodations due to the infrequency of stopovers." Not exactly the sort of town where you would expect to see a well-dressed man of fifty carefully but unmistakably stalking a cat.

It was not even a fat cat, but a gaunt-ribbed, mat-furred, rheumy-eyed sort of feline which wouldn't go a pound of stringy meat. But from the look on the well-dressed gentleman's face, there was no other reason than that.

Had he seen a riot, a golden palace, a ten-tailed dog or a parade of seals singing "Hallelujah," Ole Doc would not have been much amazed, for one sees many things strange and disorders unreasonable in a lifetime of rolling through the systems great and small. Ole Doc had been everywhere and seen everything, had long ago come to the conclusion that it wasn't even curious, but a well-dressed, obviously influential old man engaging in the stalk of a mangy cat—well!

The gentleman had crept around the corner to pursue his game and now he had a fence for cover and with it was using up the twenty-yard lead the cat had had originally. In his hand the gentleman held a butterfly net and in his eye there was hunger.

The cat was unable to locate its pursuer now and stopped a bit to pant. It looked beleaguered as though it had been hunted before and the old gentleman had it worried. It crouched warily behind a post and condensed itself anew when it saw Ole Doc some thirty feet away. This new distraction was its undoing.

Soft-footed and alert, the old gentleman left the fence and crossed the walk out of the cat's range of vision. Too late the animal caught the shadow beside it and sprang to escape. There was a swish of net and a blur of fur, a yowl of dismay and a crow of triumph and the old gentleman, by twisting the net into a bag below the hoop, struck an attitude of victory.

Ole Doc started breathing again and walked forward. The old gentleman, seeing him, held up the prize.

"A fine morsel now, isn't it, sir?" said the old gentleman. "Been three solid weeks since we've dined on good, tasty cat. Don't yowl, my good rabbit avec croutons to be, for it won't do you a bit of good. My, my, my, that was a long chase. Ten solid blocks and tortuous, too, what with thinking every instant some guttersnipe would leap out and snatch my prize from me. For I'm not as young as once I was. Dear me."

Ole Doc could see no insanity in the fellow's eyes nor find any fault other than this enthusiasm for dining on mangy cats. But, he decided suddenly, this was no time to follow the quirks of the human mind. Serious business—very serious business—was waiting for him in the wrecked hull of the *Morgue.* He glanced anxiously at his radio pack. The *tic-tic-tic* of the heart counter was very slow.

"Sir," said Ole Doc, "while I can't share your enthusiasm for cat on toast, I could use some of your knowledge of this town. Could you tell me where I might find a company known as Malbright, Diggs? They import, I think, and have their main office here in Minga."

At this the old gentleman stopped admiring his capture which was now entirely subdued. "Malbright, Diggs. Bless me!" And he removed a pocket handkerchief and blew his nose heavily. "You won't be from any town on Arphon, then."

"Be quick, man. Where can I find any member of that firm?"

The old gentleman blew again. "Well," he said, "if you've a mind for fantasy, you might try looking in heaven and then again, as their creditors would have had it, in hell. One place or the other I dare say you'll find my poor old billiard companion Malbright and his sad little partner Diggs. But Arphon isn't hell, sir. Indeed it's two stops beyond."

"The firm had failed, then. Where was it located?"

"Oh, the original Malbright, Diggs has failed, sir. But it's Air, Limited you'd have to approach to get any trace of their affairs. Malbright was the cause of it you see, poor chap. Got to needing more and more air and couldn't pay the bill out of his share. And he took to . . . well," and here he blew his nose again, "from the till you might say and one day the firm failed. Poor Malbright. Had to have the air, you see. Couldn't pay the bill. And as it was a partnership, Diggs stood ready but unable to settle the accounts. And that was the end of it. A fine, thriving business it was, too, until Malbright took to needing air. But it's all gone, all gone." And he looked around him at the autumn day as though the dismal winter snows lay heavily over the streets.

Ole Doc frowned. "Air? What nonsense is this about air? Short time ago I heard something of it. But I haven't any time. You'll remember a small extraracial clerk that Malbright had, then. Probably four-handed. Name of Bestin Karjoy—"

"Oh, dear me, no. Malbright and Diggs must have had a thousand clerks. Business ran into the billions of tons per annum, you know. Customers all over the system. Fine, rich company. Poor Malbright." And he honked again on the handkerchief.

Ole Doc was impatient. "How could a firm like that fail just because one partner needed a little air. Why, man, the whole sky around here is full of it. Air!"

"I beg your pardon, sir," said the old gentleman, shocked. "I *beg* your pardon." And before Ole Doc could think of further questions, the old gentleman hurried away, clutching his precious rabbit soup in the form of a very mangy cat, and was gone.

Ole Doc's boots were angry on the pavement. He was

struck now, as he looked for signs, with an air of decay and unhappiness about the town. There were people here and there but they were listless and incurious, like beings who have been hungry too long or who despair of any hope. Store windows were clutters of dusty junk. The theater marquee was advertising the personal appearance of a singer ten years dead. Shutters groaned in the faint wind and stairs staggered in crazy disrepair. The town looked like it had been sacked and repeopled with ghosts.

There was a city park ahead, a pitiful little thing of broken fountains and root-cracked walks and Ole Doc saw two dogs slinking through it, wary like hunted beasts, sniffing hungrily at refuse.

The town, he realized with a start, was starving. The children he saw in a doorway were bloat-bellied and unpleasant. Ole Doc turned toward them and they made a sorry effort to run away. He peered into the interior of the rickety dwelling and saw that they were now clustered around the bed of a woman who might, in other stages of economics, have been comely.

She saw his shadow and turned. Warily she tried to motion him away. "No. No more . . . I can't . . . I can't pay."

This was definitely not his business but he thrust the thought aside. "Madam, I am not trying to collect money. Here is a gold coin," and he dug one from his money pouch and placed it courteously on the table. "I want to find a man, an extraracial being of four hands, named Bestin Karjoy. Direct me to someone who will know and you shall have my deepest thanks."

She managed to understand this and then made a motion at her eldest boy. "Go, Jimmy. Go show him what he wants." But she looked suspiciously at the coin as she picked it up.

Ole Doc winced when he saw how close to the skin her bones were. He pulled a small hypo gun from his pocket, fumbled in his kit and loaded it with slugs. The jet it shot penetrated without pain and he triggered it six times before he left the room. They didn't know they had been force-fed and only stared in awe at the small gun, afraid it might be a blaster.

Ole Doc motioned to the eldest and went back into the street. But he might have found the place himself.

It was a great, gold-fronted building before which lounged Persephon guards. And over the top of the door was the mighty legend "Air, Limited" and on the panel "Big Lem Tolliver, Savior of Arphon."

Ole Doc gave the boy another gold coin and then breasted the guards. They stopped him with guttural grunts and were about to argue in earnest at his pressure when they both came up rigid, staring straight ahead. Ole Doc put the hypo gun back into his pocket, looked hard at the guards to make sure the rigor had set good and hard and would stay for a while and walked on in.

A clerk came up. "This is a private office, sir. The general entrance for the payment of taxes, rentals and bail are next door. Besides—"

"I want to see your records," said Ole Doc. "I am looking for an extraracial man named Bestin Karjoy and no second-rate town like this is going to stop me. Where are your records?"

Fatally, the clerk had new objections. There was a small snick and Ole Doc put the gun back into his pocket. "You are a trained clerk and obedient to one Lem Tolliver. It is the will of Tolliver that you find the name Bestin Karjoy in your files and give me the address."

The narco slug had bitten straight through the modish waistcoat and pink silk undershirt. "Yes, sir. Coming right up, sir. Won't keep you waiting a minute, sir. What Big Lem wants—"

"Who says Big Lem wants anything?" came hugely from the door. "I," he said, waddling closer, chin outthrust, "do not like gents who go around spieling off orders I ain't issued. Now, whoever you are, let's hear just why you impersonate a messenger for me."

Ole Doc looked at him rather wearily. He gripped the hypo gun in his pocket, but he never got a chance to use it. Some sixth sense told one of Tolliver's bodyguard that an attack was imminent and Ole Doc was seized from behind and held hard while the contents of his pockets were turned out by Tolliver.

The small meters and instruments, the minute boxes of pellets, the hypo gun itself, these meant nothing to Tolliver or anyone around him. But the gorget meant something—The solid gold ray rods of the U.M.S. which were chained to Ole Doc's throat in such a position as to protect the most vulnerable point of the jugular. Tolliver tried to yank it off, failed to break the chain and so had to stare at it.

"U.M.S.," said Tolliver. "Huh."

A clerk had come in to aid his fallen brother of the files and inkpots, for the first one, under the stimulus of the narco slug and crossed orders, had quietly fainted away. "Universal Medical Society," said the new clerk. And then he realized what he had said and jumped back, letting his brother clerk fall. He stared, mouth agape, at Ole Doc.

"Univ—" began Tolliver. And then his face went a

little white. He bent as he stared at Ole Doc. Then, dismissing it. "He'd imitate a messenger. He'd pretend anything. He ain't no Soldier of Light. Where's the crowd with him?"

"They . . . they operate alone," said the second clerk. "I . . . I read in the *Universal Weekly* that they—"

"Bosh! What would they care about Arphon? U.M.S.," blustered Tolliver, "is strictly big time. He'd never land here. Listen, you whatever-you-call-it, don't give me no stuff about U.M.S. You're here for graft and I'm on to your game. Now, let's see how good you are at crawling out of your lie. Go on, crawl!"

Ole Doc sighed. He had seen such men before. "I suppose I am addressing Lem Tollander."

"Tolliver!"

"Lem Tolliver, then. President or some such thing of Air, Limited."

"Correct. And you come here for a shakedown. Listen—" And then he stopped and looked at a new thing in the contents of the pockets. It was a slave ear tag. "Ah," he said, snatching it up from the desk, "you've been tampering with company property already. Oh, yes. That girl—so you were in that ship we blasted a few miles east of Minga, huh? Say, buddy, don't you know where to stop? A guy'd think you were kind of confused. You've already lost an old tub of a space tramp, and lucky you got out with yourself in one chunk. What kind of nerve is this—"

"Oh, do be quiet," sighed Ole Doc.

The flood of speech was suddenly dammed. It had been years and years since anyone had said such a thing to Big Lem Tolliver. Judging from the attitudes struck by the men in the office at this blasphemy, it was going to be years and years before anyone tried to say it again, too.

But Big Lem was a man of many convictions and foremost amongst them was a decided prejudice in favor of his own vast greatness. He had been honeyed and buttered and syruped so long by fawning menials that he had forgotten there were other ways to talk.

Big Lem looked more closely at Ole Doc. "Who are you anyway?"

"You seemed convinced of something else a moment ago. I'm a doctor."

"Ah," said Big Lem. He brightened and rubbed his huge paws together. "A doctor. A crooked doctor impersonating a U.M.S. soldier. Ah."

The whole thing was opened to a page he could read. He scooped up the print. This fellow had come here for a shakedown, impersonating a Soldier of Light. And because men are likely to best understand what they themselves actually are, Big Lem Tolliver was utterly satisfied.

Grinning, the president of Air, Limited, had his men search the visitor for other weapons and equipment and then with every cordiality, ushered Ole Doc into an office big enough for a ballroom and ten times as fancy.

"Sit down, sit down," said Big Lem, sprawling into the oversize chair behind his king-size desk. "Know very much about doctoring?"

Ole Doc played it patient, stilling the urgency he felt now that his small pack radio had been taken from him. He sat down in a high-backed leather chair. "Others no doubt are much better informed," he sighed.

"Where and when did you pick it up?"

"Well . . . a very long time ago. I may not know as much about modern medicine as I might."

"Went to school maybe?"

"Yes. But it was a long time ago."

"Sure, sure. And probably got kicked out of the profession for some . . . well, we all make mistakes and recovery isn't possible unless one uses his wits." He winked ponderously and laughed much beyond the need of it. "I tell you, doc, you wouldn't think to look at me that I was just a typical trans-system tramp once. Look around. Them hangings cost a fortune and them pictures is worth a cold five million. They're originals and if they ain't and I ever find out about it, God help my agents." He laughed again. "Well, doc, I guess you're wondering why I'm being so great about this thing, huh?"

"Somewhat."

"You're a cool one. I like that. I like it very much. Well, I tell you. I could use a doctor. I don't need a good one, see. You'll do just fine if you know anything at all."

"I thought there were doctors here."

"Them that was here up and went away." He enjoyed a brief chuckle and then sobered. "I had a doc as partner. He'd been a good one in his day but drink and women had got too much for him. He died about five years back and we been kind of isolated for some time, like. So, I can use a doctor. A doctor that ain't all knocked around by professional ethics."

"And what's in it for him?"

"Thousands and thousands and thousands. Oh, I can pay all right. And pay very well indeed. Taxes, fees, sales . . . I can pay. Air, Limited is just about as sound a concern as you'll ever find, my friend." He beamed jovially. "You give me quite a turn with that thingum-a-jig on your throat. The U.M.S.— Well, you knew how to back up a play. If I thought you was on the level, you wouldn't be sitting there, but I know you ain't. Not an honest pill in your pockets. No stethoscope. A blaster. Oh, I can tell a thing or two."

"Where'd I slip up?" said Ole Doc innnocently.

"Why, the blaster, of course. The U.M.S. is death on violence. Oh, I've studied up, I have. And I figure the chances of one of their big patrols coming this way is about ten million to one at least in this century. We ain't nothing on Arphon and Sun[12] is gone to pieces as a confederated system. We don't spread no germs around and we ain't in any kind of quarantine. So they won't come. But if one of them big gold ships with the hundred-men crews come around, why I want to be reasonable. So that's where we talk business. You seem to know the ropes."

"Yes," said Ole Doc. "One has to understand his fellow man to get along. Just why are you worried?"

"Well, doc, it ain't so much the U.M.S. Them Soldiers would never come here and wouldn't stay if they did. No, it's the way taxes have fallen off. I want you to do something about it. People don't pay their taxes. And then there's the fees—"

"Wait. Are you the government?"

"Well, in a way, yes. At least there ain't any other government on Arphon just now and we're a big commercial outfit. So, well, we collect taxes for the machines."

"What machines?"

"The health machines, of course." And here Big Lem began to laugh again.

"Maybe we can do business of one kind or another," said Ole Doc. "But there's one thing I've got to fix up. I want to get hold of an extraracial being named Bestin Karjoy. You let me find him and then I'll come back—"

Big Lem looked sly. "Some old partner in crime, eh? Well, doc, if that's what you want, you'll get it."

"Now," said Ole Doc.

"When we've settled a thing or two," said Tolliver. "You'll work for me?"

"We'll settle this when you've found this Bestin Karjoy for me," said Ole Doc. "It won't wait."

"I'm afraid it will, my friend. Will you sign on?"

"I'd have to know more," said Ole Doc, restraining a blow-up with difficulty and holding on to his cunning.

"Such as—"

"What taxes? What air? What are you doing?"

"We sell air," said Tolliver. "We sell it in small bombs or in cans and we get a hundred dollars for a flask big enough to keep a man a month. Now that's legal, isn't it?"

"Why air?"

"Why not?" said Tolliver. "Men have to breathe, don't they?"

"What taxes then," said Ole Doc.

"Why, the taxes to keep the machines running. Didn't you see that big machine central when you came into town?"

"I wasn't looking closely," said Ole Doc.

"Well, that's just one. We got hundreds all over the planet. And we keep them going so long as the citizens pay the tax. And when they refuse to pay it, well, we get 'em to put up a bond. And—"

"What kind of a bond?"

"Personal liberty bond, of course. If we don't collect

when it's due, then the man's liberty is over and he's repossessed by us."

"Why do you want him?"

"Slaves, of course. Nine-tenths of the people on this planet would rather be slaves than have the machines stop. So there we go."

"You mean nine-tenths are slaves by this action. See here, Tolliver, what do the machines do?"

"Why, they keep the outer spacial gases from settling down and killing people. The gases ruin the oxygen content of the air. So we run the machines and keep the gases going up, not down. That's simple, isn't it? And the air bombs we sell let men breathe when they've been hit by the gases too much."

"What kind of gases?"

Tolliver looked shrewdly at Ole Doc. The crook, thought Tolliver, was pretty intelligent. Well, all the better. "That's where I need an expert," said Tolliver. "Now if you'll just join up and take orders—"

"Let me look this thing over first," said Ole Doc. "Money is money but it just may be that I can't do a thing about it."

Suspicion was a fine quality to find in a man. Tolliver reared up and was about to call when Tinoi, sweating hard from his walk, scuttled in. He saw Ole Doc and left his prepared report unsaid.

"New recruit," said Tolliver. "They all get here, Tinoi?"

"About twelve died on the way in," said Tinoi. "Them Persephons don't have good sense when it comes to driving—"

"How much did you get?" said Tolliver.

Tinoi look aggrieved and his boss laughed.

"Well, put them in a stockade and . . . no, wait. Here. Take this man around and let him look the place over."

Tinoi twisted his head sideways at Ole Doc in suspicion, and then he caught a secret gesture from Tolliver which said, "Watch him, don't let him see too much, kill if he tries to get away."

"I need this man," added Tolliver.

Ole Doc rose. "If you'll let me know where I can find Bestin—"

"Later, later. Take him along, Tinoi."

Outside Ole Doc tried to regain his weapons and was refused. He would have made a stronger bid if he had not just then seen the slaves waiting before the door.

They were groveling in the dust, lying prone with exhaustion or looking in dumb misery at the huge gold office building which was their doom. These were the same slaves Ole Doc had seen earlier for there was the same grizzled ancient, coughing and whining in their midst, "Air! Air!"

Ole Doc took half a dozen strides and was outside. He saw what he was looking for and went sick inside. There she was, lying on a litter, moaning in semiconsciousness, twisting with fever. The beauty of her was spoiled and her spirit was shredded with pain.

With another pace, Ole Doc tried to approach her. He knew how she had been burned, why he had been lying outside in the grass. Connoly was standing hugely in his way, lordly drunk but very positive.

"Nobody gets near them slaves," said Connoly. "Orders."

"Come back here, you," said Tinoi. He scuttled down the steps and grabbed Ole Doc from behind.

Ole Doc offered no fight.

"Who's this bloke?" asked Connoly, when they had him back at a decent distance.

"Recruit, the boss said. Just what we don't need is a recruit," grumbled Tinoi. "Too many splits now. Too big a payroll. Connoly, you run these pigs into the stockade. I got to play nursemaid to this kid here. Never get to rest. Never get a drink. Never—" he trailed off. "Come on, you. What are you supposed to do?"

"I'm supposed to repair the machines," said Ole Doc.

"Well, come on, then." He scuttled away and Ole Doc followed.

The machine was above eye level which was why Ole Doc had missed it. It was a huge, gold drum and it stood squarely on top of the office building. They went up to it in an elevator and found it humming to itself.

Ole Doc had pulled his helmet on from some instinct. But he was surprised to find Tinoi getting quickly into a mask before he stepped out of the elevator.

"What's wrong with it?" said Tinoi.

Ole Doc spoke at urgent random. "The rheostats."

"The . . . well, you know your business, I guess. There's the port and there's the vats. You work and I'll stay here and rest. Walk a man's legs off and then don't even let him drink. Keep your hands out of the vats, now."

"I'll need some of the things I left in the office," said Ole Doc.

Tinoi went to the phone and called and presently a clerk came up with them in a paper bag. No pellets, no hypo gun, no blaster— Ole Doc spread out his small kit.

"Don't look like tools to me."

"I'm a chemist," said Ole Doc.

"Oh, I get you. I told him the mixture was too strong. I even get it."

Ole Doc smiled and nodded. "We'll see."

He gingerly approached a vat in the dark interior. On looking around he found a simple arrangement. There was a centrifuge in the vat and a molecularizer above it and then there were ports which carried ionized beams out into the surrounding air. He stepped up and saw that a constant stream of fluid in very tiny amounts was being broadcast through the jets to be carried by the wind all around the countryside. He went back to the vats.

With a drop of the mixture on a filter, he rapidly ruled out virus and bacteria with a pocket analyzer. Intrigued now, he made a rapid inspection for inorganic matter and was instantly in the field of naturally produced plant secretions.

He took a bit of "synthetic skin" from his case and got a very violent reaction. On the grid, the thing was an allergy product of a plant. And when he had run through twenty alkaloids, working slowly because of his impoverishment in equipment, he knew what it was.

Ragweed pollen!

He went outside and looked thoughtfully at the town below.

The beams were sufficient to carry jets of it far beyond the town limits and the winds would do more. To the east was a large expanse of greenhouse glass and a monocular told him it was surrounded by Persephon guards and a high, electrified fence. Common sense told him that ragweed was grown there in large quantities.

"Well?" said Tinoi. "Ain't I ever going to get that drink?"

"You were right," said Ole Doc. "It's too strong. I'm satisfied. Let's go."

Tinoi grunted with relief and started down. Then he changed his mind and stood aside to let Ole Doc into the elevator first. But Tinoi went just the same. He went very inert with a beautiful uppercut to hoist him and lay him down against the far wall.

Ole Doc rubbed his gloved knuckles as he turned Tinoi over with his foot. The cranial structure told him much. Tinoi had been born and bred in the slums of Earth.

"Ragweed," said Ole Doc. "Common, ordinary ragweed. And the older a race gets the more it suffers from allergies. Tinoi, Connoly, Big Lem himself—Earthmen." He was searching Tinoi's pockets now and he came up with a drug so ancient and common that at first he didn't recognize it and thought it was cocaine.

The analyzer set him right.

"Benadryl!" said Ole Doc in amazement. "Ragweed, and here's benadryl. Earthman to begin with and not very susceptible. Benadryl to keep him going and to prevent a serious case of asthma. Air—asthma—oxygen for asthma, benadryl for asthma— But it can't be air in those bombs. It wasn't benadryl."

He pushed "Basement" and descended. The door opened on a storeroom guard. He took Tinoi's blaster and put a neat and silent hole through the Persephon guard who stood outside the basement storeroom. The guard had alerted, had seen the body on the floor when the elevator opened and had not had time to shoot first. Ole Doc shot the lock off the storeroom door.

And it was there that he came afoul of another ancient custom.

A bell started ringing faintly somewhere in the upper regions of the building. For a moment he was not alarmed for he had safely bypassed all the offices in the elevator. And then he saw a wire dangling, cut by the opened door. An old-fashioned burglar alarm!

He grabbed up a black bomb with its A.L. lettering and sprinted for the elevator. But the door closed before he got there and the car went up without him, carrying Tinoi's unconscious message.

Ole Doc was shaken into the mistaken idea that this place was further guarded by gas for he began to sneeze. Then he saw that his helmet was not sealed tight and he hastily repaired it. Ragweed. He was sneezing from the solution of pollen which still stained his glove. A heavier dose would have left him gasping and as it was his eyes watered and he staggered as he fumbled for the stair door.

It crashed toward him and three Persephons leaped out of the areaway. It was not fair to them just as it had not been fair to their brothers that morning. Ole Doc gripped the searing-hot blaster, picked up the weapons of the first fallen one, stepped over the other two bodies and started on up the stairs. The top door was locked and he shot it open.

The clerks screamed and thrust back away from him for they saw murder in his old-young eyes.

Big Lem was frozen in his office entrance. The burglar alarm gonged *clang-clang-clang* with furious strength over them all.

"What's in this?" shouted Ole Doc, thrusting out the bomb.

"Put that gun down!" bawled Tolliver. "What the devil's wrong—"

Ole Doc heard in his keyed-up phone the tiny whisper of leather above the clanging gong. He spun sideways and back and the shot intended for him fired the wood beside Big Lem Tolliver.

Connoly the gunner was ponderously wheeling for a second shot. Ole Doc snapped a quick one across his chest. Connoly's face vanished in a dirty black gout of smoke. He somersaulted backwards down the front steps and landed, dead but still writhing, in the midst of the slaves he had not had time to herd away and now would herd no more.

Ole Doc was still skipping backwards to avoid a counterattack by Big Lem. The elevator door clanged shut and Tolliver was gone.

Ole Doc headed for the stairs and took them four at a time, cloak billowing out behind him. He had wasted too much time already. But he couldn't leave this building until— They weren't on the second floor. Nor the third. But the switch box for the elevator was. Ole Doc shattered its smooth glass with a shot and finished wrecking it with another. Voltage curled and writhed and smoke rose bluely.

That done he went on up with confidence. The only Persephons he found fled down a fire escape in terror. Ole Doc went on up. The roof door was barricaded and he shot it in half.

Big Lem Tolliver might have been the biggest man on Arphon but he didn't have the greatest courage. He was backing toward the "machine" and holding out his hands to fend off a shot as though they could.

"You're not playing fair!" he wailed. "You see the

racket and you want it all. You're not playing fair! I'll make it halves—"

"You'll face around and let me search you for a gun," said Ole Doc. "And then we'll get about our business. You've violated—"

"You want it all!" wailed Tolliver, backing through the door of the dome. He tried to shut it quickly but Ole Doc blew the hinges off before it could close.

The shot was too close for Tolliver's nerves. He leaped away from it, he stumbled and fell into a vat.

He screamed and quickly tried to grab the edge and come out. Ole Doc stopped, put down the bomb and dropped a stirring stick to the man's rescue.

Tolliver grabbed it and came out dripping, clothes with green scum running off them hanging ridiculously upon him. The man was trying to speak and then could not. He clawed at his eyes, he tried to yell. But with each breath he sucked in quantities of poison and his tortured skin began to flame red under the scum.

Ole Doc threw the bomb at his feet where it burst in bright green rays. He expected Tolliver to breathe then, wreathed in the climbing smoke. But Tolliver didn't. He fell down, inarticulate with agony and lack of breath and within the minute, before Ole Doc could find means of tearing the clothes from him and administering aid now that the "A.L." air bomb had not worked at all, Big Lem Tolliver was dead.

In the elevator Tinoi still lay, struggling now to come up from his nightmare. When he saw Ole Doc standing over him, Tinoi's own gun in hand, the lieutenant of the late

Air, Limited, could not be convinced that any time had passed. But he was not truculent, not when he saw Tolliver's body. He could not understand, never would understand the sequence of these rapid events. But Tolliver was dead and that broke Tinoi.

"What do you want wif me?" he sniveled.

"I want you to set this place to rights eventually. Meantime, shut off that confounded machine and come with me."

Tinoi shut it off and the ripples in the vats grew still. Ole Doc hiked down the steps behind the cringing Tinoi and so into the main offices on the ground floor.

The clerks stared at the cringing Tinoi.

"You there," said Ole Doc. "In the name of the Universal Medical Society, all operations of Air, Limited, are ordered to cease. And find me this instant the whereabouts of Bestin Karjoy, extraracial being."

The clerks stared harder. One of them fell down in a faint.

"The Univ . . . The Universal Medical Society . . ." gaped another. "The real one. I told him I thought he was a Soldier," whimpered the clerk who had first announced it. "When I read that article— Now I'll never get my weekly check—"

Ole Doc wasn't listening. He had Tinoi and another clerk by the collars and they were going down the steps, over the dead Connoly, through the moaning slaves and up the avenue at a rate which had Tinoi's feet half off the ground most of the way.

At ten thousand miles an hour, even freighted with her

passengers and the thousand kilos of Bestin and his antennae-waving father, the gig did not take long to reach the injured *Morgue.*

Bestin's father was making heavy weather of trying to unload the bundles he had brought when the gig landed and Ole Doc hurriedly helped him. The old extraracial being hobbled on ahead into the operating room of the *Morgue* and then, when Ole Doc would have come up he found himself heavily barred outside by eight hands. The door clanged shut, didn't quite meet at the bottom, bent and was shut anyway.

Ole Doc stood outside in the trampled grass and stared at the *Morgue.* The girl on her stretcher was forgotten. Tinoi and the clerk might as well have been grass blades.

Tinoi grumbled. He knew that he could run away but where could he run to escape the long arm of a Soldier of Light? "Why didn't you tell me?" he growled at the clerk. "You punks are supposed to know everything—"

"Be quiet," said the clerk.

There was a sound inside as of plumber's tools being dropped. And then the clatter of pipes. A long time passed and the sun sank lower. Ole Doc came out of his trance and remembered the girl.

She was moaning faintly from the pain of her burns.

Ole Doc timidly knocked on the door of his operating room. "Please. Could I have the red case of ointments on the starboard wall?"

He had to ask three times before Bestin's two right arms shot impatiently out with the red case. Ole Doc took it and the door clanged shut again.

The girl shuddered at the first touch and then a hypo pellet quieted her. Ole Doc worked quickly but absently, one eye on the ship. Tinoi gaped at what Ole Doc was doing and the clerk was ill.

The girl did not move, so strong was the pellet, even when half the skin was off her face and arm. Tinoi had to turn away, rough character though he called himself, but when the click and scrape of instruments didn't sound again, he faced back.

Ole Doc was just giving the girl another shot. She was beginning to stir and turned over so that Tinoi could see her face. He gaped. There wasn't a trace of a scar, not even a red place where the scar had been. And the girl was very, very beautiful.

"Feel better?" asked Ole Doc.

She looked around and saw the clearing. She recalled nothing of the in-between. She did not know she had been to Minga and back and thought she had that minute finished dragging Doc from the burning ship. She sat up and stared around her. It took a little soothing talk to convince her of what had happened.

She saw Ole Doc's mind was not on what she was saying nor upon her and she soon understood what was going on in the ship.

"Someone you like?" she asked.

"The best slave any man ever had," said Ole Doc. "I recall . . . " But he stopped, listening. "The best slave a man ever had," he finished quickly.

The sun sank lower and then at last the clicking and chanting inside the ship had stopped. The door opened very slowly and the old man came out, carrying his clumsy bundles. He put them in the gig. In a moment, Bestin came down the twisted ladder and walked stolidly toward the gig.

Ole Doc looked at them and his shoulders sagged. He rose and slowly approached the old being.

"I understand," said Ole Doc, finding it difficult to speak. "It is not easy to lose . . . to lose a patient," he finished. "But you did your best I know. I will fly you back to Min—"

"No, you won't!" howled Hippocrates, leaping down from the *Morgue.* "No, you won't! I will do it and you will tell those two stupid humans there and that woman to put things to rights in that ship they messed up. Put them to rights, you bandits! Wreck my *Morgue,* will you! She's more human than you are!"

He shook four fists in their faces and then turned to beam affectionately at Ole Doc.

The little fellow was a mass of fresh plaster of Paris from neck to belt but otherwise he was very much himself. "New pipes," he said. "Whooeee whoooo whoooo!" he screamed, deafening them. "See? New pipes."

Ole Doc saw and heard. He sat down on the grass weakly and began to laugh. Hippocrates was offended. He did not know that this was from the shock of his own near demise, from the close shave of never getting aid to him. He did not know that the biggest swindle in a thousand systems had had to relax its wealthy sway before he could be cured. He was offended.

"Clean up that ship!" he shouted, jumping into the gig. "And as for you," he declaimed, pointing at his beloved master, "don't you touch that cake. The birthday party will be at six. You invite girl but those stupid humans, never! I go now. Be right back."

And the gig shot tremendously away.

Ole Doc wiped away the tears of near hysteria and took

one of his own pills. He got up. "You better do what he says, people. And as for you, Tinoi, tomorrow morning we'll shut off and destroy those 'machines' and get this planet running again. Jump now. You heard him."

The clerk and the girl—who gave Ole Doc a lingering, promising glance—entered the ship to begin their work. But Tinoi lingered.

"Better jump," said Ole Doc.

"Sure. I'll work," said Tinoi. "But one thing, Mister Doctor . . . you're a Soldier of Light and I ain't even good enough to talk to you, I know. But—"

"Well?"

"Sir," plunged Tinoi. "It's them bombs. We had our allergy pills, but them bombs was pretty good, too. If they're so expensive to make like *he* said, how'll we ever get enough to cure up—"

"My man," said Ole Doc, "your precious bombs were one of the oldest known buncombes in medical history. A propellant and ephedrine, that's all. Ephedrine barely permits the allergy patient to breathe. It wasn't 'air' you were selling but a phony, second-rate drug that costs about a dollar a barrel. They'd take a little and needed more. You were clear back in the dark ages of medical history—about a century after they'd stopped using witches for doctors. Ragweed, ephedrine—but they were enough to wreck the lives of nearly everyone on this planet.

"Oh, get into the ship and get busy. It makes me sick to think of it. Besides, if Hippocrates gets back and finds his *Morgue* still messed up, he'll make you wish you'd never been born. Jump now, for by all that's holy, there's the gig coming back now."

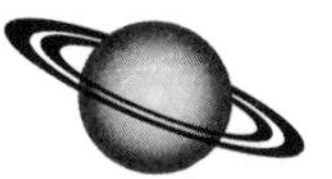

PLAGUE

PLAGUE

The big ship settled in the landing cradle, her ports agleam—and her guts rotten with sickness.

There were no banners to greet her back from her Spica run, there was no welcoming mass of greeters. The field was as still as an execution dock and the black wagons waited with drivers scared and the high yellow blaze of QUARANTINE hung sickly over all.

Five hundred and ninety-one passengers were dead. The remainder of her list would probably die. Officers and crew had contributed to the dead. And somewhere between Spica and Earth, corpses had been flung out the space port to explode in vacuum and gyrate, then, perhaps, as dark comets of putrescent matter around some darker star.

The medic at the port, authoritative but frightened, barked into the speaker, "*Star of Space* ahoy! No personnel or equipment will be given to you until a full accounting of symptoms has been given by your ship's doctor."

An officer's voice speakered out from the *Star of Space.* "The doc's dead! Let us open the ports! Help us!"

"How does the disease appear to you?"

There was a long silence and then another voice answered from the stricken *Star.* "Begins with sore throat and spots inside the mouth. Swollen throat and then steadily mounting temperature. Death comes in convulsions in about fourteen days, sometimes less. If you've got a heart, let us land. Help us!"

The group on the operations platform looked out at the defiled cradle. The medic was young but old enough to know hopelessness. The Spaceway Control Police Chief, Conway, looked uncertainly at the ship. Conway knew nothing about medicine but he knew what had happened when the *Vestal* from Galaxy 159 had brought the red death here.

"What they got?" asked Conway. "Red death?"

"I don't know. Not that." And the medic asked other things of the ship.

"You must have some idea," said Conway.

"I don't know," said the medic. He turned to a phone and called his superiors and when he came back he was haggard.

A woman had come to the ship speaker now. She was pleading between broken sobs. They were trying everything they could out there in that ship. The medic tried to imagine what it was like with those closed ports. No doctor. The ballrooms and salons turned over to dying men, women and children. The few live ones cringing in far places, hoping. Brave ones waiting on sick people. Some officer with his first command which would be his last. They had a kid at the ship speaker now.

Conway asked them for verbal messages and for an hour and a half the recorder took them. Now and then the speaker on the ship would change.

Mulgrave, president of Spaceways Intergalactic, Inc., owner of the *Star of Space,* came and looked on.

At 10:72 sidereal galaxy time, Conway took the dispatcher's mike and ordered the ship away.

There were protests. Conway did not answer or repeat his order. Slowly the protests, the pleas vanished. Sullenness marked the ship then. For a long while nothing stirred. But at 11:24 a converter began to whine. At 11:63 the tubes gave a warning blast. At 11:67 the *Star of Space* lifted from her cradle, hovered and then slowly rose spacewards, doomed.

Ole Doc Methuselah arrived on Earth at 19:95, five days after. He arrived and Earth knew it. Ole Doc was mad. Ole Doc was so mad that he bypassed quarantine and control and landed square before the hangar, gouging big chunks of dirt up with the *Morgue*'s landing blast.

A dispatcher came racing on a scooter to know what and why and he had his mouth open to become a very mad dispatcher when he saw the crossed ray rods. They were on the nose of the golden ship and they meant something. The same insignia was on the gorget at Ole Doc's throat. The ray rods of pharmacy. The ray rods of the Universal Medical Society which, above all others, ruled the universe of medicine, said what it pleased, did what it pleased when it pleased and *if* it pleased. It owed allegiance to no government because it had been born to take the deadly secrets of medicine out of the hands of governments. The dispatcher shut his mouth.

Hippocrates leaped down, making a minor earthquake, although he was only a meter tall, and the dispatcher, at the sight of this four-armed, antennaed nightmare, quickly yanked the scooter out of the way.

Not even glaring, Hippocrates went to the cab line, grabbed a bumper and pulled. He intended to coax the driver into entering the forbidden field of the ramp but the only result was the loud breaking off of the bumper.

There was an argument, but it wasn't very long. Three minutes later a cowed driver had the cab beside the *Morgue.*

Ole Doc swung down. He looked about twenty-five even

if he was nine hundred and six, that being the medical privilege and secret of any one of the seven hundred society members, and when the sun struck his gold cloak and flashed from his boots, the dispatcher, again about to protest the actions of this ship, hurriedly drew back. He was looking at a Soldier of Light and it not only awed him, it paralyzed him. He would tell his friends and children about this for the next fifty years.

Ole Doc said: "Spaceway Control Building!"

The driver gave a terrified glance at Hippocrates and shot the cab half again past its governor.

Ole Doc got down and went in so fast his cape stood out straight. He found Conway on the ninety-eighth floor in a magnificent office full of communications equipment and space charts.

Conway was bovine and leaden. He did not have fast reactions. He was a cop. He saw Ole Doc, thought of revolution, grabbed a button to bawl out a receptionist for not announcing and then stared straight into two very angry blue eyes and found that his hand had been swatted hard away from that buzzer.

"You listen to me!" cried Ole Doc. "You imbecile! You . . . you— Good Catfish! You haven't the discernment of a two-year-old kid! You . . . you flatfoot! Do you know what you've done? Do you know what ought to happen to you? Do you know where you'll wind up when I'm through with this? If you—"

Conway's bullish ire had risen and was about to detonate. He leaped up to have room for his rage and then, just as he was beginning to level a finger, he saw the ray rods on the gold gorget.

"You . . . you're the U.M.S.," said Conway, idiotically

holding the pose which meant rage but stammering like a schoolkid. Abruptly he collapsed into his chair. Weakly and with great attention he listened to the detailed faults of police and control systems in general, Conway in particular *and* Conway's children and parents and grandparents. Conway learned some pretty terrible things about himself, including his personal appearance and the slightly sub-quality of his wits. Conway would probably go around being an illegitimate imbecile for days afterwards.

"*. . . and,*" said Ole Doc, "if you don't locate that ship in twenty-four hours I'll yellow ticket this whole system. I'll yellow ticket Mars and Jupiter. I'll yellow ticket the whole condemned galaxy! You won't move a ship. You won't move a cruiser or a battle ship or a tramp! You won't even move a lifeboat for more years than I've got patience. And," he concluded illogically, "I've got plenty of that!"

"What . . . what—?" begged Conway, the mighty Conway.

"Find me the *Star of Space.* Find that ship so whoever is on her can be saved. Find her before she lands and infects an entire planet, a system and a galaxy. Find her before you kill off millions, billions, quadrillions—" Ole Doc sat down and wiped his face. Hippocrates let go of the burly police receptionist with a warning wave of a finger and came in.

"You get excited," said Hippocrates. "Very bad. Take this!"

Ole Doc reached for the pill and then, seeing it completely, struck it aside and leaped up to face the wilted Conway.

"Have the Grand Council in here in ten minutes. I don't care if they're in China or digging clams at the North Pole. Have them in here or have trouble!" Ole Doc stamped out, found a seat in a garden looking over New Chicago and composed himself as well as he could to wait. But his eyes kept straying to the blue heavens and he kept pounding a palm with a fist and swearing sharply.

Hippocrates came back in nine minutes. "Grand Council ruling Earth assembled now. You speak. But don't you get so excited. Five days to your next treatment. Very bad."

Ole Doc went in. His metal boot soles chewed bits out of the rug.

Eighteen men sat in that room, eighteen important men whose names meant law on documents, whose whims decided the policies of nations and whose intercession, arbitration or command ruled utterly the two and one-half billion people of Earth. The Army officers were imposingly medaled. The Marine commander was grim. The Navy operations chief was hard, staunch, important. The civilians might have appeared to be the most powerful men there, they were so quiet and dignified. But it was actually the naval officer who ranked them all. He commanded, by planetary seniority and the right of Earth's conquests, the combined space navies of the galaxy whenever "the greater good of the majority of the systems" was threatened.

They were grave and quiet when Ole Doc entered. They blinked a bit uncertainly when he threw his helmet down on Conway's desk. And when he spoke, they came very much to life.

"You," said Ole Doc, "are a pack of fools!"

There came an instant protest against this indignity. Loudest was that of Galactic Admiral Garth. He was a black-jowled, cigar-smoking man of six feet five, a powerful if not brilliant fighter, and he objected to being called a fool.

"You have let hell loose through the systems!" cried Ole Doc above their voices. "You've sent a cargo of death away where it can infect trillions of beings! That may be dramatic but by all that's holy, it's the truth!"

"Hold on there!" said Admiral Garth, heard because he could shake ports loose with his voice. "No confounded pill roller can come in here and talk to me like that!"

It stopped the babbling. Most of the people there were frightened for a moment. Those who had been merchants knew the yellow tickets. Those who only nominally governed saw whole nations cut off. The Army saw its strength cut to nothing because it could not be shipped and the Navy in the person of Galactic Admiral Garth saw somebody trying to stop his operations of fleets and he alone stayed mad.

"The *Star of Space* was sent away from here," said Ole Doc, spitting every word, "without medical assistance or supplies. She was rotten with disease but she got no cordon, no quarantine. She got dismissal! She went out into space low on supplies, riddled with disease, hating you and all humanity.

"Further, even though you were in communication with that ship, you did not find out the details, the exact, priceless details of that disease. You did not discover from whence she thought she received the disease or establish which passenger or crewman from what part of the Universe first grew ill. And you failed, utterly failed to find out where she intended to go!

"That's why you are fools! You should have provided her with an escort at least! But no! You, the men who supposedly monopolize all the wits on Earth, the Earth which rules the galaxy, you let the *Star of Space* go away from here to murder—yes, murder!—possibly millions and millions of human beings. Perhaps billions. Perhaps trillions! I cannot exaggerate the folly of your action. Completely beyond the base-hearted wickedness which refused that ship the help she needed, you will be evil and sinful in the eyes of all men.

"I am publishing this matter to space. The Universal Medical Society can cure anything but stupidity, and where they find that, in government, they must leave it alone!"

He sat down suddenly on the edge of the desk and glowered at them.

Hippocrates in the doorway was wondering whether or not he had put too much adrenaline into Ole Doc the last rejuvenation treatment and had about concluded that this was the answer.

Galactic Admiral Garth clamped an angry blue jaw on a frayed cigar. Pill roller, his attitude said. He'd never needed a doctor in his life and when he did he'd take a naval surgeon. Disease, bah! Everyone knew that disease warfare had almost ruined mankind. The stuff was deadly. It said so in the texts. Therefore, a diseased ship should be launched as far away from humanity as possible and left to rot. It was good sense. Nobody could fight a disease when science could make new, incurable ones at every rumor of war. It had said so in the texts for a long time, for several hundred years in fact. That made it true.

"I won't cooperate," said Garth flatly. Nobody would catch him risking any of his valuable equipment.

"Admiral," said Lionel MacBeth, Council President. "I think it *has* been foolish of us. We sent the vessel away in a senseless panic amongst ourselves, trying to save this system without regard to others. The best we can do is—"

"It was done without my advice," said Garth, "but I'd do it myself if it was to be done again. The red death got away from three army doctors"—and he glowered at the Army—"who were trying to be humane about a camp full of it. I've investigated. The *Star of Space* could get nowhere. She's branded. She had very little fuel after a run from Spica—"

"She had five hundred light-years of fuel left!" said Ole Doc.

Garth bristled. This was too much from a pill roller. "What do you know about fuel!"

Hippocrates said: "You keep quiet!" and looked mad. Fuel indeed. Didn't he know whole volumes about fuel and engines? Whole libraries? And didn't his brain belong to Ole Doc? Of course his master knew about fuels!

Ole Doc said: "I ion-beamed New Earth of Spica." He pulled out his message log. "The *Star of Space* was trying out delphi particles. She took her original weight in them. She'd have an excess of five hundred light-years above her normal reserve. She could go anywhere this side of the Hub. And when she gets where she is going, she is going to try to hide her plight. Why hasn't a general galactic alarm gone out?"

This was news to the Council. The *Star of Space* should have been completely out of fuel. Two or three nervous coughs sounded and here and there beads of perspiration began to grow.

Garth was silent. He was thinking.

"You'll have to act!" said Ole Doc. "I demand you throw out a net to intercept her, that you alert all navies to comb space, that you alarm any place she might try to land and that, in conclusion, you hold her at bay until I or another U.M.S. soldier can get there and take charge."

Seventeen heads nodded quick assent and then all attention went to Garth. Control and communication were naval functions.

Garth took out a cigar. He inspected it. He threw the frayed one away and replaced it with the fresh one. He bit the end, spat, tilted the cheroot up and looked contemptuously at Ole Doc.

"The warning will be heeded and you probably deserve some thanks for calling this to my attention. It is now in naval hands. With the permission of the Council I shall give my orders."

They gave it quickly enough.

Garth rose, shrugged into a spacecoat and started to leave.

"May I ask," said Ole Doc, "just what orders you are going to give?"

"All space navies will be ordered to an emergency standing. Patrols will search their sectors. All navy bases will be alerted. And wherever found or whenever seen, the *Star of Space* is to be blown out of existence with some well-placed shots. Good day."

The door closed behind him.

Ole Doc got up slowly.

"You abide by this?" he demanded of the Council.

They were uncomfortable.

"You do not see that if this ship is disintegrated we will have lost all possible chance of locating the source, type, course and treatment of that plague?"

They saw that but they were still uncomfortable.

"You," said Ole Doc, "are a pack of fools!" And when he had slammed the door behind him and strode off down the hall, Hippocrates was positive now about that adrenaline. Ole Doc was mad!

The first contact came when the *Morgue* was off the Carmack System and was announced as being within the Smith Empire on a planet called Skinner's Folly.

Ole Doc had guessed five years wrong and he muttered about it as the *Morgue* skimmed along under gyro control.

"We'll never make it," said Ole Doc. "That confounded System Police will get there and wreck everything. I know the Smith Empire!"

Hippocrates served soup in the lovely salon. The murals had been very specially constructed by an Old Seattle artist named Boyd who had been extremely grateful for having his life saved one afternoon when Ole Doc walked by a Venusian grog shop. The murals showed a tree of life growing all around the four walls of the room depicting the evolution of man and there were many trillionaires and kings who would have paid a planet's ransom for a duplicate. Nobody but a Soldier of Light could have kept Boyd sober that long, however.

"Monkey stage," said Ole Doc, glaring at a gibbon who was gibbering in a lifelike manner, three-dimensional and moving, it seemed, in a tree. "Few of them ever get beyond the monkey stage. Give 'em fleas to pick and they're convinced they're solving all the problems of the world."

"Too much adrenaline. This afternoon when I fix," said Hippocrates, testing the coffee for temperature before he served it, "I cut down adrenaline."

"You'll cut down nothing, you gypsum freak! I feel fine. I haven't felt this mad in a hundred years. It does a man good to feel good and mad at something once in a while. It's therapy, that's what it is."

"I cut down adrenaline," said Hippocrates. "You got bad habits. You fall in love with women and sometimes you get mad. You drink, too," he added, spitefully setting out the muscatel.

"I'll fall in love and I'll get drunk—"

"'Love is the ambition of the failed man,'" primly quoted Hippocrates. "'There is nothing,'" he continued, phonograph-record-wise, "'so nauseous under all the suns and stars as a gusty-sighing lover, painted like a clown, exchanging spittle with a predatory female under the delusion that he is most nobly discharging the highest injunctions of a divine—'"

"You heathen!" said Ole Doc. "That gibbon has more sense."

"He can't make chicken soup," wisely countered Hippocrates. "That is enough wine. At four-fifteen you be ready for treatment. Not so much adrenaline."

Ole Doc rose and looked at the telltale instruments in the cabin bulkhead. He wrote a few figures on his cuff which told him that they would be landing at Skinner's Folly by six. He went forward and tried to connect with an ion beam which would permit him to communicate with the Smith Empire. The Smith Dynasty, however, had been a very economical one and kept few beams going, depending more upon its staff of inventors than upon what was already practical and in use elsewhere.

At four-fifteen he suffered himself to be stripped and placed before a battery of ray rods, impatiently submitting to the critical ministrations of his slave. From some uncalculable system not yet discovered, Hippocrates was about as much affected by these powerful rays as a piece of lead.

The little slave found a tiny scar and that had to be fixed. He saw an off-color hair and the whole follicle system had to be treated. He fussed and clucked over a metabolism meter until he had what he thought was just right and then he shut off the rays.

"You skimped the adrenaline!" said Ole Doc, and before Hippocrates could interfere, he shut on the rheostat which blazed out with adrenal catalyst and flashed it off again. Self-righteously, he began to haul on his clothes.

Hippocrates began to quote long sections of "The Anatomy and the Gland" in a defeated tone of voice.

"Get back there and get to work!" said Ole Doc.

Hippocrates went. But he didn't go to work. He took down a tome from the library and read a long chapter on "The Reduction of Adrenal Secretion," paying particular attention to the section, "Foods Which Inhibit Adrenal Fluid." He read the lists, thus memorizing them at a glance, and made note of what to add to his stores when they reached Skinner's Folly.

But they did not arrive in time. When Ole Doc came to Garciaville, the capital city of the planet, the System Police had been there about six hours before.

From a cocky young reporter who was almost humble talking to a Soldier of Light, Ole Doc learned that the System Police, acting under advices from the Emperor Smith III, had undertaken and accomplished an unsavory mission.

At the bleak little town of Placer, the *Star of Space* had put in, landing at the Tri-System emergency field. The once great liner had made no pretense of its state but had appealed to the mayor of Placer. There was no quarantine there since no intra-galaxy traffic ever dignified the place. But the mayor had known his dangers and he had immediately ordered the liner on.

The speakers of the great ship were not functioning and a communication had been wrapped around the handle of a wrench and thrown out of the vessel. This the mayor had read. His pity had been greatly aroused and he had communicated hurriedly with Emperor Smith III without permitting the remaining people or the sick to disembark.

Smith had answered abruptly and to the point. He had advices from the Galactic Admiral of this eventuality.

It had taken two days for a runner to come from Placer to the outside. And it had taken two days to get back; due to the fifty-thousand-foot peaks around the village, no atmosphere craft cared to brave the currents. A System Police spacecraft had gone in and for four days had examined the situation, carefully keeping a cordon around the *Star of Space.*

Suddenly the mayor of Placer had come down with spots in his mouth and his temperature had begun to rise.

The mayor had talked to many people in the village. He had talked to the System Police ship officers.

The *Star of Space* had listened to the System Police band and had the decision of Emperor Smith when it was given. The liner, with its cargo of misery and death, had immediately taken off with destination unknown.

Two naval vessels had come in before the System Police craft could leave.

Twenty-inch rocket rifles had bored into the village of Placer. For five minutes the naval vessels had scorched the place.

When they left a thousand people were dead, the once

pleasant and rich valley a charred wreck. The passes were sealed through the peaks and a plague cross was painted on a dozen square miles from the air.

That was the end of Placer.

Ole Doc stood on the plain before the peaks and watched the rising smoke beyond. He had been late because he had not been promptly informed.

A thousand guiltless human beings had died.

Plague still lived in this galaxy.

It was no use to rail at Garth or excommunicate Emperor Smith.

Ole Doc went back to the *Morgue* and began anew the anxious search. Next time he had to be in at the end.

A lot depended upon it.

The *Morgue* cometed along at orbiting speed, automatically avoiding debris pockets, skipping over a dark mass here and bypassing a dead star there. Ole Doc had calculated, on the basis of information received from the Spica system, which included a list of passengers with countries—at fourteen dollars a word high space rates priority—that he had a sixty percent chance of being somewhere near the next landing place of the *Star of Space.*

He had pounded the key ceaselessly in an effort to drum up the ship herself but either he was on a course diverging faster than he could contact ion beams or the *Star of Space* had no communications operator left alive. Ole Doc gave it up, not because a naval flagship had tried to shut him off and bawl him out, but because he had suddenly shifted his plans.

He had to find that ship. He had to find her or the U.M.S. would be slaving on this disease for the next thousand years, for such are the depths of space that unknown systems and backwash towns can harbor something for centuries without notifying anyone else. The method of this notification would be grim.

Ever since the first adoption of the standard military and naval policy of "sterilization," the U.M.S. had had its grief. When men found they could take a herd of innocent bacteria, treat it with mutatrons and achieve effectively horrible and cure-resistant diseases, the military had had no patience with sick people.

The specific incident which began the practice was the operation against Holloway by the combined Grand Armies of the Twin Galaxies wherein sown disease germs by the attackers had been re-mutated by the defenders to nullify the vaccine in the troops. The Grand Armies, as first offenders, had gone unsuspectingly into the Holloway Galaxy to be instantly chopped down by the millions by what they comfortably supposed was harmless to them. With an entire galaxy in quarantine, with millions of troops dead—to say nothing of two billion civilians, the Grand Armies had never been able to recover and reassemble for transshipment to their own realms but had been relegated to the quarantine space, a hundred percent casualty insofar as their own governments were concerned.

This had soured the military on disease warfare and not even the most enthusiastic jingoist would ever propose loosing that member of the Apocalypse, PLAGUE, against anybody, no matter the heinous character of the trumped-up offenses.

Now and then some would-be revolutionist would clatter his test tubes and whip up a virus which no one could cure and so disease warfare came to have a dark character and now smelled to the military nose like an anarchy bomb.

Hence, sterilization. When you had a new disease you probably had a revolt brewing. There was only one thing the military mind could evolve. This solution consisted of shooting every human being or otherwise who was sick with non-standard symptoms; and should a community become stricken with a mysterious malady, it was better the community die than a planet.

The Universal Medical Society, operating without charter from anyone, safeguarding the secrets of medicine against destruction or abuse, had been instrumental in solving the original military prolixity for disease warfare. Indeed, this type of fighting was one of the original reasons why the U.M.S. was originated and while there were countless other types of medicines which could be politically used or abused, the germ and the virus still ranked high with the out-of-bounds offenses.

Center had contacted Ole Doc some days since, offering to throw a blanket ticket on the Earth Galaxy and stop Garth. But in that this would mean that some millions of isolated humans would probably starve, that business would be ruined and so create a panic, and that the rumor, traveling far and fast would probably demoralize a dozen galaxies or overthrow ten thousand governments, Ole Doc dot-dashed back that he would play out the hand. That was brash. Hippocrates said so. It meant Ole Doc couldn't lose now without losing face with his own fellows, the only beings in the entire Universe with whom he could relax.

And so he let the *Morgue* idle and kept all her speakers tuned to the jingle-jangle of space police and naval bands. That they were all in code did not bother him. A junior officer, back at Skinner's Folly, had gained a healed stomach and had lost, unbeknownst to him, the search code via truth drug. The junior officer would not be able to lie for two or three months, but Ole Doc had the search code memorized.

"Styphon Six . . . to . . . over . . . yawk scwowl scree . . . Hydrocan . . . roger . . . under over . . . out—" mimicked Hippocrates in disgust at the clamor which filled this usually peaceful old hospital ship. "To Command Nine . . . scree . . . Command Nine . . . swowwwww— Foolish people. Why they do all that, master?"

Ole Doc looked up from a manual of disease diagnosis. "It's bad enough to listen to those things without you parroting them."

Hippocrates stood in the door self-righteously kneading bread dough with three hands and drinking some spiced ink with the fourth. "Foolish. They should say what they mean. Then maybe somebody get something done. Go here, go there. Squadron, Flight, Fleet attention and boarders adrift! Navy get so confused no wonder we got to do their work."

"Now, now," said Ole Doc.

"Well, it may not confuse enemy," said Hippocrates, "but it sure ruin operation of own fleet." He finished the ink, popped the bread under a baking light and came back wiping his hands on an apron. "Good thing no girl you know on *Star of Space.* Then we really get in trouble."

"You leave my private business alone."

"You so full of adrenaline you maybe catch chivalry."

"That's not a disease."

"It disease with you," said Hippocrates, out of long suffering. "You stop reading now. Bad for eyes. You tell me page number and book and I quote."

He got the book all right, but he had to duck it, it came so hard. Ole Doc went back to the chartroom, which lay beyond the main operating room and its myriad bottles, tubes, instruments and bins. He pinpointed out the courses of the main units of the search fleets and wiped off a large section of the galaxy. He threw a couple of switches on the course comptometer and several thousand cogs, arms and gears made a small whirr as the ship shifted direction and dip.

Somewhere in this sphere of thinly mattered space was the *Star of Space,* or else like a drop of water under Vega's blast, she had utterly evaporated away.

Ole Doc was nervous lest he miss. Who knew how many millions of human beings might be infected by this before he was done. If only he had an exact description of symptoms!

And he sat in the "office" of the *Morgue,* endlessly speculating until:

"Scout Force Eighty-six to Command. Scout Force Eighty-six to Command. Clear Channel. Operational Priority. Clear Channel. Scout Force Eighty-six to Command. Banzo! Over."

Ole Doc whipped upright and grabbed his direction finders. He could get the distance in to that beam and know which way the command answer would travel. The nearest ion beam which was actively maintained was only fifteen seconds away. He had been traveling along it, parallel, after his last course change.

The speakers were dead except for faint crackling. The moment was tense with nothingness.

And then: "Command to Eighty-six. Command to Eighty-six. Revolve and Able. Over."

"Eighty-six to Command. Eighty-six to Command. Arcton P Lateral. Over."

"Command to Eighty-six. Command to Eighty-six. Operating Zyco X23 Y47 Z189076. Obit Banzo if Jet. Order Box Arcton P Lateral. AHDZA. ZED DOG FOX ABLE. WILLIAM GEORGE QUEEN BAKER. QUEEN QUEEN CAST FOX. Over."

There was a pause. Then. "Eighty-six to Command. Eighty-six to Command. Wilco and out."

The series of orders which began to blaze and sputter through the speakers were assembly and destination commands with the High Fleet manifesto for suspension of civil liberties on every one of the five planets of Sirius. With this the forward surge of a third of a million naval craft could be felt. Banzo was run to cover. The hunters were coming up to the hounds.

Ole Doc made a rapid scan of his charts.

Banzo, code for the *Star of Space* had been located on the ground at Green Rivers, third habitable planet of Sirius, Arcton P Lateral being the one column removal in the Star Pilot lists for Sirius. Eighty-six had orders from Garth to blow the *Star of Space* out of the heavens if it attempted to take off and to knock apart any merchantman that tried to go to or from Green Rivers. The civil authority of the Sirius System, that being a satellite of the Earth government, had been suspended and Marines were probably right now swarming down upon Manford, the capital on the planet Wales, to pick up the reins of state.

The comptometer told Ole Doc he could be at the rendezvous mentioned within two hours either way of Garth's arrival for they were now at two points of a triangle, not near but equidistant from Sirius. It all depended on the *Morgue* and she shortly began to put light leagues behind her in a way which made the galley a shambles and did nothing to improve the temper of Hippocrates.

He staggered up to control and said, peevishly: "Even if you find, you ruined the bread."

"Get out of here," said Ole Doc. "I've got several thousand fast cruisers to beat and by all that's holy, they're going to be beaten!"

From the way they skimmed the edges of clusters and plowed through systems and dodged comets for the next eight days, even Hippocrates gathered that this was important enough to put on some effort. He took to going back to the fuel chambers and helping the auto-feeders. That would have been a short and unmerry death to any human but the deadly rays seemed to like him. Hippocrates liked them. They were part and parcel of machinery and machinery, to him, was lovable. After all, wasn't it only human?

So Ole Doc rode the controls with fire in his sleepless eyes, one ear glued to the channels which would tell him if anything serious would happen before he got there and one ear to the ticking meters which said that if he kept stretching the *Morgue* out like this, she wouldn't have a sound seam in her whole, ancient hull.

It worried him because he was outrunning the bulk of the signals he would receive in case something went wrong. After you go just so fast in space, incoming stuff sounds like a Japanese record of a woman in hysterics played treble time, even when you are looping it off an ion beam.

On the seventh day they went through a space maelstrom which almost chipped Hippocrates to pieces. This phenomenon was no more than an unleashed hurricane of magnetic energies, unplotted and unpredicted. Ole Doc kept the throttle all the way down and they came through.

All during the eighth day they wore out spare tubes trying to brake. About three-thirteen s.g.t., all the port tubes went out at once and they had a wild, tumbling hour in which they passed Sirius as if it had been stabbed with a spur and then another two hours of limping while Hippocrates and Ole Doc clung to the outside plates and unjammed the fried rinds of metal which prevented reinstallation of the new linings.

It was after the succeeding two before they were at the rendezvous point and it was a very spent crew of two which came up to find fully half of the navies of the galaxy assembled in an array which would not be seen for many another day.

A hundred thousand ships, more or less, were grip to grip in squadrons, suspended majestically in scattered but orderly formations all about the space of Green Rivers.

An eye at a space port could not grasp their infinity. The light of the huge dumbbell planet blazed from their sides and made them so many jewels, for this was peace and metal was shined. Blinkers were flashing and lifeboat and gig lights were moving about until it looked, in the far distance, like a whole new galaxy had been born.

Orders were being rushed on a dozen admiralty bands. Barges cruised to conferences. Fleet train vessels moved amongst the horde with supplies and new air.

It was an imposing sight. Here lay, side by side, navies which had within the last century been searing one another out of the darkness. Here were reunions of peoples who had long since forgotten any connection with Mother Earth.

It was a blinding, majestic array.

Ole Doc was indifferent to its majesty. He wanted the flagship of Garth.

Patrol craft, as the *Morgue* cruised by the drifting lines, came out to blare a surly warning and then sheered off from the gold color of the hull without even trying to see the ray rods. Ole Doc, by naval etiquette, was entitled to priority in any anchorage. More than one spaceman of the navy heaved a gusty and hopeful sigh of relief at the sight of that hull.

But the *Morgue* had proved a better vessel than the *Tangier-Mairlicon* which had Garth's flag. In that the *Tangier-Mairlicon* was about one tenth the age of the *Morgue,* this was amazing. But the mighty, thousand-man vessel was not there. The radar did not catch her identification signal and Old Doc's flaring eye saw no blazing blue star of authority present.

He gave the controls to Hippocrates who, though this was nervous going, navy people knowing or caring no more about the rules of the road than they did, was well qualified to take them in to a safe position.

Ole Doc was satisfied that the *Star of Space* had not left Green Rivers, just as he was certain that he would be boarded and stopped if he tried to land on that planet.

He gave the sphere near them a pitying glance before he lay down in his cabin. It looked like a very pleasant planet. There would be no help for it whatever if the *Star of Space* had spread its death across its face.

Tuning up a speaker on the command channel reserved for Garth in all this babble, Ole Doc stretched out for a good sleep. The last he heard was a junior officer, officer of the deck on some cruiser trying to make headway over the control visagraph with a very snide Hippocrates.

• • •

Garth arrived full of purpose and blowing cigar smoke like a steam turbine. The voice which awoke Ole Doc was so thick with authority that it must have carried through a vacuum by itself without benefit of radio waves.

"Admirals of all Fleets, attend on the flag at sixteen-thirty hours." There was a click and that was all. Galactic Admiral Garth had spoken.

Ole Doc dressed with leisure, having bathed in hot water—a practice on which Hippocrates frowned since it would have dissolved the little slave in a splash had he neglected to grease himself up first. Old Doc pulled out a new cape, a presentation cape from Omphides on the event of his having solved a small problem for them in that system. It had a great display of jagged flashes done across it which, besides furnishing the symbol of ray rods rampant in solid gold, had actual ray reservoirs in the design which purified the air around and about. His old helmet had numerous scratches across it but that couldn't be helped. His boots were a bit scuffed despite all Hippocrates could do for them. When he thought of what those admirals would be wearing—suddenly he put the presentation cape back and got out his old one. In a very few minutes he entered his lifeboat and went across to the *Tangier-Mairlicon,* leaving the *Morgue* tethered to vacuum.

The officer of the deck, a commander, had been having his eyes dazzled enough that day, what with the flood of gold lace coming through the side, and his Marines and sideboys were nearly spent with standing to. The chief warrant bos'n saw the flashing gold but he could not spot the uniform. The O.O.D. saw the strange being coming up with this new "officer" and hurriedly grabbed a book of traditions, customs and courtesy throughout the galaxies.

Hippocrates had been there to run the lifeboat back but when he saw all these crossbelts and naked swords he became frightened. "I wait," he said.

"Return to the ship," said Ole Doc.

"You watch the adrenaline!" said Hippocrates, not daring to disobey.

The chief warrant bos'n took a breath and hoped he would pipe whatever was proper on his whistle and then, breath still sucked in, stared and blew not at all. It was the first time in his life he had ever seen a Soldier of Light and for the first time that day he was impressed.

"Belay the honors," said Ole Doc to the now stammering commander. "I want to attend this conference."

The commander gave him a Marine for a guide and then, on second thought, gave him two more. When the group had gone on, the O.O.D. turned wonderingly back to his book of courtesy.

"It won't be there, commander," said the chief warrant bos'n, for he had known the commander as a midshipman and ever afterward treated him with a hint of it the way old spacemen will. "That's a Soldier of Light."

"It isn't here," said the commander.

"Neither," said the old chief warrant, "is God."

Ole Doc entered the admiral's quarters just as Garth's fist was coming down to smite a point into his palm. The fist halted, Garth stared. Twenty-six admirals stared.

"I see," said Ole Doc, ignoring the chair his guide had stiffly pulled up for him, "that it takes a very large weight of naval metal to sterilize one poor liner today."

They regarded him in confused silence, recognizing the gold gorget, startled by the obvious youth of this man who stood before them, failing to recognize the arts which kept him young, failing also to grasp just why they were confused. But admirals or not they had been young once. They had heard the legends and tales. Some of them felt like guilty children.

"Down there on Green Rivers," said Ole Doc, "is a fragment of a ship. She is in trouble. Any still alive aboard her have a right to life."

Garth caught his breath. "How did you know," he roared, "where to find this fleet?" He could get to the roots of things, Garth. That was why he was a galactic admiral and the rest here his juniors even if his seniors in age.

"I cracked your code," said Ole Doc. "It was not a very hard code to crack, I might caution you. But then one does not need much of a code to fool one battered liner with a cargo of sick and dead."

Garth's blue jowl trembled. "Our medical men have already investigated. The disease cannot be cured. It is unknown. Nothing like it has ever been known. Do you know what has happened down there?"

Ole Doc didn't.

"Two men escaped from your precious liner five minutes after it landed. This morning there were fifty cases of that disease near Piedmont! There were nine cases in Hammerford and twelve in Hartisford! The planet lines have not been interrupted. Not even a road has been blocked. The planet is rotten with it. That means one thing and one thing only. I am here to give orders. This matter is well in hand!"

Ole Doc looked at Garth and suddenly understood why the man was fighting him. Authority. Garth had battled his way to the height of all naval ambition. Since the age-old abolition of seniority leadership, the dynamic people got quickly to the top. And although this was hard on juniors, it was wonderful for efficiency. Its only flaw was power-hunger, but nothing in all the Universe would work without that.

"What is the population of Green Rivers?" asked Ole Doc with a quiet born of his understanding.

"Nine million, the whole planet. Thirty cities and two hundred-odd towns. Are you going to weigh that against the good of all space? No, I think not. I am in charge here. I will not be bullied by a pill roller. According to regulations, this system must be sterilized and sterilize we will!"

"By?" said Ole Doc.

"By scorching the planet. By leveling everything with rays that will last for ten years. Be sentimental if you will, surgeon, but there are fifty million men in these navies. Do you want them to catch this stuff and die, too?"

"Admiral," said Ole Doc, "I have no desire to see anyone die. That is my profession. That is why I am here. The *Star of Space* needs help. She is an Earth ship, manned by officers and people like yourselves. And she has women and children aboard."

"I'd have been saved all this if she'd been disintegrated at the start!" said Garth.

"Down there on this planet, Green Rivers, there are nine million human beings or breeds. They have homes and farms and children. They have churches and projects for celebrating the harvest. They have plans and hopes. And they've carved a wilderness into something of which they are proud. And you," he said to the assembled, "are going to destroy it all."

It made them uncomfortable. They would not look at his face.

"You've forgotten," said Garth, "what happened during

the red death. I commanded a corvette under Van der Ruys. We were at Guyper in Galaxy 809 in '71. I saw what disease could do when it was not checked. Guyper is still a ruin and the stories I heard—"

"Are not half as bad as those which will be told of Green Rivers if you sterilize it," concluded Ole Doc.

"We don't want sickness in our fleets," said Garth, "and that's final. I give the orders here. At nineteen hours we cleanse this system. We have no other choice. You yourself," he hurled at Ole Doc, "admit that you have no notion of what this may be."

"You must first let me go down there," said Ole Doc doggedly.

"And come back to reinfect? No!"

"One moment," said Ole Doc. "You have forgotten something."

Garth glared.

"I am not under your orders, admiral."

"Your ship is staying where it is," said Garth. "When you go back you will find a cruiser alongside."

"He'll not dare detain me," said Ole Doc.

Garth was dangerously angry. Authority was as precious as blood to him. "If you defy me—"

Ole Doc said: "Admiral, I am leaving." He shook out a handkerchief and delicately fanned the air before his face and then restored it. "We've got warm in here, haven't we?"

Ole Doc left, went by the speechless men on the deck and was taken in a gig back to the *Morgue.*

How very small the portable little hospital looked amid

all this naval might, thought Ole Doc. The *Morgue* was tiny against the side of the attending cruiser which, it must be admitted, was having a very hard time due to an incessant demand to shift bumpers from a little four-armed being on parade.

Ole Doc went through the lock and into the cruiser. He found the commanding officer very nervous with his duty.

"I say, sir," said the captain to Ole Doc, "you've a very devil aboard, you know. He's made us do everything but wrap ourselves in silk to keep from scratching his precious ship. We've been awfully decent about it—"

"I want permission to leave," said Ole Doc. "I ask it as a formality, because I am going to leave anyway."

The captain was shocked. "But you can't! You absolutely can't! I've got orders to stay right where I am and to keep you hard alongside. The second you were sighted lying here, Admiral Garth sent me a positive injunction—" He fumbled on his mess table for it and found the radioscript.

"You would fire on a Soldier of Light?" said Ole Doc, dangerous.

"No, heavens no! But . . . well, sir, you haven't the power to pull us around and I'm afraid the grapplers are sealed."

Ole Doc looked calculatingly at the man. In Ole Doc's pocket was a hypo gun that would make this captain agree the stars were all pink with yellow circles. The second button of Ole Doc's cloak, if lighted, would fix said captain in his tracks. A capsule in Ole Doc's kit released into one ventilator of the ship would immobilize the whole crew for hours.

But Ole Doc sighed. It was so flagrantly against the U.M.S. code to interfere with an official vessel in performance of its ordered duty. And if the young man disobeyed, it would be his finish in the navy. Ole Doc took a cup of coffee from a very deferential and grateful captain. A little later he went back to his ship.

At eighteen-thirty s.g.t., Ole Doc awoke from a short nap. He looked out of the port and saw the lovely green of the planet through its clouds. He frowned, looked at his watch and then went into the operating room.

He gargled and blew antiseptic jets into his nose and dusted himself off with a sweet smelling light which incidentally washed his face and hands. He puttered for a while with a new lancet Soldier Isaac had given him last Christmas and then made short passes with it in the air as though he was cutting somebody's jugular—not Garth's, of course.

Orders. Orders were inexorable soulless things which temporarily divorced a man from rationality and made him an extension of another brain. Orders. Born out of inorganic matter contained in some passionless book, they yet had more force than all the glib conversations of a thousand philosophers. Orders. They made men slaves. Garth was a slave. A slave to his own orders.

Ole Doc opened a text on electro-deductive psychiatric diagnosis and turned to "paranoia." It was eighteen-fifty. If Garth was going to blast at nineteen—

The command speaker barked up. "Galactic Admiral Garth to U.M.S. *Morgue*. Galactic Admiral Garth to U.M.S. *Morgue*." It came over the commercial channel as well and was echoing up there in the control room.

Ole Doc went to his communications panel. He turned a switch and swung a dial. "*Morgue* to Garth. Over."

"*Morgue*. Urgent. The disease has reached the fleet. Something must be done. What can you do? Please do something! Anything!"

"Coming aboard," said Ole Doc and shut off his panel.

• • •

They almost mobbed him trying to get him aboard this time. They rushed him to the cabin. They saluted and bowed and pushed him in.

During the few hours which had elapsed, a considerable change had taken place in Garth.

The admiral was pale. Five admirals attended him and they were pale.

Garth was courageous.

"I suppose this means we are doomed," he said, trying to keep his hand away from his throat, which ached frighteningly. "The scout vessels which approached the *Star of Space* must have been infected in the air. Their captain reported to me here. He must have been the carrier. I . . . I have infected the officers who were with me today. They, returning to their ships, have exposed their crews. My own medical officer"—and it was easy to tell how difficult this was for Garth to beg a favor—"has no idea of what this can be. You must do something. You have asked for a case so that you could study symptoms. You have that case, doctor."

Ole Doc sat on the edge of the desk and swung a boot. He shrugged. "When you deal with diseases which have not been studied over a full course of sickness, you can form no real judgment. I am sorry, admiral, but there is nothing much which can be done just now."

"They've got full courses on Green Rivers," said Garth.

"Ah, yes," said Ole Doc. "But I am, unfortunately, forbidden—"

Garth was steady and stern. How he hated asking this! How he despised this pill roller despite the present plight!

"I will release you from that. If you care to risk the sickness, you are free to study it."

Ole Doc handed up an order blank from the desk and Garth wrote upon it.

"If it were not for the sake of my officers and men," said Garth, "I would not bother with this. I do not believe anything can be done. I act only on the recommendation of naval surgeons. Is that clear?"

"Orders again," murmured Ole Doc.

"What?" said Garth.

"In case of sickness, the medical corps, I think, orders the line. Well, I'll see if I know anything. Good day."

They let him out and through the side. Back in his ship, Ole Doc presented the order to the cruiser captain and the *Morgue* was freed. Five minutes later, at the controls, Ole Doc sent the *Morgue* knifing through the cloud layers and across the verdant surface of the beautiful planet.

He found the shapely towers of Piedmont with no trouble and in a short while was settled down upon the red earth of the landing field.

Within five minutes the *Morgue* was likely to be crushed by the mob which pressed to it. There was anxiety and hysteria in the welcome. Women held up their children to see the ship and hitherto accounted brave men fought remorselessly to get close enough to it to beg succor. Officials and police struggled with the crowd, half to clear it, half to get near the ship themselves. An old woman in the foremost rank, when the area before the port had been cleared, knelt humbly and began to pray in thankfulness.

Ole Doc swung out, stood on the step and looked down on their heads. The babble which met him was almost a physical force. He waited for them to quiet and at last, by patience alone, won their silence.

"People," said Ole Doc, "I can promise you nothing. I will try. While I am here you will help by giving me space in which to walk and work"—for he had been in such panic areas before—"so that I can help you. I cannot and will not treat an individual. When I have a solution, you will all benefit if that proves possible. Now go to your homes. Your radios will tell what is taking place."

They did not disperse but they gave him room to walk. He went across the field and down a tree-lined street under the directions of an army officer who informed him that the *Star of Space* was landed, partially disabled, at a flying field near the ball park.

Data was poured at him by people who fled along on either side and walked backwards a distance before him. Most of it was contradictory. But it was plain that in the last few hours a thousand cases had broken out across the face of Green Rivers.

It was a pleasant town upon a pleasant planet. The neat streets were flanked by wide gardens and trees and the heat of Sirius was comfortable. Ole Doc sighed as he realized how he stood between this homely work and a charred planet of debris.

A quack, selling a box of "fever cure," saw Ole Doc coming and ashamedly tried to stand before his sign and hide it. How the man expected to get away with any money he made was a mystery of psychology.

The *Star of Space* was a desolation. She had jammed into the ground on landing, fracturing her tubes. Bad navigation had dented her with space dust. Her sealed ports were like sightless eyes in a skull.

Ole Doc stood for a while within twenty feet of her, gazing in pity And then he cupped his hands. "*Star of Space,* ahoy."

A lock opened and a gaunt young man in a filthy uniform stood there. "A Soldier of Light," he said in a hushed voice.

A woman was crying on Ole Doc's left, holding a child cradled in her arms and when they saw her the crowd shrank from her for the child had closed eyes and was breathing with difficulty. But Ole Doc did not see her. He advanced on the *Star.*

The young man tried to say a welcome and could not. He dropped his face into his hands and began to sob soundlessly.

Ole Doc pushed on through. He was, after all, a mortal. Diseases respected no man, not even the U.M.S. It is valiant to go up against ray guns. It took more nerve to walk into that ship.

The stench was like a living wall. There were unburied dead in there. The salons and halls were stained and disarrayed, the furniture broken, the draperies torn down for other uses. A piano stood gleaming polished amid a chaos of broken glass. And a young woman, dead, lay with her hair outsplayed across the fragments as though she wore diamonds in her locks.

The young man had followed and Ole Doc turned in the salon. "Bring the other people here."

"They won't assemble."

"Bring them here."

Ole Doc sat down in a deep chair and took out a notebook. After a long while the people began to come, a few at a time, singly or in large groups. They looked at one another with fear on their faces. Not a few of them were mad.

A girl hurled herself across the salon and dropped to grasp at Ole Doc's knees. She was a beautiful girl, about twenty. But hunger and terror had written large upon her and her hands were shaking.

She cried out something over and over. But Ole Doc was looking at the people who were assembling there. Then he dropped his eyes for he was ashamed to look at their misery longer.

He began as orderly as he could and gradually pieced together the tale.

The disease had begun nine days out, with one case, a man from Cobanne in the Holloway System. He had raved and muttered in delirium and when partly conscious had informed the ship's doctor that he had seen the same sickness in Cobanne, a backspace, ruined remnant of war. He was a young man, about twenty. Twenty-one days out he died, but it was the opinion of the doctor that death was due to a rheumatic heart which the patient had had prior to the disease.

This was news enough, to find a place where a rheumatic heart was considered incurable. And then Ole Doc recalled the disease warfare of the Holloway System and the resultant poverty and abandonment of what had once been rich.

The next case had broken out twelve days after departure and had terminated in death a week later. Ole Doc took down the details and made a scan of nearly forty cases to arrive at a course.

The disease had an incubation period of something up to ten days. Then for a period of one week, more or less, the temperature remained low. Spots came in the mouth—though these had also been noted earlier. The temperature then rose rapidly and often caused death in this period. If it did not, the throat was greatly swollen and spots came out on the forehead and spread down over the body. Temperature then dropped to around ninety-nine for a day but rose suddenly to one hundred and five or more at which point the patient either died or, as had happened in two cases, began to recover. But death might follow any sudden temperature rise and generally did.

Ole Doc went back to a cabin where a currently stricken woman lay and took some phlegm. He processed it quickly and established the disease as a nonfilterable virus.

There were two hundred and twenty well officers, crew and passengers remaining on the *Star of Space*. They were without hope but their eyes followed Ole Doc whenever he moved across the salon going to patients in other parts of the ship.

The inspection took an hour and Ole Doc went then into the daylight and sat down on the grass under a tree while Hippocrates shooed people away. After a long time, it looked as if Ole Doc was asleep.

But he was not sleeping. No modern medical text contained any mention of such a disease. But that, of course, proved nothing. The U.M.S. texts were blank about it, that he knew. But it seemed, somehow, that he had heard or read something, somewhere about it.

The study of such diseases was not very modern after the vigorous campaigns for asepsis five hundred years ago. But still—Ole Doc looked at a stream nearby and wondered if it had any fish in it. Hang it, this area looked like the Cumberland country back in his native Maryland, a long, long way and a long, long time from here. Maybe if he fished—but his dignity here, right now, would not permit that. These people expected him to do something. Like that old woman, when he was a brand-new doctor up in the Cumberland Gap. Her child—

Ole Doc leaped to his feet. He grabbed the kit from Hippocrates and flung out the contents on the grass. After a short space of study he began to call for details and it was like a bucket brigade line the way Hippocrates was hustled back and forth by people between the *Morgue* and the *Star.*

He called for barrels. He called for wrapping paper. He played light on scraps of meat and he had a patient brought out from the ship and made him spit and spit again into a small cup.

The cup was treated and from the contents a drop was put in each barrel. And then the barrels were full of ingredients and being stirred under a light. And then another light, hitched to a thousand pounds of tubes and condensers, was lowered into each barrel and the mixtures left to stew.

It was crude but it was fast.

Ole Doc called for the young man—fourth officer of the *Star of Space.*

"I can catalyze the course of this disease," said Ole Doc. "I want a guinea pig."

The young man took a reef in his nerve. He stood forward.

Ole Doc made him open his mouth and poured in a deadly dose. Then he played a new electrode over the fourth officer. Within five minutes the first symptom of the disease had appeared. In ten, the man's temperature was beginning to rise.

Ole Doc grabbed a needle full of the contents of the first barrel. He gave the fourth officer a nonpiercing shot. Five minutes later the temperature was down and the man was well!

Ole Doc tried his antitoxin on five people and tried to give them the disease. It would not settle in them. They were immune!

"I want," said Ole Doc, "volunteers to write these instructions down; let me check what they have written and rush gallons of both these medicines to every part of this planet. You, you're the space-radio superintendent, aren't you? Take what I dictate here for warning to all systems and to provide them with the cure and prevention. Hippocrates, give me that mike."

Ole Doc said into the speaker, "U.M.S. to Garth. Prevention and cure established. *Star of Space* survivors will not be carriers. You may disperse your fleet. Your doctors will be furnished with information by the general dispatch."

He turned to a local doctor, a young man who, for some thirty-five minutes, had been standing there with his mouth open. "You see the procedure, sir. I would advise you to get in and treat the patients in that poor ship. If you need my further help, particularly with those who have become insane, I shall be at hand. I think," he added, "that there are trout in that stream."

Hippocrates carried the equipment back, an elephant load of it, and restored it to its proper places in the *Morgue.* Ole Doc, when he had got free of people trying to kiss his hands, push money on him and lift and carry him in triumph, climbed into the *Morgue* and stretched out his feet under his desk. He made a series of interesting notes.

> It is sometimes unwise to remove a disease entirely from the Universe. It is almost impossible to eradicate one completely from all quarters of the Universe, particularly as some are borne by animals unbeknownst to men.
>
> The human being as a race carries a certain residual immunity to many violent diseases so that these are, in time, ineffective against a group with which they have associated

but, reaching a new group, pass quickly to destructive lengths.

Diseases known to us commonly now would be fatal should we outgrow that immunity. In such a way are the penicillin-like panaceas destructive at long last.

I would advise—

A deferential footfall sounded at the office doorway. Ole Doc looked up, preoccupied, to find Galactic Admiral Garth.

"Doctor," said Garth uncomfortably, "are you busy just now? I can come back but—"

"No, no," said Ole Doc. "Come in and sit down. Have a drink?"

Garth shuffled his feet and sank gingerly into his chair. Plainly he was a victim of awe and he had a problem. "That was magnificent. I . . . I've been wrong about doctors, sir. I have been very wrong about the Universal Medical Society. I said some hard words—"

"No, no," said Ole Doc. "Come, have a drink."

"Well, the fact is," said Garth, "my doctors tell me that what my admirals and myself have . . . well . . . it doesn't fit the description. I don't mean your diagnosis is wrong—"

"Admiral," said Ole Doc, "I think I know what the trouble is." He reached into a desk drawer and pulled out a package which he gave to the admiral. "Take one every four hours. Drink lots of water. Tell your other men to do the same and keep to their quarters. Anybody else comes down, have your doctors give them this." And he wrote a quick prescription in a hand nobody but a pharmacist could read and gave it to Garth. Deciphered, it said "Aspirin."

"You're sure—" And Garth blew his nose.

"Of course I'm sure!" said Ole Doc. "Now how about—"

But Garth was uncomfortable around all this greatness

and he managed to get away, still giving his feeble thanks, still with awe in his eyes.

Suddenly Hippocrates appeared, an accusative gleam in his eyes, antennae waving with wrath. "What you give him? What you do with this out of place in the operating room?"

"Oh, by the way, Hippocrates," said Ole Doc, pulling out a handkerchief and handing it gingerly over. "Boil that when you wash. It's slightly septic."

"You did something! You gave somebody some disease! What you doing with—"

"Hippocrates, that bottle you keep stabbing at me is just common cold virus catalyzed to work in two or three hours. It's very weak. It wouldn't kill anyone. I merely put some on my handkerchief—"

Hippocrates suddenly stopped and grinned. "Aha! The admiral had the sniffles. Well, serve him right for kill all those innocent people. But sometime you get in trouble. You wait." He started to march off and then, impelled by a recalled curiosity, came back.

"What was the matter with all those people?"

"Too well cared for by doctors," said Ole Doc.

"How?"

"Hit by a disease which they hadn't contacted for a long, long time—say five hundred years."

"What disease?" demanded Hippocrates. "Not one that you spread?"

"No, no, heaven forbid!" laughed Ole Doc. "It has a perfectly good name but it hasn't been around for so long that—"

"What name?"

"Common measles," said Ole Doc.

A SOUND INVESTMENT

A SOUND INVESTMENT

The self-righteous Hippocrates was just returning from a visit to the *Alpheca* when the first blast hit him.

It was, however, not a very serious blast. The entire force of it emanated from the larynx of Ole Doc Methuselah, Soldier of Light and member extraordinary of the Universal Medical Society.

But if it came from a larynx, it was a much revered organ and one which, on occasion, had made monarchs jump and thrones totter.

"Where are my old cuffs?" howled Ole Doc.

This was a trifle unnerving to the little four-armed slave, particularly since, during the entire afternoon on the *Alpheca,* Hippocrates had been telling stewards and cooks, in the course of lying and bragging, what a very wonderful master Ole Doc was.

"You multi-finned monkey! If you've thrown out those cuffs I'll . . . I'll throw enough water on you to make a plaster demon of you! Tie into those cabinets and locate them! On the double!"

Hippocrates hurriedly began to make pieces of paper and bits of correspondence fly out of the file case in a most realistic fashion. He was innately neat, Hippocrates. He kept things in order. And like most neat people he kept things in order in very much his own way.

The items in question he knew very well. Ole Doc Methuselah possessed a horrible habit of writing on the cuffs of his golden shirts whenever he thought of a calculation of great intricacy and these cuffs Hippocrates tore off and filed. Now for some three hundred and twenty years he had been tearing off cuffs and filing cuffs and never once had Ole Doc so much as whispered that he ever wanted to look at an old one or consult the data so compiled, working always from a magnificent memory. And these particular items had piled up, got moldy, spilled over and been crammed back a thousand times without ever once serving a purpose.

Hippocrates, two weeks ago, had burned the entire lot.

"Look for them, you gypsum idiot!" roared Ole Doc.

"Yes, master! I'm looking, master. I'm looking every place, master!" And the filing cases and the office became a snowfall of disturbed papers, old orders, report copies, pictures of actresses and autographed intimate shots of empresses and queens. "I'm looking, master!"

Nervously Hippocrates wondered how long he could keep up this pretense. He had a phonograph-record-wise mind which, while wonderful in copying past situations, was not very good at inventing new ones. "They can't be very far, master. Where did you lose them?"

Ole Doc snapped up his head out of a liquor cabinet currently in search and glared hard enough to drill holes in plate. "Where did I lose them? *Where* did I lose them? If I knew that—"

"Just which cuff did you want?" said Hippocrates, antennae waving hopefully.

"The sonic notes, you featherbrained fop! The sonic notes I made two years ago last Marzo. The equations! I wrote them on my cuff and I tore it off and I distinctly recall giving it—" Ole Doc looked at the wreck of the file case in sudden understanding.

"Hippocrates, what have you done with those cuffs?"

"Me? Why, master! I—"

"Don't lie to me! What have you done with them?"

Hippocrates shrank away from Ole Doc, demonstrating the force of mind over gypsum, for Hippocrates, weighing five hundred kilos in his meter of height, could bend inch iron plates with any one of his four hands. "I didn't mean any harm. I . . . I was housecleaning. This ship, the poor *Morgue,* the poor, poor *Morgue!* It isn't as if she was human. And she all cluttered up with junk, junk, junk and I—" He gulped and plunged. "I burned them!" He shut his eyes convulsively and kept them shut.

The deck plates of the U.M.S. portable hospital, however, did not open and engorge him and the planet on which they were resting did not fall in halves. After several seconds of terrible tension, Hippocrates risked opening his eyes. Instantly he went down on his knees.

Ole Doc was slumped in a chair, his head in his hands, a reasonable facsimile of intense despair.

"Don't sell me," begged Hippocrates. "Don't sell me, master. I won't ever burn anything again. I'll let the whole place fill up with anything you want to bring aboard. Anything! Even women, master. Even *women!!*"

Ole Doc didn't look up and Hippocrates wandered in his gaze, finally rising and tottering to his galley. He looked at it as one who sees home for the last time. A phrase rose out of "Tales of the Space Pioneers" of a man saying good-bye to his trusty griffon and Hippocrates, sniffling dangerously—because it might soften his upper lip—said, "Good-bye, old pal. Many the day we've fit through thick and thin, agin horrible and disastrous odds, battlin' our way to glory. And now we got to part—"

His eyes caught on a bottle of ink and he took a long swig of it. Instantly he felt better. His spirits rose up to a point where he felt he might make a final appeal.

"Why," he said to his master, "you want cuff?"

Ole Doc dropped the dispatch he had been clutching, and Hippocrates retrieved it.

OLE DOC METHUSELAH
MORGUE
HUB CITY
GALAXY 16

WILHELM GIOTINI YESTERDAY ENDOWED UNIVERSAL MEDICAL SOCIETY WITH ALL REVENUE FROM HIS LANDS IN FOMALHAUT SYSTEM. PROCEED AND SECURE. FOMALHAUT ADVISED YOUR FULL AUTHORITY TO ACCEPT PROVISIONS OF GIOTINI WILL.

THORPE
ADJUTANT
CENTER

Appended to this was a second dispatch:

DISTRESS OPERATIONAL PRIORITY
ANY SOLDIER OF LIGHT ANYWHERE

FOMALHAUT FULL QUARANTINE UNIDENTIFIED DISEASE BEG AID AND ASSISTANCE.

LEBEL
GENERALISSIMO
COMMANDING

And yet a third message:

OLE DOC METHUSELAH
MORGUE
HUB CITY
GALAXY 16

YOUR INFORMATION WILHELM GIOTINI EXPIRED EARTHDAY U.T. OF MIND CONGESTION FOLLOWING ATTACK BY ASSASSIN USING SONIC WEAPON. AS REQUESTED BODY PRESERVED PENDING YOUR ARRIVAL FOMALHAUT.

LEBEL
GENERALISSIMO
COMMANDING

Hippocrates finished reading and memorizing—these were the same to him—and was about to comment when he found Ole Doc was not there. The next instant the automatic locks clanged shut on the hatches, the alarm said quietly, "Steady all. Take-off," and the *Morgue* stood on her tail and went away from there, leaving Hippocrates in a very sorry mess of torn papers and photographs, still clutching the dispatches.

It was not a very cheerful voyage. In the first place Ole Doc stressed to three G's above the ship's gravitic cancelators and put the sturdy old vessel into an advance twice over what her force field fenders could be expected to tolerate in case of space dust. All this made food hard to prepare, bent instruments and gauges in the operating room, pulled down a whole closet full of clothing by breaking the hold-up bar and generally spoiled space travel for the little slave.

Not one word during the next two weeks did Ole Doc breathe to Hippocrates and that, when only two beings are aboard, is something of a strain on anybody's nerves.

However, the Universal Medical Society had long since made provisions against space-neurasthenia by providing large libraries in natural and micro form to every one of its vessels and seeing that the books were regularly shifted. A new batch had come at Hub City and Hippocrates was able to indulge himself somewhat by reading large, thick tomes about machinery, his penchant.

He learned all about the new electronic drives for small machinery, went avidly through the latest ten place log table—finding eighteen errors—studied a thousand-page report on medical force fields, finished up two novels about pirates and reviewed the latest encyclopedia of medicine which was only fifteen volumes at a thousand words shorthand per page. Thus he survived the tedium of coventry in which he found himself and was able to look upon the planet Gasperand of Fomalhaut with some slight interest when it came spiraling up, green and pearl and gold, to meet them.

Hippocrates got out his blasters, recalled the legal import of their visit and packed a law encyclopedia on wills in the medical kit and was waiting at the lock when Ole Doc landed.

Ole Doc came up, belted and caped, and reached out his hand for the kit. Hippocrates instinctively withdrew it.

"I will carry it," said Hippocrates, put out.

"Henceforward," said Ole Doc, "you won't have to carry anything." He pulled from his belt a big legal document, complete with U.M.S. seals, and thrust it at Hippocrates. "You are free."

Hippocrates looked dazedly at the paper and read "Manumitting Declaration" across its head. He backed up again.

"Take it!" said Ole Doc. "You are perfectly and completely free. You know very well that the U.M.S. does not approve of slaves. Ten thousand dollars is pinned to this document. I think that—"

"You can't free me!" cried Hippocrates. "I won't have it! You don't dare! The last dozen, dozen times you tried to do it—"

"This time I am serious," said Ole Doc. "Take this! It makes you a full citizen of the Confederated Galaxies, gives you the right to own property—"

"You can't do this to me!" said Hippocrates. His mind was not very long on imagination and it was being ransacked just now for a good, telling excuse. "I . . . I have to be restored to my home planet. There is nothing here for me to eat—"

"Those alibis won't do," said Ole Doc. "Slavery is frowned upon. You were never bought to serve me in the first place and you know it. I purchased you for observation of metabolism only. You've tricked me. I don't care how many times I have threatened to do it and failed. This time I really mean it!"

He took the kit, threw the manumission on the table and stepped through the air lock.

Hippocrates looked disconsolately after his Soldier of Light. A deep sigh came from his gypsum depths. His antennae wilted slowly. He turned despondently to wander toward his quarters, conscious of how empty were his footsteps in this hollow and deserted ship.

Ole Doc paused for an instant at the lock as a swimmer might do before he plunges into a cold pool. The port was thronged by more than a reception committee for him.

Several passenger tramps stood on their rusty tails engorging long queues of refugee passengers and even at this distance it was plain that those who wanted to leave this place were frightened. The lines pushed and hauled and now and then some hysterical individual went howling up to the front to beg for immediate embarkation. The place was well beyond panic.

Beside the *Morgue* stood a car and a military group which, with several civilians, made a compact crowd of welcome for the Soldier of Light. In the front was a generalissimo.

Lebel was a big fellow with a big mustache and a big black mane. He had a big staff that wore big medals and waiting for him was a big bullet-ray-germ-proof car.

"Friend!" said Lebel. "Come with me! We need you! Panic engulfs us! There are twenty-five thousand dead. Everyone is deserting the system! We are in terrible condition! In a few days no one will remain in all Fomalhaut!"

Ole Doc was almost swept up and kissed before he recalled the customs in this part of the galaxy. He twisted expertly away to shake an offered hand. Generally he didn't shake hands but it was better than getting buried in a mustache. The crowd was surging toward him, cheering and pleading. Lebel took Ole Doc by the hand and got him into the refuge of the car. It was a usual sort of reception. The U.M.S. was so very old, so very feared and respected and its members so seldom seen in the flesh that welcoming parties were sometimes the most dangerous portion of the work.

"We have a disease!" said Lebel. "You must cure it! Ah, what a disease. A terrible thing! People die."

If he expected a Soldier of Light to instantly vibrate with interest, he did not know his people. Ole Doc, approaching his thousandth birthday, had probably killed more germs than there were planets in the Universe, and he hoped to live to kill at least as many more. He leaned back, folded his cape across his knees and looked at the scenery.

"It came on suddenly. First we thought it was something new. Then we thought we had seen it before. Then we didn't know. The doctors all gave it up and we almost deserted everything when somebody thought of the Soldiers of Light. 'Lebel!' I said. 'It is my duty to contact the Soldiers of Light.' So I did. It is terrible."

Ole Doc restrained a yawn. "I was coming here anyway. Your Wilhelm Giotini left the revenue of this system to the U.M.S."

"So I heard. But I thought that would mean a lawyer coming."

"We don't have any lawyers," said Ole Doc, easing his holstered blaster around into sight.

"But this terrible disease, it will change your plans, eh? Who would want a planetary system full of diseases. What a horrible disease!"

"Kills people?"

"Kills them! They die in windrows! They scream and then they die. But I will take you and you will see it. I have a helmet here so that I can enter infected areas. I have one for you."

"I have my own helmet," said Ole Doc.

"No, no!" cried Lebel. "I could not risk it. I *know* this helmet here is germ proof. It was tested. These germs come through the smallest, the tiniest air leak!"

"Why did you risk that crowd back there?" said Ole Doc.

"That! *Poof!* My own people. My aides. My airport people. They would not infect me with any disease! Here, try this helmet for size."

Ole Doc blinked a little at the man's terrible conceit and was on the verge of remarking that he had yet to meet a respectful germ when the first casualties caught his eye.

A street ahead was barricaded. Bodies were piled in either gutter, bodies in various stages of decomposition, of both sexes, of many races and castes. Velvet and burlap were brothers in that grisly display.

"Ought to bury them," said Ole Doc. "You'll have cholera or something if you don't watch it."

"Bury them! Who'd go near them! They are thrown out of the houses like that young girl there and nobody—"

"Wait a minute," said Ole Doc. "Stop the car!"

For the young girl was not dead. She was dressed in satin, probably in her wedding dress, for a church stood fifty feet further on, and her hair was a golden flood upon the pavement. She was pressing up with her hands, seeking to rise and falling back, each time screaming.

Ole Doc reached for the door handle but Lebel blocked him. "Don't risk it!" said Lebel.

Ole Doc looked at the frantic effort of the girl, looked at her young beauty, at the agony in her eyes and then took Lebel's offer of a helmet. When he had it strapped on—an act which prompted both Lebel, his guards and drivers to hastily do the same—he shot the bolt on the door and stepped to the pave. He gazed at the girl in satin for a moment in deep thought.

Ole Doc advanced, fumbling for the speaker buttons on the side of the helmet and finding with annoyance that the phones were squeaky in the upper frequencies. The screams came eerily through this filter. He turned down the volume in haste.

He helped her up and tried to speak to her but her eyes, after an instant of trying to focus, rolled out of concentration and screams tore up from her as though they would rip her throat to shreds. She beat at him and fought him and her gown tore down the side. Ole Doc, aware that Lebel was fearfully at his side and trying to get him away, let the girl slide back to the ground, moving her only so that she now lay upon the grass.

"Hippocrates!" said Ole Doc.

But there was no Hippocrates there and Ole Doc had to fumble into the kit himself. He laid out all the volumes of law in some amazement, holding the girl down with one hand and fishing in the case with the other, and was much wroth at all this weight. Finally he found his hypo gun and an instant later the generalissimo's aides were gripping his wrist.

"Let go!" stormed Ole Doc, too busy holding the girl to make much of a fight of it. But they continued the contest, wrenched his shoulder and made him give up what they thought was a weapon.

"Nobody draws around the generalissimo!" said the big guard, his voice shrill and squeaky in the filter of the phones.

Ole Doc glared at them and turned to his patient. He felt her pulse and found that it was racing somewhere around a hundred and forty. He took her temperature and found it only slightly above normal. Her skin was dry and pale, her blood laked in the depths of her body. Her palms were wet. Her pupils were dilated to their entire diameter. Through the rents in the dress it could be seen that no blemish marked her lovely body.

Ole Doc stood up. "Lebel, give me that gun."

Lebel looked uncertain. He had taken no part in the brief skirmish but it was plain that he was not sure exactly what the weapon was.

"Then do it yourself," said Ole Doc. "Point it at her side and pull the trigger."

"Oh!" said Lebel, seeing some parallel between this and the treatment he gave cavalry horses with wounds. He brightened and with something close to pleasure did as he was bidden.

The small hypo gun jumped, a small plume of spray-fog winding up from its muzzle. The girl quivered, stiffened and then sank back unconscious. Lebel looked in disappointment at the gun, gazed with contempt into its muzzle and threw it into the kit.

"I thought it was a weapon!" he said. "Ten—fifteen—twenty times people have tried to assassinate me. That I should fear a Soldier of Light is very foolish of me. Of course it was just a medication, eh? Well, well, let's get off this street. The sight of civilian dead worries me. On the battlefield is another thing. But civilian dead I do not like. Come!"

Ole Doc was coming but he was also bringing the girl.

"What do you mean to do with that?" said Lebel.

"I want a case history of this thing," said Ole Doc.

"Case— No, no! Not in my car! I am sick of this helmet! Leave it there where it was, I tell you! Smorg! Dallison! Put that girl back—"

The two aides didn't wait for the full command. They surged up. But Ole Doc wasn't trying to hold a struggling girl now. She quietly slid to the grass while Ole Doc's hands moved something faster.

He could have drawn and burned them to glory long before they could have reached him. He contented himself with flicking a dart from each sleeve. The action was very quick. The feathered ends of the darts fell back without their points. Smorg and Dallison stopped, reached for their weapons and froze there.

"Attention!" said Ole Doc. "You will obey only me. You can never obey anyone else again. Get into the car!"

And the two aides, like wound-up clockwork, turned around and got into the car like obedient small boys.

"What have you done?" yelped Lebel.

"They are in a fine, deep trance," said Ole Doc. "I dislike being handled by anyone, Lebel. No Soldier of Light does. We are only seven hundred in the entire Universe but I think you will find that it pays to be very polite to us. Now do you sleep or cooperate?"

"I'll cooperate!" said Lebel.

"Put this girl in the car and continue to the place you have kept Wilhelm Giotini."

The gawping driver saw his passengers and their cargo in place and then swiftly took Lebel's orders for the palace. The car rocketed through the death-paved streets, shot up the ramp of the ruling house and came to a halt in the throne room.

Lebel got out shakily. He kept licking his lips and looking around as though on the watch for guards. But he was at the same time half afraid to give any orders to guards.

Ole Doc looked at the furnishings, the golden throne, the alabaster pillars. "Nice place," he said. "Where's Giotini?"

"I'll take you up there," said Lebel. "But stay a moment. You are not going on under the misapprehension that I am trying to block you in any way, are you? I am not! My aides are jumpy. They have orders. I am jumpy. My entire system of planets is coming apart with a disease. The ruler is dead and I have only some small notion of what he meant to do.

You are the first Soldier of Light I ever saw. How do I know if you really are one? I have heard that they are all old men and you look like a boy."

Ole Doc looked at him appraisingly, planted his boots firmly on the great orange squares of the throne room and looked at the assembled guards. "Generalissimo, you are not the first to question the identity of a Soldier. Therefore I shall be patient with you. Disease is our concern. Medical research. Any medical weapon. We safeguard the health of mankind through the stars against plague and medical warfare. Several hundred years ago we organized the Universal Medical Society to combat misuse of germs and our scope is broader yet. Now if you require some proof of my identity, attend me."

Lebel walked lumberingly after Ole Doc up to the line of guards who, drawn stiffly to attention, brilliant in their palace uniforms, looked at nothing and no one. Ole Doc reached out a finger at a sergeant.

"Step forth!" said Ole Doc.

The sergeant took a smart pace forward and saluted. Ole Doc, with legerdemain which defied the eye, produced a brilliant button which fixed his subject's eyes.

"Extend your hand!" said Ole Doc.

The sergeant automatically extended his hand. He was weaving a trifle on his feet, his eyelids fluttering rapidly.

"You cannot feel anything in your entire body!" said Ole Doc. Out came a lancet. Up went the sergeant's sleeve. Ole Doc gashed a five-inch wound into the forearm, picked up the beating artery like a rope, dropped it back and pressed the flesh to stop the bleeding. He reached into a cape pocket and extracted a small rod, a ray rod of pharmacy with a Greek symbol on it. He passed the rod over the wound. It closed.

He reversed the rod and passed it once more. The scar vanished. There was nothing but blood on the floor to mark what had happened.

Ole Doc snapped his fingers to awaken his subject and pushed him back into line.

"Do you require further proof?" said Ole Doc.

The line had forgotten to be military and was a little out of rank now with slack-jawed staring. Lebel backed up, blinking. The sergeant was looking curiously around and wondering why everybody was so startled, disappointed to find he had missed something.

"I never doubted you!" said Lebel. "Never! Come right away into the south hall where we left him. Anything you say, sir. Anything!"

Ole Doc went back to the car and shouldered the body of the young girl. He was beginning to miss Hippocrates. Doing manual labor was a thing which Ole Doc did not particularly enjoy.

Wilhelm Giotini was lying on a tall bed, a scarlet sheet covering his face, his royal accouterments neglected on the floor and his crown mixed up with the medicine bottles. Any physician who had attended him was gone now. Only a woman sat there, a dumpy, weeping little woman, tawdry in her velvet, unlovely in her sorrow.

"Madame Giotini," said Lebel.

She looked up. Somewhere, in some old forgotten book of legends she had seen a picture of a Soldier of Light. Her eyes shot wide and then she came forward, falling on her knees and gripping Ole Doc by the hand.

"You come too late," she said brokenly. "Too late! Poor,

poor Will. He is dead. You have come too late but maybe you can save my people." She looked pleadingly up. "Say you will save my people."

Ole Doc put her gently aside. He laid the girl down upon a nearby couch and approached the bed. He threw back the cover and gazed at Wilhelm Giotini.

Wilhelm Reiter Giotini, unblooded ruler of Fomalhaut, creator of empires and materializer of dreams, was far past any normal succor. The fierce energy he had stored up in the streets of Earth as a gutter gamin had not served him at the last. The pride and fury of him had not staved off attack. The greatness of his mind, his beneficence to science, his bequests and scholarships had not added one single instant to his life. Here he lay, a sodden lump of dead flesh, inheritor of man's allotted ground, six-by-two-by-six just the same.

Ole Doc turned to Madame Giotini and Lebel. "Leave me."

They looked at the body and then at Ole Doc and they backed to the door. Ole Doc fastened them out and returned to the bed and stood there gazing at Giotini.

"Hippocrates!" he barked.

But there was no Hippocrates there and Ole Doc had to write his list and slide it through the door to a messenger. He went back to his thoughtful vigil by the dead.

When the girl stirred Ole Doc transferred his attention and approached the couch with a slight smile. She was, after all, a very pretty girl. He gave her a small white pill and a swallow from his flask and shortly she returned from the world of her nightmares and fixed him with pale wonder.

"It is all right," said Ole Doc. "I am a Soldier of Light."

She blinked, awed, and began to gather up her torn, white satin. "But the disease. I caught the disease. I was dying!"

"You do not have a disease," said Ole Doc. "There is none."

This was so entirely contrary to her terror that she could not digest it and looked at him with eyes of a wondrous jade hue beseeching him to tell her what he meant.

"There is no disease, no poison," said Ole Doc. "I have no further clue. But in the absence of bacteria and drugs, it is necessary that you tell me what you can of today's occurrence."

"I . . . I was bridesmaid at my sister's wedding. It . . . all of a sudden it began to get terrible. Everyone began to scream. I ran outside and fell down and there were dead people all over and I was afraid—" She caught herself back from some of the horror. "That's all I know."

Ole Doc smiled gently. "You can tell me more than that. Was anyone sick from the disease before today?"

"Oh yes. Over in the eastern quarter of the city. And on all the other planets. The disease kept spreading. There isn't anything left on Gerrybome and that had almost as many people as this world. But nobody thought it would come here today. It was awful!" She shuddered and averted her face. "My sister, her husband . . . my mother . . . is anyone left alive?"

"You will have to face this bravely," said Ole Doc. "I do not think there is. I have not been here very long."

"Is it liable to strike again? Is that why you wear that helmet?"

Ole Doc had been wondering why she didn't have as pretty a voice as she had a body. He hurriedly unstrapped the helmet and laid it aside. She gazed at him earnestly. "Could you save my family?"

"Not very well," said Ole Doc. "You were the only one

alive in that entire area that I could see. I even glanced in the church. I am sorry." He fumbled in his belt kit and came up with a cartridge for his hypo gun. He fitted it carefully. She was beginning to shudder again at the nightmare she had just experienced and paid no attention to what he was doing.

The gun, held close against her side, jerked and sent a heavy charge of neo-tetrascopolamine into her. She did not feel it but continued to cry for a little while. Then, blankness overspreading her face, she looked at him and at her surroundings.

"Who are you? Where am I?"

Ole Doc nodded with satisfaction. She had experienced amnesia for the past reaching back probably three or four days; she would not be able to recall any part of the terrible experience she had undergone.

"There was sickness," said Ole Doc, "and I brought you here to help me."

"You . . . you're a Soldier of Light!" she said, sitting up in astonishment. "A Soldier of Light! Here on Gasperand! I—" She saw her torn dress. "What—?"

"I brought you so fast your dress got torn," said Ole Doc.

"You promise you'll get back in time for my sister's wedding?"

"We'll do what we can," said Ole Doc. "Now you don't mind dead people, do you?"

"Dead—?" It ended in a gasp as she saw the body on the bed.

"That is Wilhelm Giotini," said Ole Doc. "You heard he had died?"

"Oh, weeks ago! Weeks! But there he is—ugh!"

"Now, now. No time for weak stomachs, my dear. Fix up your dress and we'll do what we can for him."

"Do what— Why, bury him, of course!" She added hesitantly and a little afraid: "You *are* going to bury him?"

"No, my dear. I am afraid I am not."

There was a heavy creaking outside the door and a knock. Ole Doc unbarred it and let six guardsmen stagger in with a load of equipment. It astonished Ole Doc. He had never thought of that equipment as being heavy before since Hippocrates had always carried it so lightly. And when they returned with a second load and stumbled with it, Ole Doc almost lost patience.

"Now get out before you break something!" he snapped.

He barred the door again and faced the unlovely thing on the bed. The girl's golden hair almost rose up in horror. "You're not going to—"

With a deep sigh which still had a great deal of compassion in it, Ole Doc showed her over to a window seat and let her sit there out of sight of the bed.

He opened the cases they had brought him and laid out a sparkling string of instruments and arctrodes, unpacked a portable generator, hooked up numerous wires, connected several condensers in series and plugged them to one end of a metal box, placing the generator at the other. Then he hefted a scalpel and a chisel and walked toward the head of the bed.

In the window seat the girl shuddered at the sounds she heard and twisted hard at the tassels of an embroidered cushion. She heard a curious sawing sound, surmised what it was and twisted so hard that the tassel came off. She nervously began to shred it, not daring to look over her shoulder. For a long time she felt ill and then became aware of a complete silence which had lasted many minutes. She was about to look when the generator took off with a snarling whine so much akin to the anger of a black panther in the local zoo that she nearly screamed with it in unison.

She could not keep away then. It sounded too bloodthirsty. But when she looked, Ole Doc was sitting on the edge of the bed looking interestedly at the metal box and, outside of a deal of blood on the golden sheets, everything seemed perfectly human.

Cautiously she approached the Soldier. "Is . . . is he in there?"

Ole Doc looked up with a start. "Just his brain, my dear."

She hastily went back to the window seat. The cushion's tassels suffered horribly when the thought came to her that she might have been brought here as a part of this experiment, that she was to be something of a human sacrifice to science. And the more she thought about this possibility the more she believed it. Wilhelm Giotini was a great man; he had built up an entire civilization on five worlds which had hitherto been given to outlaws and casual wanderers; his vast energy had been sufficient to make cities grow in a matter of weeks and whole new industries from mine to finished product in a month or two. Who was she, Patricia Dore, to be weighed in the balance against an experiment involving Giotini? This Soldier was certain, absolutely certain, to use her for his own ends.

It was a deep drop to the courtyard below and as she scouted her chances here she was startled to see that a group of guardsmen were gathering alertly at the gate below. But there were other windows and, without moving fast enough to attract Ole Doc's attention, she made her way to the next. The drop was no better nor was there a balcony and here were more guardsmen being posted. There was something about the way they handled their weapons and looked at the house which gave her to understand that they intended something against this room.

"My dear," said Ole Doc, beckoning.

She looked wide-eyed at the guardsmen and then at Ole Doc in a between-two-fires hysteria of mind. She held herself to calmness finally, the legendary repute of the Soldier of Light winning, and came back to the bed.

"There are guardsmen all around us," she said, half as a promise of reprisal if anything happened to her. Ole Doc paced to the window and looked out. He saw the troop gathered at the gate and in a burst of indignation, so obvious was their intent there, threw open the leaded pane and started to ask them what they meant.

Instantly a blaster carved a five-foot section off the upper window. A piece of melted glass hit Ole Doc on the neck and he swore loud enough to melt the remaining sash. But he didn't just stop swearing. His right hand was traveling and at almost the instant that the burn struck, his blaster jolted and jolted hard.

Three guardsmen went down, slammed back against the gate by the force of fire, the last of them spinning around and around. Ole Doc never saw him fall. Ole Doc was back and under cover just as five more battle sticks went to work on the window. A big piece of ceiling scored up and curled brown to fall with a dusty crash an instant later.

Giotini evidently had known there would be moments like this. He had big, ray-proof shutters on each window which closed from inside. Ole Doc got them shut and barred and they grew hot to the touch as people below wasted ammunition on them.

Patricia Dore made nothing of this. It had occurred to her that perhaps these guards had set out to rescue her, for she had been fed a great deal of circulating library in her youth and she had an aberrated idea of just how much men would do for one woman. Just as she was getting a dramatic notion about aiding outside to get this Soldier who was obviously now no Soldier at all—for nobody ever fired on the U.M.S.—Ole Doc told her to get out of the way and sit down and she obeyed meekly.

Ole Doc looked at the metal case, noted the meter readings and then looked at the girl. She thought he was surveying her for the kill but she flattered herself. Ole Doc was simply trying to think and it is easier to think when one has a pretty object on which to fasten the eyes.

His own helmet, with its ship-connected radio, had been left in the generalissimo's car. No other communication of orthodox type was at hand. He grabbed up a bundle of sheets, revealing a rather gruesome sight, wadded them into a ball, saturated them with alcohol from his gear, opened a shutter partly and looked cautiously out. There was a summerhouse which the wad would just reach and he launched it. He was so quick that he had drawn and fired into it and shut the shield before he got fire back. A moment later, when he peered through the slits, he saw that the blankets were on fire and busily igniting the summerhouse. There were enough roses around there to make a very good smudge. But whether Hippocrates would see it and if he saw it whether or not he would know it for what it was, Ole Doc could not possibly guess.

He went back to the cabinet. A small meter at the top was *tick-tick-tick*ing in a beg to be valved off.

He threw the switches and the yowl of the dynamo stopped, making a sudden and oppressive silence in the room which hurt the girl's ears. Ole Doc peered into the view plate, looked grim and sat down on the naked bed with the cadaver.

He began to scribble on the white porcelain top of the box, making all manner of intricate mathematical combinations, thumbing them out and making them once more. He had figured all this once on a particularly boring trip between Center and Galaxy 12 and he had written it all down neatly and with full shorthand explanation just where it should have been—on his cuff. And he had torn off the cuff and given it to Hippocrates. And Hippocrates had up and burned the whole lot of them. Ole Doc swore, forgetting the girl who held her ears and hearing swearing, was sure now that this could be no real Soldier of Light, Savior of Mankind and pale and mournful patter of suffering little children.

A thundering was begun now on the outer door and Ole Doc had to get up and double bar that. Giotini had certainly been justified in making this room strong. Unless they blew up the whole palace, they weren't likely to get in.

He figured harder, getting his thumb entirely black with smudges of erasures, reworking the equations frantically.

Far off there began a mutter of heavy cannon and he jerked up his head listening intently. The weaker rattle he knew for the *Morgue*'s battery. Hippocrates must be holding a pow-wow with them in his favorite way—and this made the chances of rescue from that quarter very, very slim.

"What's got into them people?" demanded Ole Doc of the metal box.

He erased once more and began again, making himself assume a very detached air. There was a sonic equation, a simple, embracing equation which, when he got it back again—

The girl saw how hard he was working and decided she had an opportunity to slide out the door on the side which, so far, did not seem to be attacked. She raised the bar, touched the knob and instantly was engulfed in a swirl of guardsmen.

Ole Doc came up, took three steps across the bed and fired. The flare and flash of his blaster lit up the room like summer lightning and the screams which greeted it were a whole lot louder than thunder. One guardsman went down, sawed in half. Another tangled up with the first, stood in quivering shock and then rolled out of the way to let the man behind him take one full in the face.

The girl was curled up in terror just inside the door. One shot furrowed two inches above her head and another turned the knob which she still touched so hot that it burned her. Her dress began to smolder at the hem from a ricochet.

Ole Doc was still coming, still firing. He nailed his fourth and fifth men, liberally sprayed the hall, ducked a tongue of lightning and got the door shut by the expedient of burning a body which blocked it in half. He fixed the bar.

"Now where did you think you were going?" he demanded. "Here. Listen to this." And he turned on a big radio beside Giotini's bed, flipping the cog switches for stations. But there was only one on which was just then announcing. "Sometimes," said Ole Doc, "I almost think Hippocrates was right!"

Then he went back to the case and tried to pick up the

threads of his computations. Suddenly he had it. It all came back and lay there in a scrawl looking at him.

It was the basic formula of cellular memory transmission in the neuro-sonic range, derived from the highest harmonic of nerve cell frequency and computable in this form to calculate the bracket of particular memory types as transmitted from sonic reception to audio-sonic recording cells. It was the retention frequency of audio memory.

As the nerve cell does not live long and as it is very liable to putrefaction, Ole Doc considered himself fortunate to find as much of Giotini's brain intact as he had.

He began to work with a disk recorder and mike, setting up a tangle of wires which would have done credit to a ham operator, back on Earth. The thunder was beginning at the front door again.

Vaguely through his preoccupation filtered the radio behind him. "... the complete depopulation of this planet is a certainty. No slightest signal has come from there since ten this morning at which time the recording you have just heard was taken. There is no government bulletin on this. Dr. Glendenning of the generalissimo's staff states that the disease is so virulent that it is probably capable of a clean sweep of the Planet Hass. Gasperand then remains the only populated planet in this system and a rapid survey this morning showed that the continent of Vargo and our present location alone contain any surviving beings. It is momentarily expected—"

Ole Doc looked back to his work and worked even harder. The efforts at the door grew louder and more violent.

At long last, Ole Doc made a playback, nodded and beckoned to the girl. Patricia came with great reluctance.

"You should be interested in this," said Ole Doc. "It

remarks an advance of science. I have taken Giotini's brain, preserved it and have taken from it its various memories in the audio range. Now if you will listen—"

She listened for about three seconds, her eyes saucer big with horror, and then she screamed loud enough to drown radio and battering and gunfire.

Ole Doc went to the door. "Hello out there!"

The thundering stopped.

"Hello out there," said Ole Doc. "It is necessary that I speak with Lebel. You're not going to get in here and if you keep at this too long, my relief ship will come down on you with enough guns to blow the whole planet out of orbit. Let me speak to Lebel!"

There was a very long pause and then Lebel was heard on the other side of the door. "Well? Are you going to come out and give yourself up?"

"No," said Ole Doc, "but I have built a set to communicate with my base. Unless you parley you will be a hunted man through all the stars. I have something of considerable interest to you."

"I doubt it," said Lebel.

"Come here," said Ole Doc to the girl. "Tell him what you have seen and heard."

"It's horrible!" she said. "I won't!"

"Oh yes you will!" said Ole Doc. "Tell him."

"He cut out Giotini's brain!" she cried. "He put it in a machine and he made it talk and he's got records in here of him talking! It's horrible!"

Her weeping was the only sound for several, long moments. Then Lebel, with a strangely constricted throat, said, "You . . . you made a dead man talk?"

"Stay right there," said Ole Doc, "and you'll hear about

it." He brought up his recorder and promptly turned it on full blast.

"My spies tell me—I have not long to live because Lebel has plans against me. I should never have trusted him. They say he is going to cause the death of everyone in this entire system. I have watched him lately. It seems certain to me that assassination is near. I am going to take what precautions I can but he is a devil. I should never have hired him. He is plotting to overthrow everything I have done—"

"Want to hear more?" said Ole Doc.

It was very silent on the other side of the door. The bar hinges were very well oiled. The record kept on going and suddenly Ole Doc jerked the panel in and as quickly shut it again. The bars clanged in place.

Lebel sprawled ignominiously on the floor and Ole Doc's heel was unkind in the side of his neck. He was a big man but a stamp like that knocks the largest flat and, sometimes, kills them quite dead.

Ole Doc leaned over and knocked Lebel out with his gun butt before that unworthy could stir.

When Lebel tried to sit up he was so swathed with satin strips for binding that he could not stir. He was also choking on a gag. He felt uncomfortable.

"Now," said Ole Doc with a gruesome grin, "let's get down to cases. There is only one thing which could cause death in the fashion I have seen today and that is by *extreme fear.* Do you follow me?"

Lebel glugged and struggled. Ole Doc thoughtfully fingered the edge of a scalpel and cut off a neat lock of Lebel's mustache.

"You are either flying over the planets or ground patrolling with some instrument to cause that fear," said

Ole Doc. "And that instrument is obvious to me. Why is it? Because the helmet you insisted I use had sound filters in it alive only in the upper range. Therefore it is a sonic weapon. It killed only a limited number of the people it was directed at, therefore it cannot be a common supersonic weapon. That makes it *subsonic,* something new and impossible to trace as such.

"I don't have to examine your broadcaster to know that it must be a ten to thirteen cycle note, below the range of human hearing. Sensing something which they could not locate or define, people were terrified by it, for nothing frightens like the unknown. It probably has a strength of about a hundred and fifty decibels, stronger would literally tear their eardrums and brains loose.

"It was on when I found that girl because enough of it got through to your guards and yourself to make you extremely nervous, even if you did know what it was, and you fell back to your basic fear of being assassinated. So you gave your weapon away.

"Glandular disruption in your targets often caused heart failure, adrenal poisoning and other fatal reactions all very solidly from fear, and there is no inquest when people are merely scared to death. The larger percentage of the populace is deserting or has deserted this system by means of passenger ships. You have probably helped finance that exodus as a public benefactor while your staff doctors ran about yelling news of a 'disease.'"

Lebel glugged and struggled, angry.

"Now as to why," said Ole Doc, slowly passing the scalpel a reluctant inch away from Lebel's jugular vein, "that is very, very simple. You want to knock off every living person or drive him away from the planets of this system.

That will leave you and your guards alone in possession. You heard that the U.M.S. was deeded all the revenue of Fomalhaut. You discovered that *after* you had murdered Giotini. Any government you could fight. You were afraid to fight us in any but the strictly legal field.

"You depended upon the law of salvage which says that 'any planet deserted by her populace shall become an object of salvage to whomever shall take possession.' You thought you would have us there. You would own a rich planetary system by your own galactic title, breaking Giotini's deeds of ownership and therefore his will.

"You got suspicious of me when you saw the law books in my kit. You were frightened by your own weapon which was even then turned on somewhere in the vicinity and you acted irrationally, scared by self-induced fear. Then you reached the palace and calmed down and started to play the game out once more. But advisers got the better of you, probably because they were newly in from areas where your fine terror weapon was working and you became unbalanced enough to actually tackle a Soldier of Light.

"A long time ago a fellow you wouldn't know named Shakespeare talked about 'an engineer being hoist by his own petard.' You have somebody on your staff who has done that, to himself and to you. I heard mention of a 'Dr.' Glendenning who is in your pay. He is probably no doctor but a renegade sound engineer. But let that pass. When I take off this gag you are going to sing out to cease all activity and begin instant rescue of anyone left alive anywhere in this system. Understand?"

Lebel mocked him with his eyes. Ole Doc shrugged and went for a hypo needle, dipped it in a bottle and came back.

Holding up the dripping point, very shiny and sharp,

Ole Doc said, "This contains poison. It is a fine poison in that it deprives a man of his reason gradually. There is no known antidote, save one I carry."

He jabbed the needle through Lebel's pants and drove the fiery liquid home. Lebel leaped and nearly broke the point off.

Ole Doc stood back with satisfaction. He went and filled the needle with another fluid. "This is the antidote. If not administered in ten minutes, you will be beyond all recovery."

With this cheerful news, Ole Doc went over to the window, humming a grim tune and stood there looking out a slit, needle upright and dripping.

Heels banging the floor brought him back. "Why," he said, "only one minute has gone by! Are you sure you want to give the order?"

Agony was registered on Lebel's face. Ole Doc removed the gag.

"Guard!" howled Lebel. "This madman will kill me! Recall all planes. Cease operations! Stop the agents! Rescue whoever you can! Quick, quick!"

There was an instant's hesitation outside the door but Lebel drove them to it again with renewed orders. "He knows all about it. The patrols from Hub City will come! Obey me!"

Bootbeats went away from there then and Ole Doc could relax. He could hear shouts outside the palace and turmoil within. They were carrying out orders but they were also running for their lives. They had played for their shares in a great empire and they had failed.

Ole Doc unloosed Lebel's bonds while the generalissimo regarded his incredulously.

"Go ahead," said Ole Doc, "get up. I am not sure what

is going to happen to you finally, not sure at all. But right now I am going to pay back something of what the people in these worlds have suffered. You're a fine, big fighter. You weren't shot with anything more serious than yellow fever vaccine, the burningest shot I know. Now put up your fists!"

There was a renewed turmoil outside the palace gates. It was occasioned by a big, golden ship clearly marked with the ray rods of pharmacy setting itself down with a smoking *wham* directly in the street. The vessel was charred here and there but serviceable still and about the maddest gypsum-metabolism slave in several galaxies pressed the grips on the main battery.

The palace gates caved in, the metal curling like matches turned to charcoal. The palace doors sizzled down into piles of slag and puddles of brass. A luckless company of guardsmen trying to get away from there rounded the turret at the courtyard's end, got scorched by the flames and heat and made it away with the diverted guns taking their heels off as they ran.

Then Hippocrates, girded around like a pirate and bristling with rage, stepped down from the air lock and marched across the yard, walking tough enough to crack paving blocks. He jumped the glowing pools and stalked with horrible appetite into the palace proper.

A guard, running away with a handful of jewelry without knowing of any place to run, was suddenly hauled up by his belts, suspended two feet off the floor and banged into a pillar. The jewelry fell in a bright shower and rolled away. Hippocrates banged him again.

"Where is my master?" roared Hippocrates.

The guard didn't answer fast enough, probably because he did not understand in the least what master was meant and was promptly banged so hard that he went into some other realm, there to serve other men, no doubt. Hippocrates dropped him. He grabbed at a second and missed.

Then an ominous sound came to him, the thud of bodies in combat and the breaking of furniture and he plowed his way through a milling throng like a hot knife into butter and found himself outside the Giotini suite.

The door was barred. This was no problem. He blazed away at it at a range no human could have stood and had himself a hole in it in a trice. He fished one hand through, found a bar and slammed the panels back.

There he stopped.

The bloodiest, messiest man it had ever been his fate to see was trying to crawl up from the floor. He was dripping blood from massive contusions. He was dripping rags. He was blind with fair blows and staggering on the borders of beyond. His remaining teeth were set behind lips so puffed that they looked like pillows.

And Ole Doc, standing there with his broken fists still ready, said: "Get up! Get up and fight! Get up and fight!" But Ole Doc wasn't even looking at his adversary. He couldn't see him.

Hippocrates reversed a blaster and was about to knock Lebel out with one smart blow when Lebel fell of his own accord and lay completely still.

Half an hour later, when Hippocrates had his master well healed up, the little slave turned to gather the remains of the equipment for a return to the ship. He picked up several items, rendered more or less secondhand by the combat and then laid them down, puzzled.

"What is all this, master?"

Ole Doc ranged his puffy eyes over the equipment. "Busted experiment," he said.

"What experiment, master?"

"That condemned cuff note!" said Ole Doc, a little peevish. "It sounded so good when I was working on it fifty or sixty years ago. If you could just calculate the harmonic of memory retention, you could listen to whatever a dead man had been told. But," he added with a sigh, "it doesn't work."

"But what's this record then?"

"Fake. Bait to get Lebel to the door."

"You want this junk?"

"Let it lie," said Ole Doc. "There's a silly girl around here we'll have to gather up and we've got a lot of psychotherapy to attend to where we can find anyone left alive and I've got a dispatch to send Center to tell them the state of this endowment. We've got to get busy."

"What about this?" said Hippocrates, touching Lebel with a toe.

"That?" said Ole Doc. "Well, I really don't know yet. I think I'll try him for the next couple months from time to time and then sentence him to death and then reprieve him."

"Reprieve?" gaped Hippocrates.

"So that the survivors can try him," said Ole Doc. "Then I'll pardon him and send him to Hub City to be tried."

"Drive him mad," said Hippocrates practically.

Ole Doc swished his cloak over his shoulder. "Let's get out and get busy."

Hippocrates bounced to the door and cleared it importantly.

But Ole Doc didn't pass on through. "Hippocrates, why on earth did you burn up those cuffs?"

"They didn't seem very important to me when I read," said Hippocrates, hangdog instantly.

Ole Doc gaped. "When you read . . . you mean you read all of them?"

"Yes, master."

Ole Doc laughed suddenly and laughed loudly. "If you read them, you remember them, then!"

"Yes, master!"

"But why didn't you say so?"

"I thought you just mad because I not file right. You didn't ask me."

Ole Doc laughed again. "Well, no loss at all then. *Some* of the notes may work despite this fiasco today. Hippocrates, when I bought you at that auction a few hundred years back, I think I made the soundest investment of my life. Let's go."

Hippocrates stared. He almost staggered. And then he grew at least another half meter in height. He went out into the corridor breasting a pleading, hopeful, begging throng, carving a wide swathe through them and crying out in a voice which cracked chips from the pillars in the place. "Make way! Make way for Ole Doc Methuselah, Soldier of Light, knight of the U.M.S. and benefactor of mankind! Make way! Make way!"

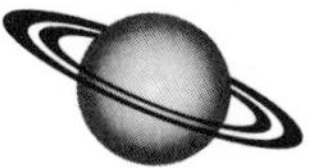

OLE MOTHER METHUSELAH

OLE MOTHER METHUSELAH

Bucketing along at a hundred and fifty light-years, just entering the Earth Galaxy, the *Morgue,* decrepit pride of the Universal Medical Society, was targeted with a strange appeal.

> ANY UMS SHIP ANY UMS SHIP ANY DOCTOR ANYONE EMERG EMERG EMERG PLEASE CONTACT PLEASE CONTACT UNITED STATES EXPERIMENTAL STATION THREE THOUSAND AND TWO PLANET GORGON BETA URSA MAJOR. RELAY RELAY EMERG.

Ole Doc was in his salon, boots on a gold-embroidered chair, head reclined against a panel depicting the Muses crowning a satyr, musing upon the sad and depleted state of his wine "cellar" which jingled and rattled, all two bottles of it, on a shelf above the coffeemaker. He heard the tape clicking but he had heard tapes click before. He heard it clicking the distinctive three dots of an emergency call but he had heard that before also.

"Hippocrates!" he bellowed. And after a silence of two days the loudness and suddenness of this yell brought the little slave out of his galley as through shot from a gun.

Four-armed, antennaed and indestructible, little Hippocrates was not easily dismayed. But now he was certain that they were hard upon a dead star—nay, already struck.

"Master?"

"Hippocrates," said Ole Doc, "we've only got two bottles of wine left!"

Hippocrates saw that the ship was running along on all drives, that the instrument panel, which he could see from where he stood in the passage, half a ship length forward from the salon, was burning green on all registers, that they were on standard speed and that, in short, all was well. He wiped a slight smear of mustard and gypsum from his mouth with a guilty hand—for his own supplies of delicacy were so low that he had stolen some of Ole Doc's plaster for casts.

"The formula for making wine," began Hippocrates with his phonograph-record-wise mind, "consists of procuring grapes. The grapes are then smashed to relieve them of juice and the juice is strained and set aside to ferment. At the end of—"

"We don't have any grapes," said Ole Doc. "We don't have any fuel. We have no food beyond ham and powdered eggs. All my shirts are in ribbons—"

"If you would stop writing on the cuffs," said Hippocrates, "I might—"

"—and I have not been fishing for a year. See what's on that tape. If it's good fishing and if they grow grapes, we'll land."

Hippocrates knew something had been bothering him. It was the triple click of the recording receiver. Paper was coming out of it in a steady stream. *Click, click, click.* Emerg. Emerg. Emerg!

Ole Doc looked musingly at the Muses and slowly began to relax. That was a good satyr Joccini had done, even if it was uncomfortably like—

"United States Experimental Station on Gorgon Beta Ursa Major," said Hippocrates. "Direct call to U.M.S., master." He looked abstractedly at the dark port beyond which the stars flew by. Through his mind was running the

"Star Pilot for Ursa Major." He never forgot anything, Hippocrates, and the eighteen thousand close-packed pages whirred by, stopped, turned back a leaf and then appeared in his mind. "It's jungle and rivers. Wild game. Swamps." And he brightened. "No women."

"What?" said Ole Doc incuriously.

"Gorgon of Beta Ursa Major. Lots of fish. Lots of them. And wine. Lots of fish and wine."

Ole Doc got up, stretched and went forward. He punched a pneumatic navigator and after divers whirs and hisses a light flashed on a screen giving him a new course departing from a point two light-years in advance of the reading. He could not turn any sooner. He settled himself under the familiar controls, disconnected the robot and yawned.

Two days later they were landing on Field 1,987,806 United States Army Engineers, Unmanned, half an hour's jaunt from United States Experimental Station 3,002.

Ole Doc let Hippocrates slide the ladder out and stood for a moment in the air lock, black kit in hand. The jungle was about three hundred feet above the edges of the field, a wild and virulent jungle, dark green with avid growing and yellow with its rotting dead. For a little space there was complete silence while the chattering gusts of the landing jets echoed out and left utter stillness. And then the jungle came awake once more with screams and catcalls and a ground-shaking *aa-um.*

Hippocrates skittered back up the ladder. He stopped at the top. Again sounded the *aa-um* and the very plates of the old ship shook with it. Hippocrates went inside and came back with a hundred and ten-millimeter turret cannon cradled comfortably over his two right arms.

Ole Doc threw a switch which put an alpha force field

around the ship to keep wild animals off and, with a final glance at the tumbled wrecks of buildings which had once housed a military post, descended the ladder and strolled after Hippocrates into the thick growth.

Now and then Hippocrates cocked an antenna at the towering branches overhead and stopped suspiciously. But he could see nothing threatening and he relieved his feelings occasionally by sending a big gout of fire from the 110 to sizzle them out a straight trail and calcine the mud to brick hardness.

Aa-um shook the jungle. And each time it sounded the myriad of animal and bird noises fell still for a moment.

Hippocrates was about to send another shot ahead when Ole Doc stopped him. An instant later a gray-faced Irishman with wild welcome in his eyes broke through the sawtrees to clasp Ole Doc in emotional arms.

"I'm O'Hara. Thank God I got through. Receiver's been out for six months. Didn't know if I was getting a signal out. Thank God you've come!" And he closed for another embrace but Ole Doc forestalled him by calling attention to the *aa-um* which had just sounded once more.

"Oh that!" said O'Hara. "That's a catbeast. Big and worry enough when I've got time to worry about them. Oh, for the good old days when all I had to worry about was catbeasts getting my cattle and mesohawks, my sheep. But now—" And he started off ahead of them at a dead run, beckoning them to hasten after him.

They had two close calls from swooping birds as big as ancient bombers and almost took a header over a tree trunk ten feet through which turned out to be a snake rising from the ooze with big, hungry teeth. But they arrived in a moment at the station all in one piece.

"You've got to understand," panted O'Hara when he found Ole Doc wouldn't run any faster, "that I'm the only man here. I have some Achnoids, of course, but you would not call those octopi company even if they can talk and do manual labor. But I've been here on Gorgon for fifteen years and I never had anything like this happen before. I am supposed to make this planet habitable in case Earth ever wants a colony planted. This is an agricultural and animal husbandry station. I'm supposed to make things easy for any future colonist. But no colonists have come so far and I don't blame them. This Savannah here is the coolest place on the planet and yet it's hot enough. But I haven't got an assistant or anyone and so when this happened—"

"Well, come on, man," said Ole Doc. "What *has* happened?"

"You'll see!" cried O'Hara, getting wild-eyed with excitement and concern once more. "Come along."

They entered a compound which looked like a fortress. It sat squarely in the center of a huge grassy field, the better to have its animal targets in the open when they attacked and the better to graze its livestock. As they passed through the gate, O'Hara carefully closed it behind him.

Ole Doc looked incuriously at the long lines of sheds, at the helio motors above each and the corrals where fat cattle grazed. A greenhouse caught his interest because he saw that an Achnoid, who more closely resembled a blue pinwheel than a man, was weeding valuable medicinal herbs from out of, as Ole Doc saw it, worthless carrots. But O'Hara dragged him on through the noisy heat and dust of the place until they stood at Shed Thirteen.

"This is the lion shed," said O'Hara.

"Interesting," said Ole Doc disinterestedly.

O'Hara opened the door. A long row of vats lined each side of the passage and the sound of trickling fluid was soothing as it ran from one to the next. A maze of intricate glass tubing interconnected one vat to the next and a blank-beaked Achnoid was going around twiddling valves and reading temperatures.

"Hm-m-m," said Ole Doc. "Artificial birthing vats."

"Yes, yes. To be sure!" cried O'Hara in wild agreement, happy that he was getting some understanding. "That's the way we get our stock. Earth sends me sperm and ova in static ray preservation and I put them into the vats and bring them to maturity. Then we take them out of the vats and put them on artificial udders and we have calves and lambs and such. But this is the lion shed."

"The what?" said Ole Doc.

"For the lions," said O'Hara.

"We find that carefully selected and properly evoluted Earth lions kill catbeasts and several other kinds of vermin. I've got the deserts to the south of here crawling with lions and some day we'll be rid of catbeasts."

"And then you'll have lions," said Ole Doc.

"Oh no," said O'Hara impatiently. "Then we'll bacteriacide the lions with a plague. Which is to say, I will. There isn't any *we.* I've been here for fifteen years—"

"Well, maybe you've been here for fifteen years," said Ole Doc without much sympathy, "but why am *I* here?"

"Oh. It's the last cargo. They send my stuff up here in tramps. Unreliable freight. Last year a tramp came in with a cargo for me and she had some kind of director trouble and had to jettison all her freight. Well, I didn't have any stevedores and they just left it in the rain and the labels came off a lot of the boxes—"

"Ah!" said Ole Doc. "You want me to reclassify sperm—"

"No, no, no!" said O'Hara. "Some of these cargoes were intended for some other experimental stations I am sure. But I have no lading bills for the stuff. I don't know. And I'm frantic! I—"

"Well, come down to it," said Ole Doc. "WHAT is your problem?"

Dramatically O'Hara approached the first vat and gave the cover a yank. The pulleys creaked. Lights went on and the glass bowls within glowed.

In this one vat there were five human babies.

Ole Doc pushed the cover up further and looked. These babies were near the end of their gestation period and were, in other words, about ready to be born. They seemed to be all complete, hair, fingernails, with the proper number of fingers and toes and they were obviously very comfortable.

"Well?" said Ole Doc, looking down at the endless rows of vats.

"All of them," said O'Hara weakly.

"And they number—?" said Ole Doc.

"About eighteen thousand," said O'Hara.

"Well, if THIS is your problem," said Ole Doc, "I would suggest a hurry-up to the Department of Agriculture back on Earth. You need, evidently, half an army corps of nurses. But as for the problem of getting these babies—"

"Oh, that isn't it!" said O'Hara. "You see, it's these condemned Achnoids. They're so confounded routine in everything they do. And I guess maybe it's my fault, too, because there are so many details on this station that if one

Earthman had to listen to them all and arrange them every day he would go crazy. So I guess I'm pretty humpy with them—the ambulating pinwheels! Well, this is the lion shed. We turn out eighteen thousand lions every three months, that being our charted gestation period. Then they go into the pits where they are fed by a facsimile lioness udder and finally they are booted out into the wilderness to go mop up catbeasts. All that is very simple. But these Achnoids—"

"When did you learn about this?"

"Oh, almost six months ago. But I wasn't terribly bothered. Not right then. I just sent a routine report through to Earth. But these Achnoids go right on with routine work unless something stops them. And the labels were all mixed up on that jettisoned shipment and they picked up phials marked with *our* code number for lions and dumped them into these vats. That's their routine work in this department. That's the only way we could ship cattle and such things, you see, because I don't think you'd like to travel on a cattle spaceship, would you? And it would be expensive, what with the price of freight. And we need lots of stock. So to avoid shipping such things as these lions—"

"I'd think it was to be avoided," said Ole Doc wryly.

"—we've developed a very highly specialized system of handling and marking. And evidently *our* codes aren't identical with the codes at the intended destination of these babies. There's an awful lot of paperwork comes off Earth about this sort of thing and frankly I didn't even know they were shipping babies by this system. I went back through all my reports but I must have misfiled something because there isn't anything on it which I've received. Well—"

"You said you messaged the department," said Ole Doc.

"Oh, heck. You know government like it is these days.

Earth has three billion inhabitants and one and three quarters billion are working for the government and they still can't keep up with the administration of colonies and stations in space."

"One billion," corrected Ole Doc.

"Well, one billion. And they still can't get our work out. So they just said that the matter had been referred through the proper channels. Then I sent them a couple urgents and they still said it was being referred to proper channels. Maybe they forgot to dig those channels. Well, anyway, that isn't what I'm getting at. By some means or other I may be able to devise ways of raising up these infants. I've got three thousand Achnoids and I can always take a hunting rifle and go grab a chief hostage until I get two or three thousand more. They train quick. I haven't got any nurses and none in sight and I have no doctors and what I know about infant maladies is zero. But six months ago I figured I could pull through."

"And now you don't?" said Ole Doc.

"Now I don't. Now this whole thing has got me. I may be indulging in mass murder or something. Will they hang me if any of these kids die or something?"

"Well, I expect that a small loss would be excusable," said Ole Doc.

"Yes, but you see I didn't pay any attention to these Achnoids. And now I think there's the devil to pay. You see, all the fluids used and the strengths used and all were for lions. And that has radically altered things. At least *something* has. I thought that just a couple had got here by mistake and I didn't know how and I got them born all right. But three days ago when I sent that emerg two things had happened. I found this whole shed full of babies and I found that they were all set to be born. And they have gestated only three months!"

"Hm-m-m," said Ole Doc, getting faintly interested. "Well, I see what you're excited about. A three months' gestation on lion fluid would be liable to upset anyone, I suppose. So—"

"Wait!" said the wild-eyed O'Hara. "That isn't the problem. I haven't showed you the problem yet!"

"Not yet!" Ole Doc blinked in astonishment.

O'Hara led them rapidly out of the shed and into a big concrete compound. There was a trapdoor in one concrete wall at the far end. O'Hara closed the gate behind them and got them into an observer's box.

"This is where I test the fighting qualities of lions," he said. "I go get a catbeast and turn him loose in here and I let a young lion in on him. It's a control test on the batch. I pick a lion at random by number and let him in. Mookah! Hey there. Mookah! Let go one catbeast!"

An Achnoid pinwheeled into view, cast respectful eyes at the observer's box and began to take the pins out of a door. There were eight pins and he removed them all at once, one hand to a pin.

"Monstrosity," sniffed Hippocrates.

The Achnoid went sailing to safety over the wall and the cage door crashed open with a bang. Out of it stalked a beast with a purple hide and enormous, sharp-fanged jaws. It bounded into the arena, reared up on its hind legs to stand ten feet tall, waltzed furiously as it looked around for enemies and then settled back with a vicious, tail-lashing snarl.

"Pleasant character," said Ole Doc.

"That's a small one," said O'Hara. "We couldn't capture any large ones if we tried. Lost about fifty Achnoids to them already, I guess. O.K., Mookah! Let her go!"

Mookah wasn't going to be down on the ground for this one. He had a wire attached to the door release which led into a shed. He pulled the wire. And out sauntered a cocky half-pint of a kid, about half the height of Hippocrates but of the physiological structure of a ten-year-old. He was clad in a piece of hide which was belted around his waist and he had a pair of furred buskins on his feet. His hair was wild and long and his eyes were wild and intelligent. Pugnacity was stamped upon him but there was a jauntiness as well. In his hand he carried a sling and on his wrist, hung by a thong, a knife.

"Whoa!" said Ole Doc. "Wait a minute! You're not sacrificing that kid just for my amusement." And he had a blaster up so fast that only a lunge by O'Hara deflected his aim at the catbeast.

The kid looked curiously at the plowed hole the blaster had made and then glanced disdainfully at the box. O'Hara, recovered from the lunge, hastily pushed a button and got a bulletproof shield in place.

"All right, all right," said Ole Doc. "I'll stand here and watch murder." But he held the blaster ready just in case.

The catbeast had scented the enemy. He got up now and began his waltz, going rapidly forward, his teeth audibly gnashing, his tail kicking up a cloud of dust. On he came. The kid stood where he was, only shifting his sling and putting something into his pocket.

The catbeast was hungry. It began to rave and its sides puffed like bellows. The stench of decayed meat floated up from it as it exhaled its breath in a thundering *aa-um.*

Hippocrates was decidedly interested. He glanced excitedly at Ole Doc and then back at the kid. But that glance had cost Hippocrates the best part of the show.

The kid let the sling spin and go. There was a sickening crunch of pierced and battered bone and the top of the catbeast's head vanished in a fountain of blood and leaping brains.

Down went the catbeast.

The kid walked forward, kicked the still gnashing jaw, grabbed what was left of an ear and hacked it off. He put the ear in his pocket, booted the convulsing catbeast in his expiring guts and turned to face the observation platform. Then, in a flash, he put a chunk of steel into his sling and whipped it at the glass. The bulletproof shield crawled with cracks and a shower of chips went forward from it.

The kid gave his "pants" a hitch, turned on his heel and strode back into the shed. The door dropped. Mookah dropped into the arena and began to call for help to get the catbeast en route to the cookshack.

"I knew he'd shoot at us," said O'Hara. "The shield was for *him*, not for you, sir."

Ole Doc let out his breath with the realization that he must have been holding it for some time. "Well!"

"Now *that's* my problem," said O'Hara. "There are eighteen thousand of them and they are all males. Sir, what in the name of all that's holy have I done *wrong?*"

"Took a job with the United States Department of Agriculture," said Ole Doc.

"First I was very loving," said O'Hara. "There were only two of them in the lion shed and I thought they'd been overlooked somehow by these condemned Achnoids. I didn't know what had happened. I was puzzled but not really upset. Strange things occur out here on these far stations. So I took them into the house as soon as they were "born" and had a female Achnoid feed them with good cow's milk. And they laid and cooed and I figured out life was a fine thing. And then I was gone on a month's trip to the next continent to see how my plant culture was doing there—planted a million square miles in redwoods—and when I came back I couldn't find the Achnoid nurse and the house was in shreds. So they been out here ever since, confound them. For a while I thought they'd eaten the nurse but she finally came whimpering back home after two weeks lying in the bayonet grass. So here they are. They evidently mature quick."

"Evidently," said Ole Doc.

"Maybe they won't be full grown for several years," said O'Hara. "But every day they get worse. That concrete blockhouse you see down there is just in case."

Ole Doc glanced down to where a dozen Achnoids were slaving in the harsh daylight, building what seemed an impregnable fortress. "Prison?" said Ole Doc.

"Refuge!" said O'Hara. "In six months or less this planet won't be safe for Achnoids, catbeasts, scumsnakes, gargantelephants, pluseagles or *me!*"

Ole Doc looked amusedly back at the Achnoids who were carting away the catbeast's body. "Well, you've got one consolation—"

An Achnoid had come up from another shed labeled "Horses" and was giving O'Hara an excited account of something. O'Hara looked pale and near a swoon.

"I said," said Ole Doc, "that you at least have the consolation that it's one generation only. With no females—"

"That's just it," said O'Hara, tottering toward the horse incubation shed.

They went in and found a cluster of Achnoids standing around the first vat. O'Hara thrust them aside and looked and grew even paler. He barked a question and was answered.

"Well?"

"Twenty thousand vats," said O'Hara. "In the third week."

"Babies?" said Ole Doc.

"Females," said O'Hara, and then more faintly, "Females."

Ole Doc looked around and found Hippocrates. "Saw a couple lakes coming in. With all the other fauna you have on this planet, fishing ought to be interesting."

O'Hara straightened as though he had had an electric shock. "Fishing!"

"Fishing," said Ole Doc. "*You* are the man who is in charge here. I'm just an innocent bystander."

"Now look!" said O'Hara in horror. "You've *got* to help me." He tried to clutch Ole Doc's cape as the Soldier of Light moved away. "You've got to answer some riddles for me! Why is the gestation period three months? Why do they develop in six months to raging beasts? Why are they so antisocial? What have I done wrong in these vats and what can I do to correct it? You've got to help me!"

"I," said Ole Doc, "am going fishing. No doubt to a bacteriologist, a biochemist or a mutologist your problem would be fascinating. But after all, it's just a problem. I am afraid it is not going to upset the Universe. Good day."

O'Hara stood in trembling disbelief. Here was a Soldier of Light, the very cream of the medical profession, a man who, although he looked thirty, was probably near a thousand years old in medical practice of all kinds. Here was a member of the famous Seven Hundred, the Universal Medical Society who had taken the new and dangerous developments out of political hands centuries ago and had made the universe safe for man's dwelling and who patrolled it now. Here he was, right here in O'Hara's sight. Here was succor. Here was the lighthouse, the panacea, the miracle he needed.

He ran beside Ole Doc's rapid striding toward the compound gate. "But sir! It's thirty-eight thousand human beings! It's my professional reputation. I can't kill them. I don't dare turn them loose on this planet! I'll have to desert this station!"

"Desert it then," said Ole Doc. "Open the gate, Hippocrates."

And they left the distracted O'Hara weeping in the dust. "Get my fishing gear," said Ole Doc.

Hippocrates lingered. It was not unlike him to linger when no emergency was in the wind. His antennae felt around in the air and he hefted the 110 mm. with three hands while he scratched his head with the fourth.

"Well?" barked Ole Doc.

Hippocrates looked straight at him. He was somewhat of a space lawyer, Hippocrates. "Article 726 of Code 2, paragraph 80, third from the top of page 607 of the Law Regulating the Behavior of Members of the Universal Medical Society to wit: 'It shall also be unlawful for the Soldier of Light to desert a medical task of which he has been apprised when it threatens the majority of the human population of any planet.' "

Ole Doc looked at his little slave in some annoyance. "Are you going to get my fishing gear?"

"Well?" said Hippocrates.

Ole Doc glared. "Did I invent the Department of Agriculture? Am I accountable for their mistakes? And are they so poor they can't send their own man relief?"

"Well—" said Hippocrates. "No."

"Then you still expect me to spend a year here nursing babies?"

Hippocrates spun his antennae around thoughtfully and then brightened up. He put down the 110 mm. and there was a blur and a big divot in the mud where he had been. Ole Doc kept walking toward the lake he had seen at the far end of the Savannah and exactly three minutes and eight seconds later by his chronograph, Hippocrates was back beside him with about a thousand pounds of rods, tackle, and lunch carried in two hands and a force umbrella and the 110 mm. carried in another. With his fourth hand he held a book on lures and precautions for strange planets and from this he was busily absorbing whole pages at a glance.

In this happy holiday mood they came to the lake, dried up a half acre of mud with one blast of the 110, pitched a canopy at the water's edge complete with table and chairs, made a wharf by extending a log over the water and generally got things ready to fish.

Hippocrates mixed a cool drink and baited a hook while Ole Doc took his ease and drank himself into a comfortable frame of mind.

"Wonder what I'll get," said Ole Doc. He made his first cast, disposed himself comfortably on the log to watch the motor lure tow its bait around the surface of the lake.

The huge jungle trees reared over the water and the air

was still and hot. The yellow lake glowed like amber under a yellow sky. And they began to catch a strange assortment of the finny tribes.

Hippocrates swatted at the mosquitoes for a while. Their beaks got dented against his hide but they annoyed him with their high whine. Finally he was seized with inspiration—direct from "Camping and Hiking Jaunts on Strange Worlds"—and unfolded the force umbrella. It was no more than a stick with a driver in it but its directional lobes could be changed in intensity and area until they covered half a square mile. It was a handy thing to have in a rainstorm on such planets as Sargo where the drops weigh two pounds. And it was handy here where it pushed, on low intensity, the mosquitoes out from the canopy and put them several hundred yards away where they could *zzzt* in impotent frenzy and thwarted rage. Hippocrates put the stick on full so its beams, leaning against the surrounding trees, would keep it in place, and devoted himself to another book he brought out of his knapsack, "Wild Animals I Wish I Hadn't Known."

And into this quiet and peaceful scene moved a jetbomb at the silent speed of two thousand miles an hour. It came straight down from a silver speck which hung in the saffron sky. It had enough explosive in it to knock a house flat. And it was armed.

Ole Doc had just hooked a pop-eyed monstrosity; Hippocrates had just reached the place where Daryl van Daryl was being swallowed alive by a ramposaurus on Ranameed, and the bomb hit.

It struck the top of the force screen and detonated. The lobes of the screen cantilevered against the trees and kicked six down so hard their roots stuck quivering in the air. The canopy went flat. The log went into the water and the jug of rumade leaped sideways and smote Hippocrates on the back of the neck.

For an instant neither Hippocrates nor Ole Doc had any idea of what had happened. It might have been a fish or a ramposaurus. But in a moment, from the smell in the air, they knew it was a bomb.

Hippocrates instantly went into Chapter Twenty-one, paragraph nine of "Tales of the Space Pioneers," socked the butt of the 110 mm. into the ground, looked at the silver image in the magnetosight and let drive with two thumbs on the trips.

The whole air over them turned flaming red. Another half dozen trees collapsed from concussion. Ole Doc dragged himself out of the water and looked up through the haze at the target.

"Train right!" he said. "Up six miles. Now left!"

But although they kept firing, the silver speck had picked up enough speed toward the zenith to parallel the sizzling, murderous charges and in a moment, Hippocrates, with the sight flashing green for out-of-range, stopped shooting.

Ole Doc looked at the upset rumade. He looked at his rod being towed aimlessly across the lake. He looked at Hippocrates.

"Missed," said Hippocrates brightly.

"Is there a force screen over the *Morgue?*" snapped Ole Doc.

"Certainly, master."

"Well, it probably needs reinforcing. Grab up the remains here and be quick about it."

• • •

While Ole Doc strode rapidly through the jungle to the old landing field, blasting his way through the creepers with a gun in each hand, Hippocrates hastily bundled the remains and scurried along at his heels.

They entered the corridor through the *Morgue*'s force field and came to the side of the ship. "At least she's all right," said Ole Doc.

Hippocrates bounced in and stowed the tattered gear while Ole Doc pulled down the switches on the battle panel. After a few minor accidents he had had a complete band of force fields installed and he turned them all on now.

He went forward to the control room and was, as usual, startled by the dulcet tones of his audio recorder. It never seemed right to him that the *Morgue* should talk soprano but he liked soprano and he'd never had it changed.

"There was a battle cruiser overhead eighteen minutes ago," said the *Morgue* complacently. "It dropped a bomb."

"Are you hurt?" said Ole Doc to the board.

"Oh, it didn't drop a bomb on me. It dropped a bomb on you."

"Dimensions and armament?"

"It isn't friendly," said the *Morgue.* "I recorded no data on it except hostility. Advice."

"O.K. What?"

"Turn on invisio screens and move me into the jungle cover."

Ole Doc threw off the switch. Even his ship was ordering him around these days.

He turned to the remote control battle panel and punched the button marked "Invisible" and a moment later a series of light-baffling planes, acting as reflectors for the ground below and so making the *Morgue* disappear from the outside except to detectors, hid them entirely. He rang "underweigh" so that Hippocrates would have warning to grab something and, without seating himself in the control chair, shot the *Morgue* toward the only hole in the towering jungle trees, a thousand yards from her former location. Lights flashed as the force screen went out and then re-adjusted itself to the natural contour of the landscape and obstacles. Ole Doc dusted his hands. The ship was safe for a moment. Now if that battle cruiser wanted to come low enough to prowl, it would get a most frightening surprise. Leaving the fire panel tuned to shoot down anything which did not clip back a friendly recognition signal, Ole Doc moved toward the salon.

But as he passed a port something caught his eye. And it also caught the eye of the alert autoturret on the starboard side. He heard the wheels spinning over his head as the single gun came down to bear on an object in the jungle and he only just made the battle panel to isolate the quadrant from fire.

There was a dead spaceship in there.

Ole Doc checked both blasters and jumped out of the air lock. He went up to his boot tops in muck but floundered ahead toward the grisly thing.

It was crashed and well sunk in the mud and over it had grown a thick coating of slime from which fed countless creepers and vines. It was not only dead. It was being buried by greedy life.

His space boots clung magnetically to the hull as he pushed his way up through the slimy growths and then he was standing at a broken port which stared up at him like an eyeless socket. He stabbed a light into it. What had been an Earthman was tangled amongst the stanchions of a bunk. What had been another was crushed against a bulkhead. Small, furry things scuttled out of these homes as Ole Doc dropped down.

The ship had been there, probably, a year. It had ended its life from heavy explosive and had been skewered through and through by five charges.

Ole Doc burned through a jammed door, going forward to get to the control room. He stumbled over some litters of boxes and his playing light showed up their mildewed lettering:

Department of Agriculture.
Perishable.
Keep under Preservative Rays.

HORSES.

Ole Doc frowned and picked his way through this decaying litter. In the control room he found what seepage and bacteria had left of the log. The ship was the *Wanderho* out of Boston, a tramp under charter to the government, delivering perishables, supplies and mail to Department of Agriculture Experimental Stations.

With sudden decision Ole Doc blew his way out through the bow and walked on logs back to the *Morgue.* He had headed for the only opening he had seen in the jungle wall ahead and that opening had been made by a killed ship.

He came back up through the air lock and opened all the switches on the battle panel except the screens.

"We can go now, master," said Hippocrates brightly. "Scanner shows nothing to stop us."

"Shut that off and fix me a biological kit," said Ole Doc.

"You're not going?" gaped Hippocrates.

"According to article something or other when the

majority of a human population on a planet is threatened a soldier has to stay on the job."

"But I said that," said Hippocrates.

"When?" said Ole Doc.

Hippocrates retreated hurriedly into the operating room and began to throw together the hundred and seventy-two items which made up a biological kit and when he had them in cases on his back he shot after Ole Doc who was already a quarter of the way back to the compound.

Ole Doc walked up the steps of O'Hara's bungalow, thrust open the office door and walked in. O'Hara looked up and gaped.

"Why didn't you tell me?" snapped Ole Doc.

"You have an accident with some animal?" said O'Hara. "I heard some shots but I knew you were armed. I thought—"

"About this jettisoned cargo!" said Ole Doc impatiently.

"What about it?" said O'Hara. "They just stacked it up and left."

"You saw them leave?"

"Well, no. The captain was in here telling me he was having trouble with his ship and when I saw they were gone in the morning I went over to see if he'd left our supplies in good shape and I found his cargo. It'd rained and the labels—"

"Was it scattered around?" demanded Ole Doc.

"Why would he scatter it around?" said O'Hara.

"What was the name of that ship?"

"The *Wanderho,*" said O'Hara. "Same old tub. The only one which ever comes. Undependable. She's about a month overdue now—"

"O'Hara, you won't ever see that ship again. She's lying over there in the jungle shot full of holes and her crew dead inside. You didn't hear a take-off a year ago. You heard a ship being shot to pieces."

O'Hara looked a little white. "But the cargo! It was all stacked up in a neat pile—"

"Precisely."

"You mean— I don't follow this!"

"Neither do I," said Ole Doc. "Have you got any force screen protection?"

"No. Why should I have? Who'd want to trouble an experimental station? We haven't got *anything,* not even money."

"No screen," said Ole Doc. "Then we may have to work fast. Can you arm these Achnoids?"

"No! And my only weapon is a hunting rifle and a side-arm. I haven't got anything."

"Hippocrates," said Ole Doc, "dismount two turrets and have them set in towers here. They won't do much but they'll stop an attack from land. And, if I'm right, that's all we have to fear."

Hippocrates looked helplessly around for a place to put down the half ton of equipment he was lugging like a mountain above him.

"Just drop it," said Ole Doc. "We're making a lab right here on the porch where it's cool."

O'Hara suddenly flamed brightly. "You mean," he cried in sudden hope, "that you're going to help me? You mean it?"

Ole Doc paid him no attention. He was already fishing in a pile of equipment for a portable ultraelectron microscope and a box of slides. He put them on the table. "Have somebody start bringing me phials out of that preservation room. One sample from every box you've got!"

In the many, many weeks which followed there was no wine, there was only work. And over Ole Doc hung two intelligences which made him very skeptical of his chances of getting out of this one alive. First was the fact that something or somebody had now supercharged the planet's ionosphere thoroughly enough to damp every outgoing and incoming message and as Ole Doc's last reported whereabouts was many a light-year from Gorgon, the chances of any relief were slender to the vanishing point—for a search party would have to look over at least a hundred planets and a nearly infinite cube of sky. Second was the sporadic presence of a silver dot in the sky, the battle cruiser, out of range, unfriendly, waiting. Waiting for what?

"I guess this is a pretty tight spot," grinned Hippocrates, all four arms deep in research assistance. "In 'Tales of the Early Space Pioneers'—"

"Condemn the early space pioneers," said Ole Doc, his eyes aching and his back cricked with the weeks of constant peering. "Give me another phial."

They had made some progress along one line. Ole Doc had taken time off to make sure he could communicate with the "infants terrible" who swarmed now, thirty-eight thousand of them, in the lion and horse pens. He had concocted a series of two thousand slides, based on the methods used for teaching alien intelligences lingua spacia, except he was teaching English. Asleep and awake, the horde of precocious "babies" were confronted by projected pictures and dinned with explanation. The projectors had to be very carefully protected and even then blastproof shields had to be renewed every few days when some enthusiastic kid bunged a slingshot pebble into it. But they couldn't hurt the screens. Those were simply the concrete walls. So willy-nilly, they learned "horse" and "cow" and "man" and "I am hungry" and "How far is it to the nearest post office?"

It was not safe to approach the pens now unless one wanted a short trip to eternity. But Ole Doc, with a force screen, managed occasional inspections. And on these he was jeered with singsong English, phrases such as, "Go soak your head. Go soak your head. Go soak your head," which, when squalled from a few thousand throats, was apt to give one, if not a soaked head, at least a headache.

On the very first day he had built five gestation vats in the bungalow and had started two females and three males on their way. And all but two of these now born had been hurriedly taken down to the main herd before they got ideas about mayhem. The remaining pair, a boy and a girl, remained in iron cages on the porch while Hippocrates took notes on their behavior. The notes were not flattering but they were informative.

When two months had passed after the birth of the experimental five from the vats, the three, properly tagged, in the lion pens and horse pens, had learned to use a small sling. But the two on the porch had not.

Ole Doc's notebook was getting crammed with facts. And now and then he saw a glimmer of knowledge about them. He had ruled out several things, amongst them the unusual radiations which might be present, but weren't, on Gorgon. Next he had crossed off machinery radiation and fluid activity.

And then, on this afternoon, little Hippocrates saw him squint, stand up and thoughtfully snap a slide into small bits.

"Maybe solution?" said Hippocrates and O'Hara in different ways but almost in the same instant.

Ole Doc didn't hear them. He turned to the racks of paraphernalia and began to drag down several bottles which he began to treat with pharmaceutical ray rods.

"You maybe poison the whole batch?" said Hippocrates hopefully.

Ole Doc didn't pay him any heed. He ordered up several flasks and put his weird stew into them and then he drew a sketch.

"Make a catapult like this," said Ole Doc. "One on every corner of the pens. That's eight. With eight flasks, one for each. Trigger them with a magnet against this remote condenser so that when it is pushed, off they go into the compounds."

"And everybody dies?" said Hippocrates expectantly, thoughtful of the bruises he had had wrestling these "babies."

"Rig them up," said Ole Doc. "Because the rest of this is going to take another day or two."

"What's the sudden rush?" said O'Hara.

Ole Doc jerked a thumb at the sky. "They were about a hundred miles lower today."

"They were?" said O'Hara anxiously. "I didn't see them."

"You missed a lot of things," said Ole Doc dryly. And he picked up a bundle of ray rods and began to sort them. He took a look into the yard and saw a chicken contentedly pecking at the dirt.

"Bring me that," he said. "By the way, where's Mookah?"

O'Hara looked around as though expecting the overseer to be right behind him. Then, suddenly, "Say, he hasn't been around for three days. He's supposed to make his report at two o'clock every afternoon and that's an hour ago."

"Uhuh," said Ole Doc.

"Golly, no wonder you guys live so long," said O'Hara. He climbed off the porch and came back with the chicken.

Ole Doc took the bird, pointed a rod at it and the chicken flopped over on its side, dead. Presently it was under a bell jar with more rays playing on it. And then before the astonished gaze of O'Hara the chicken began to change form. The feathers vanished, the shape vanished and within ten minutes there was nothing under the jar but a blob of cellular matter. Ole Doc grunted in satisfaction and tipped the mass into a huge graduate. He stuffed a ray rod into the middle of the mass and left it.

"Another chicken," he said.

O'Hara closed his mouth and ran into the yard to scoop up another one. It squawked and beat its wings until a ray rod was aimed at it. Then, like its relative, it went under the bell jar, became jellylike, turned into a translucent mass and got dumped into another graduate.

Five chickens later there were seven graduates full of cells, each with a different kind of ray rod sticking out.

"Now," said Ole Doc. "we take that first baby. The boy."

O'Hara repressed a shudder. He knew that medicine could not make scruples when emergency was present, but there was something about putting a baby, a live, cooing little baby—if a trifle energetic—under a bell jar and knocking it into a shapeless nothingness. But at that instant a howl sounded from the pens and O'Hara was happy to assist the now returned Hippocrates in slapping the vigorous infant on the face of the operating table.

O'Hara expected to see the bell jar come down and a ray rod go to work. He was somewhat astonished when Ole Doc began to strap the baby to the board and he began to fear that it was going to be a knife job.

But Ole Doc didn't reach for a scalpel. He picked up a big hypo syringe, fitted an antisepticizing needle to it and took two or three cells out of the first graduate. He checked it and then turned to the child.

He made a pass with a glowing button and then plunged the needle into the baby's spine. He withdrew it and made a second pass with the button. Rapidly, in six separate places, he injected cells into the infant anatomy. And then O'Hara's eyes bulged and he went a little sick. For the seventh shot was rammed straight into the child's eye and deep into its brain.

Ole Doc pulled out the needle, made a pass with the button again, and stood back. O'Hara expected a dead baby. After all, it had had needles stuck in the back of its head, its spine, its heart and its brain. But the baby cooed and went to sleep.

"Next one," said Ole Doc.

"There isn't going to be a next one," said a cool voice behind them.

They whirled to find a leathery-faced, short-statured character in leather garb who stood indolently leaning against a porch post with an undoubtedly lethal weapon aimed in their general direction.

"And who are you?" said Ole Doc.

"The name is Smalley. Not that you'll be very interested for long. All done playing with the kids? Well, stand away so you're not in line with those cages and we'll get this over with."

Ole Doc looked at Hippocrates and Hippocrates looked at Ole Doc. It would have taken a very good poker player to have told what passed between them. But Ole Doc knew what he wanted to know. During his chicken treatments his orders had been carried out. He laid his hypo on the table with a histrionic sigh and carelessly thumbed the button on the magnetic release. Very small in the distance there were slight, pinging sounds.

"You know," said Ole Doc, "I wouldn't be too much in a hurry, Smalley."

"And why not?"

"Because I was just giving this kid a treatment to save his life."

"Yeah. I believe you."

"Happens to be the truth," said Ole Doc. "Of course I didn't have any idea that their friends would be along so soon, but I just didn't like to see kids die wholesale. If you'll call up your medico, I'll show him what's to be done—"

"About what?"

"About this illness," said Ole Doc. "Strange thing. Must be a lion disease or something. Very rare. Affects all the nerve centers."

"Those two kids look all right to me!" said Smalley, getting alert and peering at the cages on the porch.

"These I've practically cured, although the girl there still wants her final treatment. But down at the pens—"

"What about the pens?" demanded Smalley.

"There's thirty-eight thousand mighty sick babies. And it's going to take a lot of know-how to heal them. Left untreated, they'll die. But, as you're the one who's interested—"

"Say, how do you know so much?" snarled Smalley.

"I happen to be a doctor," said Ole Doc.

"He is Ole Doc Methuselah!" said Hippocrates with truculence. "He is a Soldier of Light!"

"What's that?" said Smalley.

"A doctor," said Ole Doc. "Now if you'll bring your medico here—"

"And if I don't have one?"

"Why, that's surprising," said Ole Doc. "How do you expect to keep thirty-eight thousand kids whole without a doctor?"

"We'll manage! Now get this, doc. You're going to unbuckle that blaster belt right where you stand and you're going to walk ahead of me slow to the pens. And you'd better be telling the truth."

Ole Doc dropped his belt, made a sign to Hippocrates to gather up the graduates and stepped out toward the pens.

Here, under the slanting yellow rays of the afternoon sun it became very obvious that there wasn't an Achnoid in sight. Instead there were various beings in disordered dress who held carefully ordered weapons commanding all avenues of escape.

"Thought you'd land tomorrow," said Ole Doc.

"How's that?" snapped Smalley.

"Oh, the way the Achnoids acted. And a detector that's part of my operating kit which said you'd already come down twice before last week to the south of here."

"Just keep walking," said Smalley. "You might get past me but you won't get past the gate or get near your ship. We've had that guarded for two months hoping you'd show up."

"Lucky I didn't, eh?" said Ole Doc. "Your harvest here would be dead."

They stood now near the concrete wall of one pen. Smalley, keeping an eye out behind him and walking with caution, mounted up the ramp. But contrary to Hippocrates' fond expectation, no pellet knocked the top of his head off. He stiffened and stared.

Ole Doc went up beside him and looked down. As far as these pens reached they could see kids lying around, some inert, some twitching, some struggling but all very, very ill. And obvious on the first of them were big red splotches.

Smalley yelled a warning to his guards to stay clear and then faced Ole Doc.

"All right. They're sick. How they goin' to get cured?"

"Why, I was all set to cure them right here," said Ole Doc. "But if you're so anxious to shoot me—"

"That can wait! Cure them! Cure them, you hear me?"

Ole Doc shrugged. "Have it any way you like, Smalley. But I'll need the rest of my equipment over here."

"All right, you'll get it!"

Ole Doc dropped down into the first pen and Hippocrates handed him equipment. From his cloak pocket Ole Doc took a gun hypo which did not need a needle to penetrate. He fitted a charge in this and shot the first kid. Then he rolled the infant over and got to work with his hypo needle.

Smalley looked suspicious. He kept his place at a distance and kept down the visor of his space helmet. Two of his guards came up and, some distance from him, received further orders and went back to watch from the gate.

The first kid got seven shots and then another charge from the hypo gun. The red splotches began to vanish and the child was asleep.

It was assembly line work after that with O'Hara and Hippocrates slinging kids into place and holding them and Hippocrates quadridextrously administering the before and after gun shots.

Night came and they lighted the pens and the work went on. Ole Doc stopped for food after he reached the thousand mark and came back to where Smalley was watching.

"Give me a hand up," said Ole Doc.

Smalley had watched child after child go peacefully to sleep and the blotches vanish and despite his air, he was too confused about Ole Doc not to obey the order. Ole Doc gripped the offered hand and came up over the ramp.

He was nearly back to the bungalow, with one of the guards tagging him, when Smalley screamed. Ole Doc went back.

"What's the matter?" he asked solicitously.

"I'm poisoned!" screamed Smalley, sagging down and clawing at his helmet. His face was already turning red; his hands were covered with blotches.

"Well, before you pass out," said Ole Doc, "you'd better tell your guards that I'll have to treat you so they won't think I'm killing you and shoot me out of enthusiasm for their commander."

"Don't shoot him! Don't shoot him whatever he does!" screamed Smalley.

The guards stood well back, eight of them. It made them very nervous when Ole Doc had Hippocrates pass up a hypo gun and a syringe. It made them more nervous when Ole Doc started to ram Smalley's spine and brain with that long, glittering point.

The first gun cured the blotches, the last gun put Smalley to sleep. And then Ole Doc went on into the bungalow to get himself some food and a little rest.

The following many hours were hectic indeed for it was enough to simply treat thirty-eight thousand kids suffering from skin allergy without the other labors. And to complicate things, members of the hostile ship kept coming down with it, one by one. A scribbled message from Smalley's fourth successor, for instance, finally carried it back to the ship itself. And when the crew tried to bring up the ailing members for treatment, *they* came down.

Shoot with a hypo gun to cure the blotches. Shoot seven times with seven different things in seven different places for each patient. Shoot again to put them into a few hours' slumber.

Ole Doc didn't sleep. He kept himself going on multithyroid, which Hippocrates said was very bad for him indeed. But O'Hara keeled over in nervous and physical exhaustion before they had reached the ten thousandth case. They put him under the influence of the second hypo gun and left him in his own lion pen to snooze it off.

And Hippocrates and Ole Doc went on.

It takes a long while to handle thirty-eight thousand babies and one hundred and ten crewmen, much less treat them. But within three days they were done.

Ole Doc stood up and looked at the still snoring acres of babies. And at the rows of sleeping crewmen. And at the five who, nervously aloof, still covered the gate with powerful weapons and barred any escape.

Ole Doc pondered giving them something. But he was too tired to take off. He went into the bungalow and stretched out and soon was sleeping the sleep of the innocent and just.

Eighteen hours later, fully refreshed, he rose and washed his face. He looked out of the window at the vigilant guards and sighed.

"Hippocrates, go gather up our gear."

"We leaving?"

"On the double," said Ole Doc.

With a *swish* and a *swoosh* the little being collected their scattered equipment into a portable pile.

"Now go gather up O'Hara and bring him along," said Ole Doc.

Hippocrates swept off to get the chief of the experimental station and came back lugging him with ease. Then he took up the mountain of heavy equipment in his other two hands and with O'Hara's heels trailing in the dust, tagged after Ole Doc, who walked, buckling on his blasters.

The five at the gate were wary. They had been on the post, in the two enfilading towers, when all the illness began and they weren't going to tolerate anything now. But they were apprehensive because they could not be sure that their leader and other people would wake up.

"Stop or we shoot!" barked their squad leader.

Ole Doc negligently fingered his first cloak button. It hummed a little. He kept on walking.

"Stop!" cried the squad leader. "Stop and go back until I'm sure they're going to recover or we'll kill you!"

Ole Doc stopped. He looked sadly at the five on the wall above him. And then he suddenly dived to the right and drew in a blur which flamed before it could be seen. He fired rapidly.

Three shots came at him. Three shots ricocheted off his portable force screen. Five guards went down in charred heaps where the ashes lay amid glowing bits of metal.

Ole Doc looked alertly across the Savannah, glanced back to make sure the screen had protected Hippocrates and then struck off for the *Morgue.*

There was no guard there now since that guard had been changed from the ship. Ole Doc swung in, indicated a couch where O'Hara was to be tossed and walked through the vessel to check her for ascent. But she had not been harmed and in a few minutes he could sink with confidence behind his controls and buckle his belts.

He rang for take-off and got Hippocrates' cheery O.K. back. And then the *Morgue* hurtled upwards to an altitude of three miles.

It looked so peaceful down below. The dark green of the jungle bounding the silver of the lakes was pretty to his appreciative eye. And then he dived and put five big, solid charges into the battle cruiser and left her a curling, smoking mass of wreckage. And he dived again at another place to the south and slammed two shots into a mountainous stock-pile of structural materials and munitions and saw how prettily their black smoke rose, interspersed red with exploding shells.

That gave him a great deal of satisfaction.

He skipped upwards then through the atmosphere and out into the black comfort of absolute zero and set his course and speed for home.

"Calling Center," he said into his mike. "Calling Center. Methuselah. Methuselah. Calling Center—"

"Come in! Hey! Come in!" said Center, a tenth of a galaxy away.

"Methuselah with a report."

"Methuselah is enough!" said Ole Doc Cautery at Center. "We have had five navies and the marines looking for you for months. We've had six empires scared 'til they can't spit. WHERE have you been?"

"Got a report," said Ole Doc. "Turn this on confidential."

"Circuits on. Begin report."

Ole Doc spoke into the five-wave scramble which had defied cryptographers since the U.M.S. had adopted it two hundred years before. "Alien extragalactic race attempted foothold for jump-off attacks on Earth. First independent space flight originators met so far. Stature about three-quarters Earth normal. Carbon people. Almost a duplicate of man but missing several tissues essential of emotional balance including one brain chord intimately related to kindness, worry and judgment. Established depot of supplies but unable to transport workmen and soldiers in quantity and so made use of Department of Agriculture Experimental Station vats on Gorgon, wrecking freighter and substituting its phials. Very sentient. Obviously well informed intelligence at work in this galaxy. Leaders conditioned to enterprise and spoke English. Detectable by uncommon strength. Life period very short, reaching maturity at about six years of age due to emotional imbalances and early development of gonads and so easy to detect in society by rapid aging.

"Treatment and handling of case: Developed the formulae of their gene patterns and isolated missing development cells. Synthesized cells and injected them into proper areas where they will harmonize with bodies. They succumb easily to a strawberry allergy and are painfully affected by it. All beings so located and all artificial gestations infected so that they could be treated. All treated and left in a stupor except five who could not be reached with strawberries.

"Recommendations: That you get hold of the Department of Agriculture of the United States as soon as possible and inform them as follows: Their vessel *Wanderho* destroyed. Their station on Gorgon deserted but undamaged; the Achnoids there were bought by the aliens and are no longer to be trusted; inform them that the Gorgon Station is now inhabited by about thirty-eight thousand aliens *converted to human beings* and that a relief expedition should be sent to take care of them since they will none of them be found over twelve years of age and the bulk of them a human five or six months, needing care. Expedition should be armed but should also contain several dozen expert nurses. Gorgon can now be considered to be humanly populated.

"Proceeding at normal speed to base to refit. Please have somebody air out my quarters, preferably Miss Ellison. That is all."

As he threw the switch he heard a gasp behind him. "That's all!" said O'Hara. "You convert thirty-eight thousand one hundred and some odd extragalactic invaders to human beings and you say, 'that's all'! Man, I've heard legends about the Soldiers of Light, but I never realized what superboys you fellows really are."

Ole Doc gave him a very bored look and then and thereafter ignored him.

"Hippocrates," said Ole Doc, "we're almost home. Let's open those last two bottles of wine."

ABOUT THE AUTHOR

Born in 1911, the son of a U.S. Naval officer, L. Ron Hubbard was raised in the state of Montana when it was still part of the great American frontier. He was early acquainted with a rugged outdoor life and as a boy earned the trust of the Blackfeet Indians who initiated him as a blood brother. He became the nations's youngest Eagle Scout at the age of thirteen.

During his teens, L. Ron Hubbard made several trips to Asia, carefully recording his observations and experiences in a series of diaries, as well as noting down story ideas resulting from his many adventures. His travels were extensive, including Malaysia, Indonesia, the ports of India and the Western Hills of China. By the time he was 19, he had logged over a quarter of a million miles on land and sea in an era well before commercial air travel.

Returning to the United States, he enrolled at George Washington University where he studied engineering and participated in the first classes on atomic and molecular phenomena. He was also an award-winning contributor to the University's literary magazine.

While still a student, he took up "barnstorming." He quickly gained a reputation as a daring and skilled pilot of both gliders and motorized planes and became a frequent correspondent for "The Sportsman's Pilot."

His intense interest in understanding the nature of man and the different races and cultures of the world took him once again to the high seas in 1933. This time he led two expeditions through the Caribbean. He was subsequently awarded membership in the prestigious Explorers' Club and would carry their flag on three more expeditions.

Drawing from his travels and first-hand adventures, L. Ron Hubbard began his professional writing career in 1933. He went on to create an amazing wealth of stories in a variety of genres which included adventure, mystery, detective and western. Ron produced a broad catalog of entertainment which attracted a huge readership, and in 1935, at age 25, he was elected president of the New York Chapter of the American Fiction Guild. During his tenure as president, the Fiction Guild membership included many renowned authors such as Raymond Chandler, Dashiell Hammett, Edgar Rice Burroughs and other notables who were the life-blood of the American literary marketplace.

Ron was invited to Hollywood in 1937, where he wrote the story and scripted 15 screenplays for Columbia's box office serial hit "The Secret of Treasure Island." While in Hollywood, he also worked on screenplays and story plots for other wide-screen productions.

In 1938, fully established and recognized as one of the country's top-selling authors, he was approached by the publishers of Astounding Science Fiction Magazine to write for them. They believed that in order to significantly increase the circulation of their speculative fiction magazines, they would need to feature real people in their stories. L. Ron Hubbard was the one writer they knew who could deliver this better than any other. The upshot was a wealth of celebrated science fiction and fantasy stories, which not only expanded the scope of these genres, but established Ron as one of the founding fathers of the great "Golden Age of Science Fiction."

During this period, Ron wrote the classic tale FINAL BLACKOUT, a gripping novel of unending war. "Not half a dozen stories in the history of science-fiction can equal the grim power of this novel . . ." stated Astounding's editor, John W. Campbell, Jr. A short time later, Hubbard's story FEAR appeared, setting a whole new standard for horror fiction and influencing generations of writers. Stephen King calls FEAR a true classic of "creeping, surreal menace and horror."

With the advent of World War II, L. Ron Hubbard was called to active duty as an officer in the U.S. Navy. The course of this brutal war effectively interrupted his writing career and it was not until 1947 that he was once again turning out exciting stories for his many fans. These included the benchmark novel TO THE STARS—a powerful work centering on the impact of space travel at light-speed—and his critically acclaimed story, THE END IS NOT YET. It was during this same period that Ron wrote the ever-popular OLE DOC METHUSELAH stories. Published under the pen name René Lafayette, a byline which Ron reserved for the captivating series, the adventures of Ole Doc and his companion Hippocrates quickly became a reader favorite.

In 1950, with the culmination of years of research on the subject of the mind resulting in the publication of DIANETICS: THE MODERN SCIENCE OF MENTAL HEALTH, L. Ron Hubbard left the field of fiction and for the next three decades, he dedicated his life to writing and publishing millions of words of non-fiction concerning the nature of man and the betterment of the human condition.

However, in 1982, to celebrate his 50th anniversary as a professional author, L. Ron Hubbard returned to science fiction and released his giant blockbuster, BATTLEFIELD EARTH, the biggest science fiction book ever written. BATTLEFIELD EARTH became an international bestseller with millions of copies sold in over 60 countries. In the U.S. alone, it appeared on national bestseller lists for over 32 weeks.

Ron followed this singular feat with an even more spectacular achievement, his magnum opus—the ten-volume MISSION EARTH series, every one of which became a New York Times bestseller. MISSION EARTH is not only a grand science fiction adventure in itself, but in the best tradition of Jonathan Swift and Lewis Carroll, is a rollicking, satirical romp through the foibles and fallacies of our civilization.

L. Ron Hubbard departed this life on January 24, 1986. His prodigious and creative output over more than half a century as a professional author is a true publishing phenomenon. To date, his books have been published in 90 countries and 31 languages, resulting in over 104 million copies of his works sold around the world. This vast library includes over 330 popular fiction novels, novelettes and short stories (all of which are planned to be republished in the years to come) as well as hundreds of non-fiction publications, establishing L. Ron Hubbard as one of the most acclaimed and widely read authors of all time.

"I am always happy to hear from my readers."

L. Ron Hubbard

These were the words of L. Ron Hubbard, who was always very interested in hearing from his friends and readers. He made a point of staying in communication with everyone he came in contact with over his fifty-year career as a professional writer, and he had thousands of fans and friends that he corresponded with all over the world.

The publishers of L. Ron Hubbard's literary works wish to continue this tradition and would very much welcome letters and comments from you, his readers, both old and new.

Any message addressed to the Author's Affairs Director at Bridge Publications will be given prompt and full attention.

BRIDGE PUBLICATIONS, INC.
4751 Fountain Avenue
Los Angeles, California 90029